Dann McDorman is an Emmy-nominated TV news producer. He's also worked as a newspaper reporter, book reviewer, and cabinetmaker. He lives in Brooklyn with his wife and two children.

West Heart KILL

Dann McDorman

RAVEN BOOKS
LONDON · OXFORD · NEW YORK · NEW DELHI · SYDNEY

RAVEN BOOKS
Bloomsbury Publishing Plc
50 Bedford Square, London, WC1B 3DP, UK
29 Earlsfort Terrace, Dublin 2, Ireland

BLOOMSBURY, RAVEN BOOKS and the Raven Books logo
are trademarks of Bloomsbury Publishing Plc

First published in 2023 in the United States by Alfred A. Knopf,
a division of Penguin Random House LLC, New York
First published in Great Britain 2023
This edition first published in 2024

A catalogue record for this book is available from the British Library

ISBN: HB: 978-1-5266-6622-2; TPB: 978-1-5266-6623-9; PB: 978-1-5266-6628-4;
eBook: 978-1-5266-6621-5; ePDF: 978-1-5266-6618-5

2 4 6 8 10 9 7 5 3 1

Typeset by Scribe, Philadelphia, Pennsylvania
Designed by Anna B. Knighton
Printed and bound in Great Britain by CPI Group (UK) Ltd, Croydon CR0 4YY

To find out more about our authors and books visit www.bloomsbury.com
and sign up for our newsletters

For Caroline

"That corpse you planted last year in your garden,
Has it begun to sprout?"

THURSDAY

This murder mystery, like all murder mysteries, begins with the evocation of what the reader understands to be its *atmosphere*, the accumulation of small, curated details to create a shared myth of mood, time, and place—though not all at once, of course, that is important. The writer of murder, like all writers, must be a miser, conceding revelations bit by bit; for every novel is a puzzle, and every reader a sleuth.

Not all mysteries begin with the protagonist, but this one does. He is riding in the passenger seat of a car; these opening sentences don't reveal the year, model, and make, that would be too simple, but you do see the protagonist pushing an 8-track into the dashboard, *Wings at the Speed of Sound*, music bounces out—"Let 'Em In." The protagonist is smoking something, a joint, passing it back to a new character, the driver, whose presence was implied at the start of this paragraph but never explicitly stated . . . The two men—yes, both men—are dressed similarly, in clothes of an era that is not your own but that you recognize from film and television: the clues accumulate . . .

And now a crucial moment, the first bit of dialogue:

"What do they hunt at this hunting club?"

"Deer, mostly. Pheasant. A bear, once in a while."

"People?"

"Only each other."

They laugh, but you are thrilled; you think, perhaps, of the plot of "The Most Dangerous Game," in which a rich eccentric lures unsuspecting men to his island, to hunt for sport . . . Is this to be *that* kind of story? But listen, they are speaking again:

"My family is one of the poorest here. We're really only allowed to stay because we were originals, founding members."

"How many families?"

"Maybe three dozen? More? They all have their own cabins, all over the property. Every few years, a member leaves, a new one is added. The dues are steep."

"And what does all that money get you?"

"Hunting grounds. A lake stocked with fish and canoes. The clubhouse. Meals prepared for big parties."

"Like this one."

"Yes, fireworks on the Fourth of July. Also, Memorial Day . . . Labor Day . . . New Year's. Any excuse, really, to drink too much and ogle other people's wives."

"There are less expensive ways to have an affair."

"These people have money to burn. Or did. But what they're really paying for is separation. Privacy. Miles and miles of empty trails. Graves in which to bury their secrets."

"Will you get any reaction for inviting a bum like me?"

"No, they'll view you as a new toy, something to toss from one paw to another and then be condescending about later, over drinks."

"Sounds wonderful."

"It's worth it, just to get out of the city. It's falling apart. And too goddamn hot right now. You said you didn't have any work, anyway."

"I did get one case."

"What is it?"

"Nothing interesting. Not in the city."

"Fine, don't tell me. Anyway, I think the women will like you . . ."

The joint has burned down to the roach; a state-police cruiser passes, and both men's eyes dart warily to the rearview mirror—shit, did he see them, is he going to turn around, lights and siren blaring . . . And it's only now that the dialogue's clues begin to click into place; you're convinced, though nothing thus far indicates one way or another, that the protagonist is the stranger who's been invited up for the weekend, and that the driver is the one dropping all those artfully foreshadowed details about the hunting club. You now know the date, perhaps the decade, too; the socioeconomic status of this hunting club; and perhaps also something about the moral character of its members. These insinuations of sex don't disturb you, you're no prude, though it's not exactly what you're looking for from a mystery; in fact, you're hoping this is not one of those books where the author embroiders or obscures the story with sex or violence or gimmickry. The real writers, the ones you trust and return to again and again, have no need of such cheap deceits.

The police cruiser continues out of sight, and both men relax. They switch on the radio, which is broadcasting an ominous weather report, and their talk turns to matters that need not concern us here: old friends, politics, film, music . . . You sense they knew each other quite well, long ago, but haven't talked much in recent years, and you wonder why, now, they have become reacquainted. You sense that this, too, might be part of the mystery.

But you are also pondering that earlier word *case:* is our protagonist, then, a private detective? You feel the book settle into the comfortable formula of its genre. Of course there is a detective, there *must* be a detective. Very well, then. You can perceive the contours of the plot ahead, anticipate its false clues and blind alleys, the ways in which this writer will try to conceal the truth in plain sight, like a purloined letter on a mantelpiece; you just hope that the rules of the form are followed, because a mystery that cheats is the worst kind of fraud.

But we'll return to those rules later; for now the car's wheels are crunching on gravel as it turns off the main highway and onto the unpaved road that must lead to the hunting club and, you antici- pate, to death . . . Orange NO TRESPASSING signs are nailed to trees along the road, each emblazoned with the name of the club—West Heart—and its insignia: a bear's head with two rifles crossed behind it, resembling, you can't help but think, a skull and crossbones.

After a long drive up the dirt road and across an old wooden bridge spanning a small creek, the two men begin to pass . . . *cabins*, is what the driver called them, but in fact they are large, well-built houses: second homes, no doubt, or third or fourth homes, city wealth slumming in the country. A lake shimmers through the trees; the men can see children splashing in the water and shining, oiled women in fashionable sunglasses lying on the sandy beach . . . and then they are at the West Heart clubhouse.

"Didn't expect it to be this big."

"Something like fifty rooms. Could be a nice hotel, if this place ever fell apart."

"Is that likely?"

A shrug, which, you note with studied interest, is not an answer . . . your trained gaze following the eyes of our protagonist as he studies the clubhouse, a three-story monument of wood and stone built to evoke the famed lodges of a former era, with a massive wraparound porch, girded by sturdy logs, draped with patriotic bunting for the weekend's festivities. Inside, wandering around a labyrinthine inte- rior of wood paneling and dark corners, he will discover a main floor that holds the dining hall, kitchen, and a great hall with an enormous fireplace that, he is told, is tended by the caretaker to burn virtually uninterrupted from November to March. On the second floor are the library, study, and several guest rooms, with more guest rooms taking up the entire third floor. The basement is used principally for storage, although it also holds the club wine cellar—a detail, you think, surely designed to feint toward Poe's "The Cask of Amontillado."

But our protagonist learns all of this later, for now there is a "Sixer" under way, so named for the hour when the club members emerge for their first drinks of the day, at least the first public drinks: there are well-worn jokes about whether certain members are thought to enjoy private "Fivers" or even "Twelvers." Perhaps a dozen people are on the porch, cocktails in one hand, cigarettes in the other, trading anecdotes, scoffing at the tragedies, and nodding gravely at the jokes. The dialogues that follow include references to Gerald Ford, peanut farming, the PLO, the Concorde, and the rising cost of fireworks during this Bicentennial year—those raw ingredients of verisimilitude that construct an ersatz world within which characters will act out pantomimes of death for the purposes of entertainment. No effort is made to provide any backstory, at least not yet, and the confused snatches of conversation that you're permitted to overhear seem designed to keep you off-balance, guessing, groping blindly in a room in which the lights have not yet been turned on . . .

Still game for the hunt tomorrow?

Is he here?

How many acres are they going to cut?

Did you see her this morning at the breakfast?

What time? I have a new rifle.

Who?

I heard everything on the far side of the bluff.

She looked like hell.

Six?

The applicant . . .

Must be a thousand acres.

Julia saw her swimming, naked, in the lake last week.

Better make it seven. Might be a late night.

Honestly? I don't like him.

It's a shame. Have we ever sold off logging rights before?

I'm afraid she's gone to seed, poor thing.

Should we invite others?

Neither do I. He doesn't . . . fit with West Heart, if you know what I mean.

Decades ago, I think. Such desperation.

One must keep up appearances, if nothing else.

I'll ask Ramsey and Duncan.

John only wants him because he has money.

It's unseemly.

Can you imagine her medicine cabinet? It must be like a pharmacy.

Not Otto?

I doubt one man can "save the club," if that's what he's thinking.

Of course, trees grow back. Better than selling the land.

I would say Duncan should do something for her, but, of course, he's tried.

It's too much walking for him. With the leg.

Of course, some think it's not worth saving.

We might have to do that, too, before the end.

We've all tried, haven't we . . . ?

And then there are introductions, during which you finally learn that your protagonist's name is Adam McAnnis; the driver's name, James Blake—followed by several paragraphs whose purpose is to introduce you to the principal cast, characters with names that also help evoke the upper-class Anglo-Saxon mise-en-scène, names you might discover on a melancholy walk in the rain through a forgotten New England graveyard . . . Mayer, Garmond, Caldwell, Burr, Talbot . . . each character totemized by a physical trait to help you keep them apart: the woman with the scar at her temple that she attempts to cover with her hair, the jowled man with the sallow complexion, the younger man with a limp, the woman with a streak of white in her otherwise dark hair. Of course, you know that each description is also a question. How did she get that scar? Does he have jaundice from drinking? What accident or injury caused the limp, and does it still fill him with regret? What tragedy or terror shocked that lock of hair into whiteness?

You are alert—as a veteran of murder, you know that one of these new characters is likely to be the killer, but which one? You hope this writer is skilled enough to avoid too heavy-handed a clue; even the wrong adjective, or adverb, or the subtle rhythm of a sentence or phrase can tip off a canny reader to the ultimate conclusion. In fact, while you wish this was one of those old-fashioned mysteries that list the dramatis personae at the front of the book, you also fret about its perils: For example, how shall the writer resolve the knotty dilemma posed by a character who is not who he claims to be? Or the two characters who in reality are just one person assuming a second identity, perhaps in pursuit of some devious and decades-long plot of revenge? Would not a dramatis personae listing two such characters individually register, after the final revelation, as a dishonest trick? Ultimately, does not every dramatis personae lie to you, if only by omission?

×

Dramatis Personae

The Garmond Family

JOHN GARMOND. West Heart Club President. ▮▮▮▮▮▮▮▮▮▮▮.

JANE GARMOND (NÉE TALBOT). Sister of Reginald Talbot. ▮▮▮▮▮▮▮▮▮.

RAMSEY GARMOND. Son. ▮▮▮▮▮▮▮▮.

The Mayer Family

DUNCAN MAYER. ▮▮▮▮▮▮▮▮▮.

CLAUDIA MAYER.

OTTO MAYER. Son. Walks with limp due to ▮▮▮▮▮▮▮▮▮.

The Blake Family

DR. ROGER BLAKE.

MEREDITH BLAKE.

JAMES BLAKE. Son. College friend of Adam McAnnis.

EMMA BLAKE. Daughter. Newly graduated from college.

DR. THEODORE BLAKE. Deceased. Roger Blake's
father. ▇▇▇▇▇▇▇▇.

The Burr Family

WARREN BURR. ▇▇▇▇▇▇▇▇▇▇▇▇▇▇▇▇▇▇▇▇▇▇▇.

SUSAN BURR. ▇▇▇▇▇▇▇▇▇▇.

RALPH WAKEFIELD. Nephew.

The Talbot Family

REGINALD TALBOT. West Heart Club Treasurer. Brother of
Jane Garmond. ▇▇▇▇▇▇▇▇▇▇▇▇▇▇▇▇▇▇▇▇▇.

JULIA TALBOT. Pregnant.

The Caldwell Family

ALEX CALDWELL. Widower.

AMANDA CALDWELL. Deceased. ▇▇▇▇▇▇▇▇▇▇.

TRIP CALDWELL. Son. Deceased. Killed
in ▇▇▇▇▇▇▇▇▇▇▇▇▇▇▇.

ADAM MCANNIS. College friend of James Blake's. Private
detective hired by ▇▇▇▇▇.

JONATHAN GOLD. Prospective West Heart
member. ███████████████████████████.

FRED SHIFLETT. West Heart caretaker.

×

You're reviewing this list of names carefully when you realize that
McAnnis has slipped away to explore the clubhouse, empty but for
the rattle of plates and the chatter of staff in the kitchen. He clutches
a half-empty drink in his hand as a token or excuse, an outward
symbol of belonging, the very casualness of it all denoting nothing
more sinister than a man who has idly wandered away from a party,
certainly not a professional sleuth bent on discovery . . . And it's in
this quiet moment that the sentences finally turn to describing this
protagonist: McAnnis is thirty-five but looks older, with tousled
black hair, curling long over his ears, and a dark mustache that
stamps his face with what he thinks is a faintly sinister cast, useful
in some circumstances, a liability in most others. The crows have
scratched their feet at the corners of his eyes, lines not from smiling
but from skepticism, the habitual grimace or squint of a man weary
of betrayal. He has light-blue eyes—"my mother's eyes," he sometimes confides to the women who comment on them—and it's those
eyes that give the game away: sad and wary and wounded, the way
someone looks at you when you're obviously lying, an embarrass-
ment and disappointment to you both. His nose is slightly crooked
from a punch years earlier that McAnnis knows he should have seen
coming. On the back of his left hand is the round white puckered
scar of a cigar that had been extinguished on his skin—a reminder,
as if he needs one, of poor choices and risks not worth taking.

McAnnis still believes in suits as a necessary evil for the job,
and not one of those damned leisure suits, either; a real suit, however cheap and threadbare, would usually suffice to open doors
or get people talking, especially when he flips his wallet to flash a

shield whose authenticity would stand up to all but the most rigorous inspection. McAnnis wears his ties loose; on the nights when he remembers to undress for bed, the ties stay with the shirts he takes off.

For this trip, he is wearing a brown number with a yellow shirt and an orange-and-tomato tie; after a few hours in the car, it's clear that the entire ensemble is quite obviously not, despite JCPenney's claims to the contrary, *wrinkle-free.*

McAnnis has climbed the stairs to the second floor. The library is dark in the fading sunlight. A small brass plate next to the door reads: *In gratitude to Dr. and Mrs. Blake, for the donation of their private collection. December 1929.* Charitable tax deduction, you expect McAnnis is thinking. After the Crash of '29. Most of the library consists of leather-wrapped tomes. One shelf is devoted to hunting and fishing. Another is filled with what appear to be West Heart records, including decades of the club newsletter, printed and bound. One wall has no shelves, featuring instead two massive mounted deer heads surrounded by nearly two dozen brass plaques listing the names and years of the club presidents, each evidently having served a five-year term. McAnnis is studying these thoughtfully when a club member intrudes. It is Reginald Talbot, the treasurer. He is a short, fidgety man with glasses and a receding hairline and a habit, McAnnis discovers, of blinking nearly incessantly.

"Hello—you're that detective, aren't you? McAdams."

"McAnnis. Adam McAnnis."

"Of course. I overheard you talking to James. Are you looking for the Necessary?"

"The what?"

"The bathroom, sorry. It's the term up here."

"Funny. No, I was just looking around."

"Not investigating something, I hope?" asks Reginald Talbot, eyes fluttering.

"No, not at all," says McAnnis. "If I had a clock, I'd be off it."

"You may not be looking for crimes, but perhaps they're looking for you?" ventures Reginald Talbot. "That's how it seems in all the mystery novels. Detectives on holiday when a fellow hotel guest turns up missing?"

"Or dead, usually," says McAnnis. "But no, I don't generally stumble across bodies in my spare time. Right now, I'm just looking for a refill." He holds up his drink.

"I'm sure we can help you with that."

"Though I am curious . . ." McAnnis adds.

"Yes?"

"Do these plaques cover all the club presidents?"

"I think so, why?"

"I'm wondering what happened in the thirties?"

"What do you mean?"

"All these plaques cover five-year stints. But 1935 to 1940 is missing. We have Horace Burr, 1930 to 1935, then Russell Caldwell, 1940 to 1945."

Reginald Talbot leans in. "You're right. Odd."

"Any explanation?"

"No clue. You could ask one of the old-timers, if you're really interested. Though I can't imagine why you would be."

"I'm not. Just habit."

"A detective detects."

"Something like that."

"Good. Let's get you another drink, then. After all"—Reginald Talbot moves smoothly toward the door, feigning nonchalance like an amateur actor overplaying a part—"we can't have strangers wandering around unchaperoned, unearthing all our secrets."

×

Out on the porch, the Sixer is in full swing, tongues loosened by the first or second or third drinks of the evening. McAnnis is sipping his refurbished Pimm's, studying the celebrants, trying to match these people to the names in the club dossier he'd prepared for himself, its manila folder hidden beneath swim trunks in his small overnight luggage.

The Sixer attendees are dressed in the browns and oranges and yellows and baby blues of the day, a collective aesthetic that this writer evidently thinks is best described by proper nouns and trademark symbols: Wear-Dated® Acrilan® trousers with Sansabelt® technology, lightweight Orlon® acrylic sweaters, Fortrel® polyester jeans, PERMA-PREST® double-knit slacks of cotton and Dacron® polyester with Ban-Rol® waistband lining, Trevira® and Kodel® polyester slacks, Ban-Lon® polos, jerseys of mercerized Durene® cotton, Ultriana® knit button-up shirts, Arnel® triacetate print short-sleeve shirts, Avril® nylon skirts, Nyesta® double-knit tops of Antron® nylon, Qiana® silk blouses, SANI-GARD® socks inside wedge-heel Kraton® thermoplastic rubber-sole shoes, Porvair® poromeric gator-look vamps . . .

Most of the men sport variations of the Izod Lacoste or Brooks Brothers polo, although a few, adopting the mode of the new libertine, are trying to seem at ease in tight Huk-A-Poo shirts, generously patterned and unbuttoned to a greater or lesser degree. The older generations are sweating in Bill Blass pink or canary sport coats, checked pants too slim for the paunch at the beltline.

The women, as you would expect, are more imaginative, in peasant blouses, maxi dresses, and sleeveless numbers from Lilly Pulitzer; Austin Hill princess jumpers with matching silk headscarves; Skyr orange floral blouses; Meadowbank slacks, Herman Geist jerseys, and pull-on culottes from Gordon of Philadelphia . . . and it's only now, surveying these brands from another age, that you realize you've been distressed by the absence of women in this mystery so far—curious, since so often women are the victims, or the murderers, or the motives, for the crime. Even for the misogynistic Sherlock Holmes, Irene Adler, who appeared in exactly one short story, proved over the years to be invaluable: *the woman*, in Holmesian lore, adding some rouge to the cheeks of an otherwise sexually colorless canon. So now you are pleased to see Adam McAnnis talking to Jane Garmond, her blond *Klute* hair partially concealing the scar at her temple. She is an attractive woman perhaps a decade older than McAnnis, with hazel eyes and fair skin, wearing a green wraparound Diane von Furstenberg dress. She has what writers like to describe as a *hint of sadness* around her mouth and is the sort of woman whose family, centuries past, would find after her death a journal of poems that no one knew she'd been writing her whole life, or a perfumed packet of fading letters from an ill-fated love who'd been dead for decades.

"Your husband is John," says McAnnis. "The club president."

"Yes."

"Does that make you the First Lady?"

Jane Garmond shakes her head. "Hardly. The job is more a hassle than anything else. Paperwork. Truth be told, it's just sort of handed off from family to family. Passing the conch around the fire."

"*Lord of the Flies*, right?"

"Very good. Anyway, it's not very special. There are lots of ex-presidents floating around."

"Like who?"

"Oh, Dr. Blake was one, for example. Also, Duncan Mayer."

"So—you married into this place?"

Jane Garmond takes a slow, careful sip, the ice cubes she'd dropped in to keep her white wine cool rattling in the glass. "Do you always interrogate your hosts?" she asks.

"It's called conversation!" protests McAnnis.

"I'm teasing you. No, I did not. I am a lifer. I was born into this. I'm originally a Talbot. Reg Talbot is my brother."

"I just met him in the library."

"Yes, I saw you two coming out. So I've been here forever. I've known some of these people since we were children. We all spent summers here, up through our teenage years."

McAnnis falls silent. You recognize this technique; like any good interrogator, he knows that silence encourages the subject to fill the gap. Especially when made uncomfortable by guilt, suspects are desperate to smooth out any awkwardness, thinking it makes them seem more natural and innocent, when in fact the opposite is true. It is a sad vulnerability of human nature to try to please, which any detective or grifter can exploit.

"That's how I got this scar," Jane Garmond says, touching her forehead. "Duncan Mayer used a slingshot on me. It bled like hell."

"Jesus. I hope he got in trouble."

"If you knew his father, you wouldn't say that. We could hear Duncan's screams as he got whipped all over the lake."

McAnnis tries to press his advantage, but they're abruptly joined by others—Meredith Blake and Claudia Mayer, of the white-streaked hair, along with two younger men, Claudia's son, the limping Otto Mayer, and Jane's son, Ramsey Garmond.

McAnnis, while parrying questions with polite small talk, is quietly examining these new acquaintances, trying to add some color to the dry, lifeless facts in his club dossier. He'd gathered the dates and details from birth certificates and school records and, in Ramsey's case, an innocent one-item rap sheet from an Ivy League prank that had gone wrong and ended up before a bad judge, or maybe a good judge on a bad morning. Otto Mayer is dark-haired and tall but ungainly; his shoulders look uneven, as if his crippled leg had tightened a screw one quarter-turn to twist his torso around his spine. Ramsey Garmond is his opposite: blond with slate-blue eyes, handsome and well built—he probably rowed crew, McAnnis thinks—and when they shake hands, he claps the detective on the shoulder as if they were old chums. He smiles easily, a young man certain that he's walking into a bright and dazzling future.

McAnnis remembers from his files that Otto and Ramsey were born just a few months apart. They must have grown up here together: summers, weekends, holidays. They have the shared ease of brothers or at least lifelong friends, but to McAnnis, they look like the two sides of a fateful coin flip.

". . . detective?" Ramsey Garmond is asking.

"Yes?"

"So will you?"

McAnnis realizes that he's missed something.

"Sorry," he says. "What was the question?"

"What's it like to be a detective?"

"It's not like in the movies," says McAnnis.

"It's more exciting than being a tax lawyer," observes Ramsey Garmond.

"Depends on the taxes," says McAnnis.

"Ramsey works with his father," says Jane Garmond. "John. Believe me, it's not exciting."

"Don't hold back on us," says Otto Mayer. "Tell us a detective story."

McAnnis sighs. Most of his business consists of tragedies of the most mundane sort: infidelities, embezzlements, missing persons (also, in one particularly desperate period, a missing cat). But occasionally it's more interesting. Once, a father asked if McAnnis could "work with his sources in government" to engineer his son's return from Vancouver, after the young man burned his draft card live on the local news. Another time, a woman asked how much it would cost for McAnnis to kill her husband. Last year, a sad young man asked him to track down his birth mother.

Every now and then, McAnnis would be visited by representatives of insurance companies, if they were stretched thin. They didn't like to do it. They seemed to think it was slumming. He remembered one insurance agent in his office, glancing about distastefully, holding his card lightly between thumb and index finger as if it carried some contagion.

"It's a fire case, Mr. McAnnis. A small department store. Family-owned."

"Accidental, but you suspect arson."

"Of course."

"Why?"

"Because it's always arson," the insurance agent said.

McAnnis also sometimes had the odd corporate job, masquerading as a private matter: a lawyerly man in a fine-tailored suit hiring him to find proof of another man's infidelity.

"Your wife?"

"Of course not."

"Then why do you care?" asked McAnnis.

"We don't. But we believe in having some security."

"Who's *we*?"

McAnnis didn't get an answer. But he discovered that the cheating man was a top executive at a large bank that was in the midst of a complex and expensive acquisition. The executive was stupid and indiscreet. McAnnis got the dirty photos that the lawyer wanted. The acquisition, he read later in the papers, fell through.

And then he also got problems of the most personal, intractable sort: a father who wanted McAnnis to get his son off heroin.

"Not my usual line of work," McAnnis had said. "You need a doctor. Or therapist. Maybe a priest."

"I'll get those, but first I need to cut off the supply. My son has a friend . . . a bad influence. He's the supplier. The pusher."

McAnnis sensed where this was going. "And what do you want me to do?"

"I want you to persuade this friend that my son is not worth the effort."

That word—*persuade*. Such a flexible word. Layers of significance and deniability. McAnnis knew what it meant. Brass knuckles, a weighted leather sap. Waiting in the shadow of a doorway for the target to emerge from the bar or restaurant: a quick, decisive blow to a crumpling knee, the target's wailing promise that he'd do whatever was asked. McAnnis was offered this type of wet work often, but he never said yes. This father, though, was so desperate and plaintive that McAnnis conceded that he'd "look into it." Turned out the son was the dealer, not the friend.

You sympathize with McAnnis's reluctance to share these case studies; your favorite detectives are taciturn creatures, terse, tight-lipped, paid to be both inscrutable and discreet, but you know it would be counterproductive to frustrate anyone who might be useful to him. He needs them talking, and sometimes that means he talks, too. Every detective, therefore, must have a story to sate the appetites of the curious. It need not be true, but it must feel so, and must also convey certain elements that will help with the subsequent investigation and questioning of any who hear it. And so this is the story McAnnis tells now to the group, which in his own mind he's always thought of as:

The Cult Job

This case was a nasty one, parents hiring him to locate and extract their daughter from a cult in California. Weeks of stakeouts, undercover work. Revolutionists stockpiling rifles in basements. Children injecting heroin in the People's Park. The guru was called Ayuva Daeva but his real name was David Sherwin, of Manhattan. This was his second attempt at starting a religion; the first, McAnnis was able to ascertain, had dissolved when he was indicted for writing bad checks. The daughter, he learned, had once been friends with Angela Atwood, a.k.a. "General Gelina"—the "voice" of the Symbionese Liberation Army, who had burned to death when the SLA safe house in Los Angeles caught fire during a police shootout on May 17, 1974. *It could be worse*, he wanted to tell the girl's parents, though he didn't, once he found her. The guru was pocketing the checks and other gifts sent to California by worried, loving parents back east, ostensibly to support their liberation from the sufferings of this illusory reality. In truth, it was all funneled into a bank account under the David Sherwin name. Hashish, LSD, and heroin were utilized to keep the girls compliant. McAnnis had had one cult case before, and he knew what didn't work—words. What did work was kidnapping. He grabbed her off the street in broad daylight—she was walking with just one other Ayuva Daeva devotee, on the way back from the Berkeley Grocery Collective, paper bags in hand—and shoved her into his rental car, placed handcuffs around her wrists—*Pig! Fascist!*, she screamed at him, despite his longish hair and mustache, *Fucking asshole motherfucker!*—and took her to the rented, remote bungalow in the hills where her parents anxiously waited. But that's where things went south, because, instead of the expert psychologist and cult deprogrammer he'd been told would be there, the father—a doctor—simply plunged a needle into the girl's arm, and had her committed to a mental institution in Napa, where, as far as he knows, she remains. *Send me the invoice*, the father had said, before driving off in a spurt of gravel and dust . . .

×

"That's terrible," says Claudia Mayer, dismay flashing across her pale face. She has delicately arched eyebrows and high cheekbones and seems awkward around the others, McAnnis observes, as unsure of herself as an actress who's been thrust onstage in a play for which she never learned the lines.

"What did you do next?" asks Otto Mayer.

"I cashed his check."

"You didn't try to help her?" asks Jane Garmond.

"What could I do?" McAnnis says. "Her parents were the legal guardians. She was a drug addict and cult member. The courts like to send off pretty young girls like that, to try to restore their virginity. Metaphorically speaking."

"You should have tried to help her," says Claudia Mayer, quietly.

"I do my best," says McAnnis. "What's the line? 'Down these mean streets a man must go who is not himself mean.'"

"What's that?"

"Raymond Chandler. On how the private detective must be a man of honor. Of course, he had never been one. Dashiell Hammett was one, and he had different ideas."

"I'm so glad that you came up with James," says Meredith Blake, with the ease of a hostess adept at redirecting conversations. To the others: "We haven't seen Adam in what . . . ten years?"

"More."

"And what made you two connect?"

Meredith Blake is smiling and polite but shrewd: she has a grandmother's face with a lawyer's eyes, the way Lady Macbeth might have looked, McAnnis thinks, if she and her husband had survived the witches of their ambition. Her sand-gray hair is tucked up into a bun, and she's wearing a floral-patterned dress best described as "sensible." McAnnis remembers her vividly from weekends when he and James would take a cab to the Blakes' sprawling apartment in what the doctor half-jokingly called "God's country" in the East Sixties, carrying dirty laundry and the expectation of a home-cooked meal. Once, at a cocktail party to celebrate Dr. Blake's ascension to department head, McAnnis watched her gliding around the library offering hors d'oeuvres and refilling drinks while silently itemizing the guests; he always thought she was the smart one in the family—certainly smarter than her husband. He knows what she's really asking now: *Why are you here?*

"Actually," says McAnnis, "I reached out to James."

"Yes, he mentioned that," says Meredith Blake. "He didn't say why, though."

"I saw someone we both used to know."

"A girl?" asks Otto Mayer.

"An ex-roommate. He asked how James was, and I realized I didn't have an answer. So I placed the call."

"How'd you get his number?" asks Meredith Blake.

McAnnis smiles. "I'm a detective."

Meredith Blake nods, unsatisfied. "Of course. Well, you're in for a big weekend. The bonfire, the greased watermelon, the egg toss, the fireworks. Assuming, of course, that this storm doesn't wash it all out. We moved everything up a day because of it."

"We heard something about the storm on the radio," says McAnnis. "It's supposed to be bad, right? When does it start?"

"Not tonight," says Claudia Mayer.

"Tomorrow night," says Meredith Blake. "Late. After fireworks. Apparently, the club could lose power. We have generators, of course. But the roads might be a problem. They're all dirt and gravel, you see. There's been talk of paving some of them, but we just never seem to get to it. And there's also the bridge. It's old, very old."

"You might be trapped here," warns Ramsey Garmond.

"God help me," says McAnnis, to laughter.

×

Later, McAnnis finds Claudia Mayer at the quiet end of the porch, beneath a Betsy Ross flag that had been hung from the timbers for the occasion, a half-empty bottle of white wine on the table next to her. She's wearing a lilac print sundress that went out of style a few years ago. He guesses that she's in her late forties, perhaps a bit older, but her black hair is already graying around that white forelock. She's a thin woman. Perhaps too thin. When she looks up at him, McAnnis has the peculiar feeling that she is peering out from behind her eyes like a prisoner gripping the bars of a jail cell window.

"Mind if I join you?"

"Not at all," says Claudia Mayer, gesturing toward an empty chair with her wineglass. "They can be a bit much, can't they?"

"They seem all right."

"You need to get to know them better," she says. "Duncan always shames me into attending these things."

"Sixers?"

Claudia Mayer smiles fleetingly, and McAnnis sees a flash of a different woman, the woman she might have been or perhaps once was. *What changed?* he wonders. "You're getting the lingo," she says. "Do you know about the Necessary?"

"I do. Fortunately."

"There's a certain . . . *language* here at West Heart. A vocabulary that's meant to exclude. Or I should say, I don't know if that's what it's meant to do. That's just what it does. Difficult for outsiders to comprehend. You can learn it, you can speak it, eventually, but you're never quite *fluent*, if that makes any sense. Duncan, of course, was born to it."

"It's the language of money," says McAnnis.

"Perhaps. Though the club is not what it once was."

McAnnis pauses, giving her time and space to elaborate. But she doesn't, so McAnnis says: "I'm sorry if my story upset you."

"Was it just a story?"

"You mean, was it real?"

"Yes."

"Would it make you feel better if I said it wasn't real?"

"No."

"It's a true story," says McAnnis. "Unfortunately."

"It's so easy to lock someone up," says Claudia Mayer, "if you really want to do it. Like that father did to the girl. Simply say that they're crazy. A danger to themselves. It's for their own good. Et cetera. These are irresistible arguments, don't you think? Exploiting someone's desire to do good as a way to do evil."

"I try not to think in terms of good and evil."

"What else is there?" she asks. She empties her wineglass. "You're not a religious man, are you, Mr. McAnnis?"

"Not particularly," he says.

"I was without faith, then I had it, then I lost it again."

"Losing faith once is a tragedy," says McAnnis. "Losing it twice smacks of carelessness."

Claudia Mayer smiles again. "A joke."

"Yes."

"Do you avoid the terms *good* and *evil* because you don't know on which side of the line you fall?"

"How very forward of you, Mrs. Mayer," says McAnnis. "We've only just met."

"Forgive me."

"I'm joking again. Or trying to. I'll stop."

"It's okay. Sometimes I forget . . . how you're supposed to act. There are so many rules and expectations, aren't there? It's difficult to keep up with it all. So easy to make a mistake. And then you get the stares, the people whispering behind their hands. There she goes again, they'll say. Poor Claudia. Poor Claudia is talking to herself again. Poor Claudia is naked in the lake again. And of course all these rules change depending on the time, the place, who you're with, the weather, the position of the stars . . . Are you into astrology, Mr. McAnnis?"

"Honestly, no."

"Neither am I, really, but sometimes I can't help but wonder if there's something else, somewhere, that governs our condition. Think of the moon, for example. A trillion tons of rock just hanging there, right over our heads, weighing down on us, pulling apart the tides . . . How could it *not* affect us? Does it shape how we sleep? How we bleed? What else does it do that we don't know about?" She stops abruptly, seeing the detective's befuddled expression. "Apologies. I do go on."

"It's quite all right."

"I forget myself sometimes," Claudia Mayer says absently. "What a curious phrase. *I forget myself.* How does one, precisely, forget one's self? Do you ever forget yourself, Mr. McAnnis?"

"Not as often as I would like."

The evening breeze flutters the bunting along the rail. It's pleasant in this corner of the porch; in the quiet, away from the Sixer, they can hear birds chirping above the creek running by the clubhouse. Wind chimes hanging from the beams over their heads are tinkling softly.

"I made those," says Claudia Mayer, following the detective's upward glance.

"They're beautiful," says McAnnis.

"I used to play piano. Now I make wind chimes. One pipe is in C. Another in D. Also F, G. If the wind is right, they almost—almost—play Beethoven's 'Ode to Joy.' But of course they never play it perfectly."

"Sounds good to me."

Claudia Mayer pours herself more wine. "I imagine that being a detective is a lonely occupation."

"I talk to lots of people."

"You interrogate lots of people," says Claudia Mayer. "It's not the same thing."

"No, it's not," admits McAnnis.

"You spend a lot of time alone, don't you, in your work?"

"Yes."

"What do you think about then, on those long . . . What do you call them?"

"Stakeouts?"

"Yes. Stakeouts. Seems to me that solitude like that would lead a person to think, think, think, endlessly . . . That's what it does to me, anyway."

"You can be alone but not lonely," says McAnnis.

Claudia Mayer smiles. "Very true. Of course, the opposite is true as well. The loneliest I've ever been is in a crowd. That's why I enjoy it up here during the week. You can walk for hours in the woods and not see anyone. Once, I didn't speak for three days. I was almost afraid that I'd forgotten how. But, in truth, I enjoyed it. I felt like a monk, in seclusion, studying some esoteric secret."

"I think I know what you mean," says McAnnis. "I've spent most of my working life studying secrets."

"Other people's secrets are easy. It's our own that are hard," says Claudia Mayer, looking at him with the unblinking gaze of a child or a fanatic: curious, brazen, seemingly unaware or uncaring of the impropriety. McAnnis stares back in what feels like some sort of test of faith. "Anyway. I should be off. A busy night. Enjoy your time here at West Heart. I expect," she adds cryptically, "that you'll have your hands full."

Claudia Mayer drifts away, and McAnnis, left in the wake of that oracular pronouncement, thinks, *What a strange woman.* But he can't deny that her words hit close to the bone. How often is he both lonely and alone, suspicious of everyone, accepting betrayal as the rule, not the exception? The deceits that begin to unfold the moment the client walks through his office door. Nights spent in parked cars watching illicit silhouettes behind shaded windows, receipts pulled from dripping trash bags, a five-dollar bill waved between two fingers before a junkie's fixed gaze . . . the debased work of hundreds of cases, a file cabinet full of tragedies and comedies and tales too ambiguous to categorize.

Sometimes, during long bleary nights when he's had too many

of his little pills, or too much whiskey, or both, McAnnis imagines that all these separate cases are really just one case, no matter how random and disconnected they seem, each a piece in a puzzle that will take a lifetime to assemble. What he's really investigating, McAnnis thinks with a false and razor-edged Dexamyl clarity, is himself.

He is walking back to the front of the clubhouse when a scream suddenly pierces the air . . .

×

A scream suddenly pierces the air. Startled glances are exchanged on the porch, a drink is spilled, a baby begins to cry, and your muscles tense; you sense this is one of those plot leaps that writers use to punctuate and propel the narrative, like those bursts of biological creativity that scientists claim shock evolution into action. But you are unsettled; just pages into the book, is it too early? Should a mystery unfold in a more demure fashion? Aren't the suspense and anticipation the real secret thrill of the book, rather than (let us be honest) the all-too-often disappointing dénouement, the magician turning over his cards for an audience that realizes, bitterly leaving the theater, that they've been had?

But you set aside these doubts, at least for now, and follow the crowd around the corner of the clubhouse to where the body of a dog lies in the driveway behind a car. A man kneels next to him: the widower, Alex Caldwell.

"I'm so sorry," he says. "I didn't see him. I didn't know he was there."

Duncan Mayer steps forward, red-faced, fists clenched. "You bastard."

"It was an accident. I didn't mean to do it."

"You're a goddamn liar." No one else speaks. "I said you're a goddamn liar."

The kneeling man stands. "That's enough, Duncan."

"Get away from him," snaps Duncan Mayer. Alex Caldwell

takes a step back. "This was no accident. You meant to do this. You wanted to find a way to hurt me, to hurt Claudia and Otto, and now you did."

Alex Caldwell looks at the people gathered in the driveway. He lifts his hands, palms out, the way a man might when trying to retreat from the brink of a bar fight: *Look, I don't want any trouble.* "He's wrong." He turns to the club president. "John, you know I wouldn't do this."

John Garmond steps forward slowly. "It might just be best if you went home, Alex," he says with a quick glance at Duncan Mayer. "I can call you later. Let us deal with this here."

"I swear I didn't see him."

"Just go home, Alex."

Alex Caldwell hesitates, evidently uncertain whether going home will register as an admission of guilt, quite literally leaving the scene of the crime—but at the same time, he must be repelled by the corpse, driven by the ancient taboo that sparks the desire to flee death, to want to bury it, forget it, fear it . . . He quietly mutters something to John Garmond, then gets into his car, announcing one more time to the crowd before he drives off: "It was an accident. I'm so sorry."

By now Otto Mayer has limped forward and is kneeling in the dirt. Jane Garmond hands him a picnic blanket, which he lays across the dog's corpse.

Duncan Mayer turns to John Garmond. "Can you watch him a moment? I have to get my truck."

"What are you going to do?" asks John Garmond.

"Bury him."

"I meant to Alex."

Duncan Mayer's eyes betray nothing. He turns and walk away.

×

McAnnis has been observing the scene—and observing the others observe the scene, like a veteran gambler looking for a tell.

Ramsey Garmond has put his hand on the shoulder of his friend Otto Mayer. James Blake is whispering something to his mother. Jane Garmond is speaking urgently to her husband. The jaundiced man, to whom McAnnis has not yet been introduced, is smiling as if at some private joke. Next to him is a chestnut-haired woman who turns her head to stare at McAnnis; he feels like a voyeur who catches another pair of binoculars gazing back from a darkened apartment window. Her frank gaze sends a jolt down his body: not quite a *come hither*, but neither is it a reproach; rather, a challenge, an opening that requires him to accept the gambit or to make one of his own. McAnnis stares back long enough to send what he hopes is a series of signals communicating interest, sophistication, self-awareness, wry amusement; though he's so rusty at this game that he's not sure what message, if any, is received.

The detective steps away from the crowd and glances back at the clubhouse. On the porch, alone, stands Claudia Mayer. Her hands are methodically tearing apart a cocktail napkin; she absently watches the shreds drift away in the evening breeze. McAnnis takes a step toward her, but she turns abruptly and is gone.

×

On the way back to the Blake house, to prepare for dinner, Adam McAnnis and James Blake run into a man loading tools into the back of a pickup truck. You note the outward signifiers—dungarees, sweat-stained work shirt, dirty hands, scraggly beard—of a different socioeconomic class, a workingman, and you guess this is Fred Shiflett, the caretaker, a guess proved correct in the brief conversation that follows, touching on various club matters seemingly of no great import—a bear spotted in the creek by the bridge, the need for a new tennis net, the lightning-struck oak tree blocking Talbot's Way—but you are hardly listening. You are distracted by the murderous arsenal in the back of this man Shiflett's truck, half covered by a tarp: chainsaw, crowbar, ax, machete, even a drum of some sort of pesticide or poison . . . all filthy or rusted, but all still more than capable, you note, of disappearing from this truck, plucked by gloved hands in the dead of night, and used to snuff out a life before being thrown into the lake, to reappear—if ever—only after days of dredging by police. Or perhaps this caretaker, resentful from years of tending to the whims of the rich, suffering their thousand injuries in silence, finally decides to exact some small measure of revenge himself.

You could be wrong, of course; the Chekhovian principle of a gun in the first act being fired by the final act need not always apply, and in fact an artful author can exploit that expectation as its own kind of ruse. But in the end, you think, isn't the real gift of the mystery novel the premonition usually accessible only to mystics and fanatics, the belief that the world is infused with an inner fire of meaning? Who knows what mortal secret links the aging spinster and the cracked mirror in the attic? The hidden packet of illicit letters and the child's headstone? Readers of murder must zealously knot these strands together until the pattern becomes clear, for otherwise they may note the rifle hanging over the fireplace, for example, and the antics of the brash teenager a scene or two later, but fail to suspect that they will soon be savoring the ancient delights of patricide . . .

This is, you reflect, one of the consolations of the genre: any respectable practitioner must follow the rules in making the truth— however skillfully camouflaged by lies—accessible to all.

×

Rules

T. S. Eliot had five. Jorge Luis Borges had six. Ronald Knox had ten (the famous "Decalogue"). S. S. Van Dine had twenty. Agatha Christie, of course, knew all the rules and broke most of them, brilliantly.

The mystery, virtually since its inception, has invited rule-making and rule-breaking. Borges articulated the crux of the writer's dilemma in a 1945 essay describing the construction of detective novels in terms so daunting that one wonders if he thought anyone ever truly succeeded:

> Everything in them must prophesy the outcome; but those multiple and continuous prophecies have to be, like those of the ancient oracles, secret; they must only be understood in light of the final revelation. The writer is thus committed to a double feat: the solution to the problem posed in the initial chapters must be necessary, but it must also be astonishing.

The key rule is a sense of fair play—the reader must not feel cheated. The murderer must be someone present throughout the story, with motives and means that are accessible to the reader, suggested by clues honestly presented. Some mysteries actually pause the narrative, near the end, with a fourth-wall-breaking direct challenge to the reader: *You now have all the clues necessary to solve the crime* . . . In the short-lived *Ellery Queen* TV series of the mid-1970s, the actor playing the detective would stop and turn to the camera to say something like:

> The important things to remember—besides what happened to the door—are the brandy snifter on the carpet and the bruise on Manning's knee. Have you got it now?

Hercule Poirot, in the film version of *Evil Under the Sun* (though not the novel), performs much the same trick, though more elegantly directed at another character, by rattling off the clues he has pieced together into a solution for the baffled delight of one of the suspects: "a bathing cap, a bath, a bottle, a wristwatch, the diamond, the noonday gun, the breath of the sea, and the height of the cliff." In *The Riverside Villas Murder* by Kingsley Amis, the dust jacket challenges readers to "pit their wits against the author's and solve the mystery for themselves" with a careful "study [of] pages 61, 82 and 160."

This level of fair play requires significant architecture, and, indeed, Agatha Christie's notebooks reveal that she made endless lists of possible motives and methods of murder, page after page of the stuff. (Out of context, a horrified reader might think she had stumbled upon a psychopath's recipe book.) Italo Calvino, as part of a 1973 exercise titled "The Burning of the Abominable House," imagined a computer that could solve or create crimes, if only you could properly input the data (his story proposed twelve different possible crimes that had occurred in the house, which he calculated could lead to 479,001,600 different combinations). Decades later, an online Mystery Plot Generator promised a million different story combinations built around a few key pivots: Protagonist, Secondary Character, Plot, and Twist! (always with the exclamation point).

The Oulipo school of writers, of the 1960s French avant-garde, devised elaborate architectural tortures for themselves: Georges Perec wrote an entire novel without the letter "e" (a void that echoes his characters' search for a missing person) and another built around a complex formula he called his "story-making machine." Jean Lescure invented a conceit called "S+7," in which every noun is replaced by the seventh noun that follows it in the dictionary (obviously, results will vary according to the dictionary consulted). Here is one S+7 version of the opening paragraph of this novel:

> This murder nag, like all murder nags, begins with the example of what the reaper understands to be its atrophy, the acid of small, curated detours to create a shared napalm of moral, tinder, and plague—though not at all once, of course, that is important. The wrong of murmur, like all wrongs, must be a mishap, conceding reveries blackguard by blackguard; for every nude is a pyre, and every reaper a slob.

Obviously, the reader's patience is tested, if not soon exhausted, by this sort of play. But for the writer of murder, a principal interest of the Oulipo school lies in how one prominent member (Raymond Queneau) described them: "Rats who construct the labyrinth from which they plan to escape."

×

Adam McAnnis is unpacking his clothes in his room at the Blake house. Swim trunks, clothes for a hike, nicer attire for dinner. The manila folder with his club file. And, of course, his Colt Detective Special, series three—a bit old-fashioned, honestly, these days, but he's always been one for tradition. Sensing a presence at the door, which he'd forgotten to close, McAnnis slides the revolver under some underwear and turns with exaggerated nonchalance. A young woman is watching. Did she see? He thinks not.

"Do you have any weed?" she asks.

McAnnis blinks. "Why do you ask?"

"Because you smell like weed."

"Isn't it polite to knock?"

"The door was open." She mimes rapping on the empty air. "Knock knock."

"You must be Emma."

"We've met before, you know," she says accusingly. "You don't remember."

"Apologies."

"I'm devastated."

McAnnis does in fact remember her, from a trip to the Blakes' apartment in the city, during college, but she was just a kid then, with the full horror show: braces, acne, awkwardness. But now she is an altogether different creature . . . and you think, as you read the passage that follows, of how all novelistic descriptions are essentially exercises in voyeurism and fantasy, especially when, as here, the words evoke the tropes of what academics call the *male gaze:* tanned thighs, ripped jean shorts, star-spangled red-white-and-blue-bikini-topped breasts, blond shag framing cheeks dotted with summer freckles . . . descriptions that, you've always suspected, reveal more about the writers than the characters they've invented.

"Sorry, can't help you."

"With the weed, you mean."

"Yes."

"Disappointing," says Emma Blake. "Narcs nailed my dealer back in the city, and I haven't found a new one yet."

"A tragedy," says McAnnis. "Anyway, I'm not sure James would want me doping up his little sister."

"Little? He's more of a child than I am. I've had an abortion. I've been to Europe twice. Slept on the beach in L.A. Did cocaine once with John Belushi."

"Your parents must be so proud."

"Catch them between their pills and their wine and their vodka and you could ask them." She fixes him with a curious stare. "Why did James get in touch with you again, anyway? After so many years?"

McAnnis hesitates, and when he does reply, it is with a certain half-reluctance, as if he isn't sure he's chosen the right option. "Actually, I reached out to him."

"Why the hell would you do that? He hasn't gotten *more* interesting since college."

McAnnis senses that the answer he gave Meredith Blake earlier— a chance encounter, a phone call out of the blue—won't work with her daughter, so instead he just says: "You must find it boring up here."

"*Boring* is not the word I would choose," says Emma Blake. "Anyway, if you change your mind on the weed, let me know. See you tonight."

×

And now the table is set for dinner—an important moment, you know, for any tale of murder. You might want to pour yourself another cup of tea or coffee, mute the phone, close the door, for this will require your full attention. You must carefully observe who enters, who leaves, and at what time; who has reason to drink too much, and why; what is said and left unsaid; and, most of all, what this writer chooses to describe: what *sharp glances* are exchanged, whose *cheeks suddenly flush*, whose laughter might be said to be *nervous* . . .

Dinner will be staged outside at a long table on the Blakes' stone terrace, overlooking the lake. Night has fallen. A pleasant breeze sways the pine trees. The frogs murmur at the water's edge. The sounds of a Neil Sedaka record on the hi-fi drift outside. The hosts are Dr. and Mrs. Blake, joined by their children, James and Emma. The guests are: John and Jane Garmond. Warren and Susan Burr. A boy named Ralph Wakefield, scribbling in a book on the couch in the corner of the living room. Adam McAnnis. And another stranger: Jonathan Gold, a stern-looking man wearing a tie and an air of cold bemusement.

Susan Burr is the woman who stared back at McAnnis outside the clubhouse; she arrives wearing a red-lipped smile of promise and peril, Bakelite bracelets jangling as she shakes hands with the detective, her eyes, smoky with mascara, fixing him with an appraising stare—*What might you have to offer?*

"So nice to meet someone new," she says a few moments later, when they find themselves alone at the bar by the record player in the living room. "And who might you be investigating?"

"No one."

"That's a bit boring, isn't it?" says Susan Burr.

"Should I have said I was investigating you?"

Susan Burr shrugs. "I feel like I'm always under suspicion, for one thing or another."

"That one yours?" McAnnis gestures toward the boy hunched over a workbook on the couch.

"God, no. Do I look like a woman who has children? He's my sister's kid. She's in France for a month."

"What's he doing?"

"Some sort of math problems. Not for school. For fun. He's a bit touched, as we used to say."

"Special."

"Exactly."

Susan Burr is attractive, McAnnis thinks, and knows it. Long, straight chestnut hair with Jane Birkin bangs and brown eyes to match, an effect she accentuates with black eyeliner and the afore-mentioned mascara. She's wearing a pistachio Ultrasuede shift that's probably too fancy for this affair, though McAnnis suspects that Susan Burr stopped caring long ago about the looks she elicits from other women.

"So what does one do, at a club like this, for entertainment?" asks McAnnis.

"Well, it should be a classic West Heart weekend," says Susan Burr. "If you're into that sort of thing. Bonfires and fireworks. Booze. The younger set will refuse to share their drugs. The rest of us will be forced to fall back on more . . . classical diversions."

Her husband calls her name from across the room. Susan Burr makes a face, then leaves the detective alone at the bar, trailing the scent of perfume in her wake. McAnnis is still trying to iden-tify it—Halston? Chanel?—when Meredith Blake guides him by the elbow outside to introduce him to Jonathan Gold, hands the newcomer his bitters and soda, then flees immediately afterward, as hostesses invariably do with strangers at a party. Jonathan Gold is pale, nondescript, with an undertaker's thin lips and an economy of movement. As he speaks, you realize he's the kind of man whose every word is tinged with a delicate, humorless irony.

"So you're a detective," says Jonathan Gold.

"Yes."

"Are you on a case right now?"

McAnnis glances across the terrace. The other guests are close—close enough, he thinks, to be wary. "I am," he says quietly.

"How exciting," says Jonathan Gold. "What are you investi-gating?"

"I'm afraid I can't discuss it," says McAnnis. "Not here, anyway."

"Of course, of course. I understand."

Jonathan Gold pauses to sip from his highball glass. McAnnis notes that he's the only one here not drinking alcohol. Invariably a sign that a man either cares very little for booze, or cares too much.

"Perhaps at least I can ask how it's going?" continues Jonathan Gold.

"It's early yet," says McAnnis. "But I'm confident. I don't think it will be too difficult."

"That's interesting." Jonathan Gold inclines his head, as if struck by an idea. "You know, I've just thought of something."

"What?"

"You could be investigating me, and I wouldn't even know it," says Jonathan Gold, with a faint mocking smile. "Perhaps I'm a suspect?"

McAnnis is silent a moment. Then he says: "You have no reason to be nervous, Mr. Gold. Unless, of course, you've done something wrong."

Instead of answering, Jonathan Gold looks up at the sky. Even diminished by the lanterns on the terrace, the stars are glorious in the night. He begins to talk of constellations—"a childhood passion, I must admit"—pointing out Ursa Major and Minor, Draco, Cassiopeia . . . But McAnnis sees none of it. To him, the lines in the textbooks had always seemed arbitrary. You could make any picture you liked, he thinks, by randomly linking any given star to another. The pattern in the sky was just a lie.

"The rabbis of my youth liked to lecture us about God's great works," reflects Jonathan Gold. "Of course, God is dead now. *Time* magazine told us so."

"I don't keep up with the news," replies McAnnis.

Their stilted conversation continues, allusive, opaque, and you sense an emptiness in their dialogue, things unsaid and, you note, unasked . . . McAnnis doesn't pursue the questions begging to be put to this stranger Jonathan Gold: Who is he? Why is he here? It could be that this writer is careless with details; it may also be the case, you reflect, that people don't ask questions to which they already know the answers.

"Enjoying West Heart?" asks John Garmond, joining the two men. The club president is handsome, late forties, with expensively cut hair, graying at the temples, and the deep tan of a man who's spent many work hours on the fairway swinging a 5 iron, or on the tennis court practicing his toss while squinting into the sun. His white polo shirt is tight enough to suggest the vanity of a washboard stomach.

"Yes, thanks," says McAnnis.

"Nice to be back," says Jonathan Gold.

"We do the holidays well. Bring in some help from town. Make a whole weekend of it." John Garmond turns to Jonathan Gold. "I don't want to speak prematurely, but you should feel optimistic about your membership application."

"Good to hear. I hope others feel the same."

"If not now, I'm sure they will soon," says John Garmond. "Have you submitted your paperwork yet?"

"Not just yet. My accounts are somewhat diverse; it takes time to pull it all together."

"Of course."

"Is there any rush?" asks Jonathan Gold.

"Not at all, not at all," John Garmond says quickly. "But let me know if there is any way I can help."

Dr. Blake emerges from the living room, bottle of Dom Pérignon in hand, to pose the eternal question: "Shall I open some champagne?"

The doctor has, McAnnis thinks, hardly aged since he saw him last. The same smooth white hair, the same unflappable, casual manner. Strangers might describe him as having a face that *crinkles with kindness*, but McAnnis has always felt it was a bit of an act. "The only problem with being a doctor," McAnnis imagines him confiding to a colleague over a Scotch and soda, "is the goddamn patients." On those rare occasions when he lets his guard down,

Dr. Blake is brusque and imperious; he exudes the arrogant nonchalance of a man convinced that he's earned his success—and others, their failures.

"What are we celebrating?" asks Jane Garmond.

"Everything. Anything. Nothing."

"Does one need a reason?" asks Susan Burr.

"One does not."

"Just remember poor Donald Caldwell," advises Meredith Blake.

"What happened?" asks McAnnis.

"Alex Caldwell's uncle. He tried to saber a bottle of champagne on New Year's Eve. Lopped off a thumb."

"Good God."

"No great loss," mutters Warren Burr. "I was surprised he had opposable thumbs to begin with."

"Warren!"

"Where did he get a saber?" asks McAnnis.

"He didn't. He used a butcher knife."

Dr. Blake opens the bottle with a hushed pop. "A nun's fart," he says in satisfaction.

McAnnis glances questioningly at Emma Blake.

"Apparently, only savages blast the cork across the room," she explains, pulling a chrome cigarette case of Virginia Slims from the back pocket of her jeans. "A properly opened bottle should sound like a nun's fart."

"However you open it," says McAnnis, "I'm pretty sure it goes down the same."

×

Before dinner, McAnnis wanders back inside the house to find the bathroom. As he passes the Blake master bedroom, he's struck by the urge to slip inside, search the closet, tap the walls. Slide his hands beneath the mattress. Check for an envelope taped to the underside of a nightstand drawer. It's a compulsion or an instinct he's come to recognize, an itch demanding to be scratched. But laden with risk. After a moment's hesitation, McAnnis continues to the bathroom, where, door safely shut behind him, he opens the medicine cabinet. He's astounded, as always, at the secrets people willingly leave exposed on those shallow little shelves.

Since every reader is, by definition, a voyeur, you don't hesitate to peek over the detective's shoulder as he rotates the drug bottles to read the labels. Noting evidence of the affluent insomniac: Aspirin. Valium. Flurazepam. The merely embarrassing: Preparation H. Vagisil. The expected: Minoxidil. Premarin. And the intriguing: Ritalin. Quaalude-300. A writer so inclined, you reflect, could build a biography based solely on the contents of a person's medicine cabinet. You think, also, that an overdose of sleeping pills is a frequent, if unreliable, method of murder.

On his way back outside, McAnnis overhears voices in the kitchen. His hosts.

"I'm telling you, I don't want him here," hisses Dr. Blake.

"We had to invite him," says Meredith Blake. "John begged me to."

"I don't like him in our home."

"Why?"

"You know why."

"It's just a couple hours."

"It's a lot more than that. He's trying to become a *member*!"

The voices are moving toward him, so McAnnis quickly makes his way into the living room, where he finds the boy, perhaps ten years old, still hunched over his workbook, on a green Naugahyde couch facing a massive stone hearth. He's wearing flared jeans, a blue-and-white rugby shirt, and red Jox sneakers. His straight brown hair obscures his face as he scribbles on the page.

"So you're Ralph," McAnnis says.

"My name is Ralph Wakefield," the boy says without looking up. "But everybody calls me Ralph."

"What are you doing there, Ralph?"

"Math. Word problems."

"I hated word problems when I was your age. Are they hard?"

The kid shrugs. "Not for me."

"And you're doing this for fun? Not for school?"

"There is no school," Ralph says peevishly. "It's summer."

"Of course," says McAnnis. "Have you been enjoying your summer vacation?"

"I don't know."

"Spending some quality time with your aunt and uncle?"

"I don't know." Pencil still scratching across the page. "She doesn't like him very much."

"Is that right," says McAnnis, trying to keep himself from smiling. "Did she say something?"

"No. But I can tell." The boy looks up for the first time. "Are you really a detective?"

"How do you know that?"

"I heard you talking earlier."

"So you were eavesdropping."

"What's that?"

"That's when you listen to other people's conversations. Sometimes you hear things they didn't want you to hear. That's what detectives do."

"I thought detectives catch bad people."

"That too. Occasionally." McAnnis notices a creased, smudged piece of paper next to the boy on the couch. "What's that?"

"What's what?"

"That."

The boy glances down. "It's just a map. I drew it."

"Do you mind?"

The boy doesn't say anything, so McAnnis picks up the paper. At first he doesn't understand it. The lettering is tiny and the lines on the page look vaguely like the schematics of Egyptian tombs that he'd seen in a *National Geographic* once—he kept stacks of magazines in his back seat, for stakeouts—but then the image resolves, like the optical illusion of an old crone turning into a young woman, and McAnnis realizes what it is.

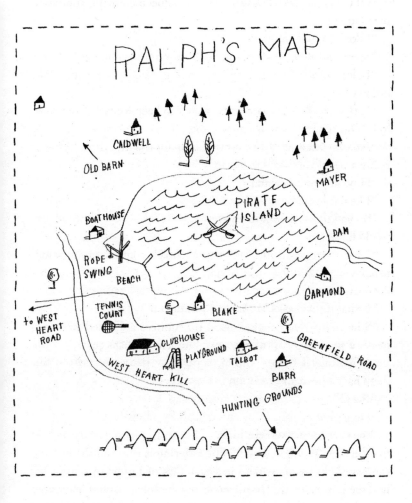

"So this is a map of West Heart?"

"Of course."

"It's good," says McAnnis.

"Thanks," says Ralph Wakefield. "You can have it if you want."

"Really?"

"I don't need it anymore."

McAnnis studies the map again, then carefully folds it and slips it into his pocket.

"Thanks."

"When you find a bad person, someone who killed someone . . ." Ralph shakes his head and starts over. "I mean, when you find the person who did it, do you have to kill them, too?"

"Not usually. Not if I can help it."

"Who kills them, then?"

"What do you mean?"

"If you kill someone, then someone should kill you. Nothing else would be fair."

"A lot of people think that," says McAnnis. "Other people think that two wrongs don't make a right."

"A negative times a negative equals a positive," says Ralph.

"Is that right?" asks McAnnis. "I didn't know that."

"So who kills the person who killed someone? The judge?"

"In a manner of speaking, yes. The judge or the jury. But the actual killing, if there's killing, is done by people in prison. But there hasn't been an execution in over a decade."

"Why?"

"I don't know," McAnnis says truthfully. "Legal stuff."

"So what happens to the killers?"

"They go to prison. Usually for a long time."

"I would kill someone, if I had to, if they were trying to kill me," says the boy, returning to his workbook. "Anyone would."

"I think you're right," says McAnnis. "But people also find other reasons to kill."

Dinner is clams casino (brought from the city, on ice, in a Coleman cooler McAnnis had noticed in the back seat of James Blake's car), cold sour-cherry soup, and Cornish hens stuffed with wild rice. The wine, a few bottles of a young Grüner to start with and then a seemingly endless supply of a 1970 Bordeaux. The atmosphere, strained. McAnnis can sense the decades of history surrounding him, the weighted sentences, the words left unvoiced because everyone is already thinking them . . . He feels like he's fallen into a long-running in-joke for which they've forgotten the setup and can no longer bring themselves to laugh at the punch line.

"So, detective," says Meredith Blake, turning to her guest as a neutral source of table talk. "Tell us about yourself."

"Yes, dance for your supper," says Warren Burr, smirking at McAnnis.

"Warren, please," rebukes Dr. Blake.

"I'm all out of stories," protests McAnnis.

"Not about the work," says Meredith Blake. "About you. Are you married?"

"No."

"Ever been married?"

"No."

"Ever been close?"

"Sure. Every Saturday night."

"Ever regret being single?"

"Every Sunday morning."

"Adam was in college with James," Meredith Blake explains to the table. "But you left before graduating—that would have been what, thirteen, fourteen years ago?"

"Give or take a couple lifetimes, yes."

"Were you a detective that whole time?"

"Most of it. I did some odd jobs."

"Like what?"

"An oil rig in Texas. A timber company in Washington. A Filipino fishing boat. Opium transport in the Golden Triangle," says McAnnis, ticking them off on his fingers. "I also ran security for a nightclub in Singapore. Of course, all of that was before I fell in with the Japanese Red Army."

"You're making fun of us," Meredith Blake says sternly, her eyes flashing with an unmistakable message: *Knock it off.*

"Not at all," protests McAnnis. "Just trying to be an interesting dinner guest."

"Did you go to Vietnam?" asks Jane Garmond.

McAnnis hesitates. "No, I was lucky," he says. "I have a heart murmur."

"I wouldn't call that lucky," says Dr. Blake.

"It might kill me someday," says McAnnis. "But not today. Or, hopefully, tomorrow."

"Or the next day, or the one after," says Susan Burr, raising her glass in a mock toast.

"Every year, without knowing it, we pass the date of our death," declares Jonathan Gold, eyes flitting around the table. "How would our lives be different if we knew that date? If we could observe it properly? Celebrate it?"

An awkward hush. McAnnis takes a drink.

"That's rather ghoulish, isn't it?" Emma Blake says finally, pouring herself more Grüner. McAnnis notices Meredith Blake staring reprovingly at her daughter's tanned shoulders above the white peasant blouse.

"It might make the other three hundred sixty-four days easier to get through," replies Jonathan Gold.

"I don't believe," says John Garmond, "that I would like to know."

"Me neither," says his wife.

"I would," says Warren Burr.

He's perspiring slightly, a big man on a warm summer night, thick but not fat. He has a faint sallow cast to his skin, and you realize this must be the character alluded to earlier at the clubhouse: the Jaundiced Man, you think, like some character from a tarot deck. He has abandoned the wine in favor of a double Scotch.

"I'd throw a party," continues Warren Burr. "If I died, then it would turn into my wake. If I didn't, it would be a celebration of making it through one more year. Either way," he adds, "we'd drink."

"Save us, Mr. Detective," says Emma Blake, "from this morbid conversation."

"I'm curious about West Heart," McAnnis says obligingly. "I saw the list of presidents in the clubhouse. It goes back a long time."

"End of the last century," says John Garmond. "There were four founding families. All of whom you see represented here. The Garmonds, Blakes, Burrs, and Talbots. They bought the land when it was still cheap."

John Garmond goes on to explain that Heart, New York, was a utopian Shaker community founded more than a hundred years earlier, back when the Shakers would actually *shake*—twitching and writhing and dancing in ecstasy during services. Now it was just a few forlorn houses on either side of the new highway, and a plaque bearing the town name that kept getting stolen by lovestruck teenagers. There was an East Heart, too, consisting of an old quarry, now abandoned, and a still-robust roadhouse that once served the miners.

West Heart was the name adopted by the founding families for the woodland parcel they bought in 1896. It was originally just nine hundred acres but increased over the decades, reaching its present size shortly after the Second World War.

"And everyone hunts?" asks McAnnis.

"We all have guns," says Warren Burr. "What we do with them varies."

"And the closets are full of skeletons, I presume?" asks McAnnis. "Secrets buried under the floorboards, that sort of thing?"

"Isn't it your job to find that out?" asks Emma Blake.

"I don't have a job at the moment," says McAnnis.

"I think, Mr. McAnnis," says Dr. Blake, "that you think we're more interesting than we really are."

"I'm sure he agrees that everyone has a story," says Susan Burr. "It's just a matter of finding the right way to tell it. Isn't that right, detective?"

McAnnis nods, raising his glass. "Here's to the people of West Heart," he says. "And their stories."

"The club is not what it once was," mutters Warren Burr.

"But it could be again," says John Garmond, with a sharp glance.

"If we win the lottery, maybe."

"It's gauche to talk about money at dinner," says Meredith Blake.

"And in front of strangers," adds her husband.

"Politics, then?" asks Jonathan Gold. "Religion? The religions of politics?"

"The only topics worth our time are the classics," declares Susan Burr. "Love. Hate. Sex. Death."

"I would argue those are really just one topic," says McAnnis.

"Now it seems like we're talking about religion," warns Meredith Blake.

Jonathan Gold leans forward. "I would be the first Jew at West Heart, would I not?" he asks.

The table falls silent, except for the boy, Ralph, who's been humming to himself throughout the meal. Then Dr. Blake says: "I haven't the faintest idea."

"I'm surprised," says Jonathan Gold. "That's the kind of thing I would think would be known. Discussed. Wouldn't you agree?"

"I assure you, Mr. Gold—"

"Jonathan. Please. After all," he says, smiling, "we are to be neighbors."

"Yes. Well," says Dr. Blake, "I assure you, Jonathan, that there have been no conversations like that at all. Regarding your application."

"But it *is* a change for the club? Unless I'm mistaken?"

"These are different times," says Dr. Blake.

"Of course," says Jonathan Gold. "I just want to be sure I'm welcome."

"Don't be ridiculous," interjects John Garmond. "Of course you're welcome."

"Good. The world outside is changing," says Jonathan Gold. "But in some places, change comes more slowly. Behind closed doors, surrounded by the ghosts of your ancestors, things can feel different."

Warren Burr laughs theatrically. "I guess it's time we reveal our big secret," he says to the table. "We can't hide it any longer."

"What are you talking about, Warren?" Dr. Blake asks coldly.

Warren Burr ignores him. "You deserve to know the truth," he says to Jonathan Gold. "We are not a hunting club. Never have been. We are, in fact, a cell of Marxist revolutionaries. We've stockpiled our weapons. Tomorrow we rob a bank. To finance the people's revolt. We've drawn lots. Your initiation will be to kill the security guard."

"Knock it off, Warren," says John Garmond.

"You'll have to excuse my husband," Susan Burr says to Jonathan Gold. "He considers himself a great wit."

"Just having some fun," says Warren Burr, with a menacing smile. "Someone has to. But, Jonathan—excuse me, may I also call you Jonathan?"

"If you insist."

"So, Jonathan, I agree with my neighbors here. Times are changing, even here at West Heart. These days, apparently, we are broad of mind and generous of spirit. Always eager to try out new people." Warren Burr glances down the table at his wife. "Isn't that right, Susan?"

"If you say so," says Susan Burr.

"Susan loves meeting and entertaining new people. Especially the entertaining." He turns to the Garmonds. "How is it in your household. Is there much . . . entertaining?"

"Not especially," says Jane Garmond.

"Odd. I thought you two were more sociable."

"You're mistaken," says Jane Garmond. Not gently.

"Apologies," says Warren Burr. Then turning to the two visitors: "I myself am a bit of an anti-socialite. In case you couldn't tell. And now, I think, it's time for another drink."

Warren Burr pushes away from the table and lurches inside

toward the bar. You recognize the type: he's the guest who blackens a party like a blot upon a page, and for whom the lights always seem to dim when he enters a room. You feel sorry for his wife, even as you recognize that this was one of the intentions of the dinner scene, an episode littered with crumbs of clues left at the table: the insinuations, the premonitions, the comments that *just don't feel right*, the carefully planted seeds that might sprout later, or not, the backstory that's slowly being filled in . . .

But, still, you are wary of this man Burr. As a general rule, in murder mysteries, the least likable character is the most likely to die. But devious writers can anticipate your knowledge of this cliché and thrust a character like Warren Burr into early prominence to surprise you, later, with an entirely different victim. Or, perhaps, more devious still, circle back and kill him off in a double bluff—destined to die all along, exploiting and perverting your expectations from the start. Of course, some writers, among them not the least skilled, use much the same trick to mask and unmask their murderers . . .

×

The evening ticks forward. People cease to pay attention to what they're drinking, or how much of it. Spirits replace wine, to the general detriment of all. Guests squint groggily at the glasses before them, trying to figure out which is theirs. Food is neglected; the strawberry cheesecake that Meredith Blake had ordered from the bakery in the nearest town, twenty miles away, is prodded by distracted forks. When dinner finally ends, the table is a ruin: empty wine bottles, cracked glasses, the tablecloth stained with red-black wine, bony chicken parts next to cigarette butts mashed into dinner plates, a practice that McAnnis, not fastidious in other matters, has always found repulsive. He volunteers to help Meredith Blake clear the table—"No, I insist"—which, though this was not his intention, allows him to lurk behind the kitchen door and overhear snatches of what seems to be an argument that John Garmond and Warren Burr are having by the bar.

"Have you made up your mind yet?" asks Warren Burr.

"Not yet," says John Garmond.

"Soon it will be too late. We can't hold the wolves at bay forever."

"It's a lot to think about."

"Don't be sentimental."

And then, on the detective's next trip:

"You really think that this new man can save everything?" sneers Warren Burr.

"It's worth a shot."

"Is he that wealthy?"

"So it would seem."

"We're in trouble. Reg made some idiotic choices."

"The whole board signed off on them," says John Garmond. "Including yourself."

"I don't trust him."

"Many would say the same about you, Warren."

"And they'd be right. I wouldn't trust me, either."

"Bottom line, I'm still thinking about it."

"You're running out of time, John."

"Aren't we all?"

×

By now, McAnnis is drunk enough to be bored. He idly peruses the spines of the books in the living room, walks into the screened-in porch on the other side of the house, takes a few steps into the yard . . . He realizes he's looking for Susan Burr. A familiar pungent odor lingers in the warm night air; he follows it to find her around the corner, smoking a joint.

"You caught me red-handed," says Susan Burr, leaning against the chimney's stone exterior. "There's a war on drugs, I don't know if you've heard. So I have to indulge my vices in secret."

"Secret vices are my specialty," says McAnnis. "I am the soul of discretion."

Susan Burr smiles. "How old are you?"

"Thirty-five."

"A child," she scoffs. "How old would you say that I am?"

"A dangerous question," says McAnnis.

"Be honest."

"Forty?"

"But don't pander."

"Forty-five?"

"I am three months shy of my forty-sixth birthday," says Susan Burr. "That puts you and me on different planets. Eisenhower was my first vote for president. Kennedy, poor Kennedy, was my second. I haven't voted since. By the time the Pill came, I was already married. The sixties were what happened to other people. The dreams of a bright new future were what you read about in magazines. I skipped all of that. Which was fine. When it all went to shit, I didn't feel like I'd lost anything. The saving grace, of course, was that I never had children."

"Me neither," says McAnnis.

"That you know about."

"That I know about," he acknowledges.

He's been expecting her to pass the joint, but instead she reverses her hand and holds it out expectantly—she intends for him to smoke it from her fingertips. Her eyes remain locked on his as McAnnis inhales, aware of the warmth of her skin against his lips.

"So what did you do?" asks the detective.

"When?"

"When you were sitting out the sixties. When the rest of us were blowing up government labs and selling mescaline and plotting the revolution."

"Did you do any of that?" she asks, bemused.

"No."

"Of course not. What did I do?" Susan Burr sighs reflectively. "I spent money. I took tennis lessons. I read trashy novels. I got on a first-name basis with the makeup girls at Bergdorf's. I watched Ingmar Bergman films at the Ziegfeld. I started at brunch and drank my way to dinner. I made friends. Then I lost them. I bought a new living-room set every few years. I went to Club Med La Caravelle a week ahead of my husband. What was I supposed to do? Sometimes," she concludes, "it feels like life is just something that you do to pass the time."

"You could divorce," says McAnnis.

"Sure. But to do what?"

McAnnis takes the plunge. "Is this the moment when you press a room key into my hand and whisper a time?"

Susan Burr holds her breath for a long moment. Judging him. "Unfortunately, Mr. McAnnis," she says finally, "we are not a hotel. At least not yet."

"Of course."

"But there are rooms in the clubhouse," she continues smoothly. "Empty rooms, unlocked, on the third floor. Room 302 is somewhat less unacceptable than the rest. A man too restless to sleep might, at midnight, find some diversion there."

McAnnis nods. "Midnight."

"There's really nothing left to say, then, is there? After all," adds Susan Burr, "if you talk more, I might change my mind." She stubs out the joint on the side of the Blake house and walks away like an actress accustomed to applause every time she exits the stage.

×

The moon has risen above the trees—red maple and black birch in this part of the club, though balsam firs dominate elsewhere—milk-white and full and shimmering across the surface of the lake. McAnnis waits outside a few minutes, hoping to slip back unobserved; but the moment he returns to the terrace he's flagged down by Warren Burr. The detective hesitates, then reluctantly walks over, wondering if this husband is the jealous kind. Does he know or suspect where McAnnis has been? Does he care?

"We haven't had a chance to talk all night," says Warren Burr. The big man sits slumped in an Adirondack chair, White Owl Demi Tip cigar in hand. "Just you and I."

"Well, I'm here now," says McAnnis.

"You're a private detective."

"That's right."

"What do you detect?"

"Right now? Subtle condescension."

Warren Burr's eyes narrow. Then he laughs, loudly. "That's good. I like that," he says, in a way that leaves no doubt he does not. "I suppose you're not allowed to discuss past cases, then. Professional ethics and so forth."

"Something like that."

"But in general, though," presses Warren Burr, "you do—what? Divorces? Wives cheating on husbands? Spend your nights snapping dirty photos through windows?"

"Why? Are you looking to hire someone?"

What is left of the smile drops. "You have wit, which is a good thing," Warren Burr says coldly. "And a mouth, which is not. Up here, of course, we are all friends. Gentlemen. But back in the city, that wit and that mouth could get a man into trouble. If he's not careful." Warren Burr smiles at the detective. "McAnnis, is it? Adam McAnnis?" As if committing the name to memory, to be written down later, inside a matchbook, or on the back of an OTB ticket, and slipped into the gloved palm of a man who will *take care of it* . . .

"That's right," says the detective.

"Pleasure to talk with you. Now, if you'll excuse me . . ." Warren Burr raises his empty glass and retires inside to the bar.

James Blake, who had been observing the scene, crosses the terrace, shaking his head. "Careful, Adam. He's not a man to mess with."

"Is that so."

"Warren Burr runs a private financial firm, very discreet; nobody knows who his clients are, but they are thought to be 'not nice people,' if you get what I'm saying," warns James Blake. "People who need to put their money in quiet places that the government won't notice. I heard him once talking to my father about having a man who could 'fix things.'"

"You're saying he might try to 'fix' me?" asks McAnnis.

"I'm saying be careful. That's all."

James Blake continues to talk about the professions of various West Heart men, but it's information that McAnnis already has in his files, so instead of listening he studies his old friend and thinks about how easy it was to maneuver an invite for the weekend. James was always like that: trusting and generous, to a fault. While others at Columbia avoided the blue-collar kid from the boroughs, James did the opposite, adopting McAnnis as one takes in a stray. He was unembarrassed to find McAnnis working at the dining hall, wearing the blue-gray uniform of the help, cleaning up after other students who left behind piles of dirty dishes because of course *there are people who do that*. James has gotten a bit heavier, he has a blond-brown mustache now, several shades darker than his hair, that makes him look like *Sundance*-era Robert Redford. Otherwise, he looks the same. He's still unmarried; James's bachelorhood, the detective suspects, is the source of much irritation to his parents, and of gossip to others. Whatever secrets he discovers in that vein, McAnnis thinks, don't need to go into the report to his client.

"Can I ask you something?" asks McAnnis.

"Depends."

"Is the club in financial trouble?" asks McAnnis.

"Why do you ask?"

"Things I've heard."

"Right," says James Blake. "Well, I don't really know much about it. But yes, I think so. Not sure why. Apparently, there's a push by some to sell the club. Some disagree. Some don't know what to think."

"What do you think?"

"I don't."

"You don't have an opinion?"

"I don't have a right to an opinion. I'm not a member. Only my parents are," explains James Blake. "Once you reach adulthood, you lose membership. I'm just a visitor here."

"Like me."

"Exactly. If I want to join, then I have to buy my own house, pay my own dues. Or I suppose," says James Blake, "I could just wait until my parents die."

×

The Burrs were the first to leave. Susan Burr hadn't even glanced at McAnnis when she left, slowly shadowing her husband's swaying form as he lumbered down the path toward the road. Jane Garmond followed soon after—"If I don't leave now, I'm going to pass out on your couch," she'd told Meredith Blake. Her husband had stayed behind. And so now, when McAnnis sees John Garmond alone on the terrace, nursing an Armagnac, the detective knows that it's the opportunity he's been waiting for.

"You handled that situation earlier deftly, I thought," says McAnnis, walking up behind him.

"What situation?"

"The dog."

John Garmond grimaces in distaste. "Right. That whole situation has gotten very ugly."

"What do you think happened?"

"I don't know."

"You must have a theory. Or an instinct."

John Garmond stares down into his acorn-shaped glass, then takes a sip. McAnnis notices that he's spilled some of the cherry soup onto his white polo. "I think any man, or any woman for that matter, looking in a rearview mirror, given a chance for revenge, might take it."

"So you think it was deliberate."

"I think not even Alex Caldwell may know for sure," says John Garmond. "A motive is a funny thing. My wife enjoys detective novels, and in those books there is always a clear motive. Love. Hate.

Greed. Et cetera. But I imagine you've found, in real life, in your work, that people can have all sorts of reasons for wanting to kill. Some of which they don't admit even to themselves."

"Perhaps," says McAnnis. "I've found that, generally, we are most hurt by those closest to us. Especially those we love, or who love us in return."

"I would agree with that," John Garmond says somberly. "I suppose all this," he adds, gesturing at the club property, "seems old-fashioned to you. Out of date."

"I'm not sure," McAnnis says cautiously.

"Out of step with the times."

"In times like these," says McAnnis, "perhaps that's not a bad thing."

"It's a vulgarity, these days, to talk about tradition. But thank God I have a son. My grandfather helped create this place. I hope it's still here when Ramsey is a grandfather." John Garmond runs his fingers through his hair, the sort of tic, McAnnis thinks, that reveals more than he would like. McAnnis has had clients like him before: successful men whose lives have proceeded exactly as planned but who are now struggling to identify the source of a vague, unsettling feeling that something, somewhere, has gone wrong. Their partners' accounts aren't adding up. The old gifts no longer amuse their wives. The news anchors describe a world they don't recognize. These men have everything but secretly worry that it means nothing, and they're paying McAnnis because they're too proud to see a shrink or a priest.

"Things feel hollowed out, don't they?" continues John Garmond. "They look the same, maybe even feel the same, on the surface. But a tap reveals the emptiness inside. Knock hard enough and it will all shatter."

"Are we talking about West Heart?"

"We're talking about everything." John Garmond sighs. "Do you know what I miss? New York. The old New York. I used to love the city. Jane and I would go to restaurants, museums, theater. We had Ramsey in a public school. You could walk in Central Park after dark. But then it all changed. I don't know how it happened. I don't know that it was anyone's fault. Or maybe it was everyone's fault. But the city stopped working. The garbage wasn't getting picked up. Ramsey was mugged three days in a row. Novelists were running for mayor. Our neighbors asked if we were swingers. People I knew, solid people, started having nervous breakdowns. Now the city just saddens me. It limps along like some gut-shot beast lumbering through the woods, unable to understand that it's already dying."

"'Ford to City: Drop Dead,'" quotes McAnnis.

"Exactly."

"And you think of West Heart as a bulwark against that?"

"Or refuge," says John Garmond. "Look, I have no illusions about this place. I know it's easy to caricature. I can imagine how it looks through your eyes. It needs to change; there's no question. But it's worth fighting for. And you don't need to burn it all down to change it."

"Are we still talking about West Heart?"

John Garmond smiles morosely. "We're still talking about everything."

He leans forward. McAnnis follows his gaze. A shadow is moving through the woods in the direction of the clubhouse.

"Hello?" cries John Garmond. "Hello!"

No answer.

"Maybe they didn't hear," says McAnnis.

"They heard," says John Garmond.

"Who was it?"

"One of our resident drunks, lost in his own woods. Or Fred Shiflett, maybe. He doesn't answer anyone if he doesn't have to."

They continue to talk, quietly, and you sense that the mood has softened, a movement into a minor key. The notes describing John Garmond are now tuned at a different pitch—a *lined* face, *tired* eyes, shoulders that are *bent*—which you suspect is meant to induce empathy, if not sympathy. The two men listen while a bird somewhere chirps in the night, a song that at this hour likely means a predator is near, and you suddenly fear very much, in these pages, for the fate of John Garmond.

The club president sighs.

"Good night, Mr. McAnnis."

"Good night, Mr. Garmond."

McAnnis glances at his watch: 10:25 p.m.

×

Ten minutes after midnight. The windows of the clubhouse are all dark. McAnnis slips inside carefully, wary of his trespass. There is no explanation for his presence here, and certainly no presumption of innocence. Main floor. Second floor. Third floor. Room 302. His hand reaches for the doorknob, but it turns on its own, the door opens quietly inward, and there is Susan Burr. He steps into the room. For a moment they do nothing, enjoying the thrill of these final moments before the leap: the pleasure of delay, the awareness of their own pounding heartbeats. Then they kiss. They still haven't spoken. They fall onto the bed.

Later, she whispers: "Open the window."

McAnnis rises obediently, pulls aside the curtains, and slides the window open. Moonlight floods into the room. He shivers slightly as the night air meets the sweat on his skin. He'd felt her fingertips tracing the puckered scar that traverses his rib cage, and he knows that she can see it now. He shakes a Winston from his pack and climbs back into bed.

"I know what you're thinking," Susan Burr says softly.

"Do you read palms, too?" McAnnis says, voice also quiet.

"You're thinking, Does she pick a new one every weekend?"

He shakes his head. "Not at all. Really, just wondering how she chooses her prey."

"You'd like to know my criteria?"

"I'm curious."

"Tall. Dark. Handsome. Not afraid of being murdered by a jealous husband."

"Is that likely?"

She shrugs. "Depends on the man."

"Does he want to sell the club?"

"Why do you ask? And why do you care?"

"Just curious. Something I overheard."

"You'd have to ask him."

"I don't think he'd be eager to explain."

"For a man like Warren," says Susan Burr, "business is borrowing and spending. You spend right, you pay back what you owe, with plenty left over. You spend wrong, and you're having some unpleasant conversations with unpleasant people."

"He needs the money, then."

"There's another criterion," Susan Burr says, changing the subject. "Very important."

"What's that?"

"It relates to the law of supply and demand. My demand was very high. But the supply was very low. You were, I'm afraid, the only option. Albeit a good one."

"You could have picked the new man, the lawyer."

"I try to avoid my husband's associates."

A long pause—too long. McAnnis says, carefully: "Warren knew Jonathan Gold? Before he applied to join the club?"

Susan Burr turns on her side. "It's a poor detective who uses all his pillow talk to ask about the husband. Aren't there more exciting secrets to extract?"

"Sure. I have questions."

"Such as?"

"Do you only pick strangers? Or do you have diversions here at the club, too?"

"I do."

"Who?"

"Can you guess?"

"John Garmond," says McAnnis.

"Why would you say that?"

"Because of the way he looked at me when I was looking at you."

"The famous policeman's instinct?" asks Susan Burr. "But you're not a policeman."

"I have other questions."

"Go ahead."

"Why would everyone assume that Alex Caldwell would want to kill Duncan Mayer's dog? Why is there a plaque missing—"

"Shhh," interrupts Susan Burr.

"What is it?"

"Listen."

From another room down the hall—the low buzzing of voices. A groan or sigh. Silences that leave much to the imagination.

McAnnis isn't familiar enough with the voices to identify them. But Susan Burr obviously can.

"Who is it?"

"If I just came out and *told you*," she says, "wouldn't that spoil the fun of all your sleuthing tomorrow?"

"I'm not here to investigate anyone."

"Of course not."

The bodies in the other room fall into a familiar rhythm. McAnnis can hear Susan Burr's breathing quicken.

"Again?" she says.

×

McAnnis wakes up. Something must have disturbed him. Then he hears it again: A creak outside the door. A floorboard's betrayal. Someone creeping down the hall. The words describing the footsteps—*delicate, halting, cautious*—suggest a woman, though you know that could simply be a writer's feint, the soft lie of misdirection. McAnnis lies still, listening. The footsteps pad down the hall and pause at the door of the other rendezvous, and now you have questions of your own. Will she go in? Stand quietly at the foot of the bed, watching the lovers sleep, unaware of the danger? Does she have a gun? Will she have the fury to use it? Will her hand tremble as she aims? Which one will she shoot first?

McAnnis has to choose a course of action. But it all depends on whether he hears the click of the doorknob, the squeak of the hinges. He waits. And waits. Finally, the footsteps shuffle unevenly to the stairwell at the other end of the hall.

×

Adam McAnnis is walking back to the Blake house. He'd risen from bed quietly with some thought of pursuing the woman, the person, in the hall, and slipped on his clothes. He'd turned to find Susan Burr watching him from the twisted sheets.

"I'm usually the first to leave," she'd said.

"Me, too."

"Tomorrow is the bonfire."

"It's already tomorrow."

"Tonight, then."

"I'll see you there," McAnnis had said.

"I wouldn't expect too much," Susan Burr had said. "It's just another West Heart tradition. We have so many. This one is a kind of pagan throwback. The burning expiation of our sins."

He'd bent toward her for a final kiss. When she rolled over, he noticed a bruise on her lower back, as large as a tennis ball, blue-black in the moonlit shadows.

McAnnis is near the Blake house when he sees, or thinks he sees, a figure on the dirt road far ahead. Like him, without a flashlight. But, unlike him, familiar with the road. McAnnis can't tell if it's the same person as earlier that evening. But he thinks not. The figure disappears into one of the trails that crisscross the club's many acres. McAnnis glances at his watch: 2:56 a.m.

He slips into the Blake house like a burglar, creeps into his room, and collapses on the bed, fully clothed. His head is thick with booze and sex and the promise of the morning's hangover. He is too tired to reflect on the men and women introduced earlier, so you do it for him, one by one, as if counting sheep . . .

Jane Garmond, who tries to hide her scar.
Reginald Talbot, who patrols the library.
Warren Burr, who likes to make threats.
Jonathan Gold, who is not the stranger he pretends to be.
Alex Caldwell, who has (or is thought to have) a vendetta.
Claudia Mayer.
John Garmond.
Susan Burr.
The lovers in the other room.
The shadow in the hall.
The walkers in the wood.

×

Word Problems

1) She weighs 135 pounds. The bottle at her bedside contains 25 sleeping pills of 10 milligrams each. The flask of vodka is half empty. It is 74 degrees outside, the sky is darkening, she has barely left her cabin in 3 days. *Calculate the probability that she will be alive in the morning. Show your work.*

2) The woman's husband crouches in a deer stand 10 feet off the ground. The prospective killer is 50 yards away, holding a Winchester 70. The wind is blowing southwest at 5 miles per hour. Back on her porch, the woman pulls a strand of hair from her eyes, beautiful as the day they first met. *Does he shoot?*

3) A woman has been married for 25 years to a man she doesn't love. For 8 of those years, she has secretly met, for the purposes of sexual congress, her neighbor down the road, who has been married to his wife for 24 years. They see each other for dinner, with their spouses, on

average, every 6 months. As the years pass, the hope of a happy resolution asymptotically approaches zero. *What is the limit of their desire?*

4) The knife was manufactured in Canada 7 years earlier. The blade is 6 inches long, serrated, with a 300 BESS sharpness. It's been in the kitchen drawer for 5 years. She has come to despise weekends at this house. *How much total time, measured in minutes, has she spent fantasizing about plunging the knife into the back of his neck?*

5) A couple's son died 5 years earlier in a car accident. The driver's blood-alcohol level was found to be 0.17%. He was going 30 miles over the speed limit but was wearing a seatbelt. Their son was not. They were best friends with the driver's parents. *What is the minimum ratio of hatred to grief needed for the pain to finally, mercifully, ebb away?*

6) The private detective is sleeping among strangers at a remote locale, 16 miles from the nearest law enforcement. The closest hospital is 22 miles away. He is surrounded by *x* suspects with *y* motives. There are 102 firearms on the property. *Does he comprehend the danger?*

×

"Because," said the doctor, frankly, "we're in a detective story, and we don't fool the reader by pretending we're not."

FRIDAY

I woke up with a nasty headache and a mouth of ash and the sun shining mercilessly through an open window, ice picks in my eyeballs. Still wearing last night's clothes. I smelled like booze and sex, and the sheets were soaking wet, which meant that the night terrors had come. I could usually keep them at bay with drugs or whiskey, but sometimes nothing worked, and especially in the miserably hot summer months in the city, I could tell by their eyes when my neighbors had heard everything.

Once, the man who sometimes slept in the apartment of the women next door stopped me as I left the building. He was smoking a cigarette, sitting on top of a garbage can.

"Hey, man."

"Yeah?"

"You got a cigarette?"

I looked at him. "You smoke two at a time?"

"Nah, man," he laughed, exhaling smoke. "I'll save it for later."

He may have been a pimp. Maybe he was just a snappy dresser. I don't know. I gave him a cigarette. He tucked it into his hat.

"Hey, man."

"Yeah?"

"What's with the screaming, man?"

A question to which I had no good answer. Not everyone came home the way I did. Especially back in the early days, when no one was paying attention. Before the protests and the marches and the children placing daisies in the barrels of the rifles of the National Guardsmen. Before Allen Ginsberg levitated the Pentagon. Before Walter Cronkite's epiphany and napalm explained in *The New York Times* and the whole goddamn mess. Before anyone could understand what the hell was wrong with me, why I would sweat through the sheets, women I'd just met leaping out of bed, waking me up—*You've got a serious problem, you know that?*—and the ladies next door staring at me with those hooded eyes.

I sat up, cradling my head in my hands. Had the Blakes heard? What would I say to them if they had?

I lit a cigarette, trying not to think about the bigger problem: the likelihood that my newest client, currently my only client, had not been straight with me. The job was described as *simple*, though *well paying*, and certainly *worth my time*. The directive, suspiciously vague.

"Keep your eyes and ears open."

"For what?"

"Anything unusual. Or undesirable."

"What I may desire, or not, may be very different from what you do," I'd said.

"True. But words are constraints. They limit or prejudice your thoughts. 'Don't think of an elephant' and so forth. If I say what I think you should be looking for, then unconsciously your mind will filter out everything else. I don't want the filter. You are my *tabula rasa*, Mr. McAnnis. An innocent sent to kick the hornets' nest."

"Sounds terrific."

"Good luck with your investigations. And be careful . . ."

The job felt off to me, but I had no other work, the New York summer was curdling into shootings and smack, so I said yes. The next step was simple. As my new client suggested, I reached out to an old college friend, James Blake. A few well-placed comments about the city heat and the upcoming holiday led to an invitation to West Heart, which I accepted with surprise and gratitude. An afternoon at City Hall and in the main branch of the library at Forty-second Street provided some background on the club. A few additional days for discreet inquiries about my client, and the clients of my client—a standard, and often enlightening, precaution. Then, yesterday morning, James Blake leaning against his car outside my apartment building on the Lower East Side, shaking his head in dismay as I stepped across a sidewalk filled with trash and discarded condoms and shattered syringes.

"I can't believe you live here."

"I'm undercover."

"For how long?"

"About a decade."

"You would've been better off as a cop, like your old man," said James Blake.

"So he liked to tell me."

And now—here I was. Nursing a hangover in a country house, plotting my next move.

The monologue continues in this new claustrophobic perspective, the "I" of the first-person protagonist, a point of view you have viewed with suspicion ever since your first innocent reading of Agatha Christie's *The Murder of Roger Ackroyd*. In general, you find it to be a technique of frustration. You are inside this detective's head, but parts of his mind are "walled off," so to speak, including the parts with information you would dearly like to know: Who hired him? How did they find him? How did they know about James Blake? Why West Heart?

But at least now you know that it was important for McAnnis to be here at the hunting club this weekend, and in fact he may have been hired explicitly *because* of his connections to the Blake family. You are also saddened to suspect that his night with Susan Burr may have been strictly an act of manipulation; many detectives justify sleeping with potential witnesses or suspects on professional grounds, but you generally prefer to think that's just a cover story, a lie they tell themselves. The truth, you want to believe, is that detectives pursue these seductions because desire is electrified by risk, because they walk into a woman's life not as themselves, but as every sleuth she's ever read about in a book or watched on film. Once the crime is solved, the detective leaves and she returns to her everyday life with a secret to nurture for the remaining years or decades she has left. Unless, of course, she is the murderer . . .

McAnnis has been shuffling around his bedroom while you've been wrestling with these thoughts; you notice fingernail scratches on his back as he changes shirts. From the top bureau drawer he pulls out a small plastic container of pills, grimacing as he swallows two without water. He staggers into the kitchen. The rest of the Blake household is still asleep. The appliances baffle McAnnis, so he slips out to retrace the prior night's steps toward the clubhouse, in search of coffee.

×

It was quiet. I could smell bacon frying in the kitchen. From the foyer I could hear female voices and a coarse laugh that I recognized as the caretaker, Fred Shiflett: the chatter of the help when they're certain their employers are still sleeping it off. I climbed upstairs to the library for no reason in particular other than that the club treasurer, Reginald Talbot, hadn't wanted me there.

I stood in front of the shelf stacked with bound volumes of West Heart newsletters. When you don't know what you're looking for, you can start anywhere. I began pulling them down at random, skipping haphazardly around the decades. The hemlines on the women getting shorter. The hair on the men, longer. In a 1971 issue, I saw the first (and only) photo with a black man—a guest?—smiling next to James Blake. Then I remembered the missing years from the president plaques—1935–1940—and turned to the older books.

A June 1931 article about how, "in light of the current economic crisis and its effect on member finances, the club has begun selling trees to a lumber concern, to help offset operating costs." A practice they'd resorted to once again, judging from the logging trucks I'd seen in the clear-cuts on the way in.

A March 1932 article about a guest lecture by the "illustrious" Dr. George Roberts, for the presentation of his "wondrous" invention that unlocked the mysteries of the human body's electrical system. His "oscillophore" measured vibrations: Irish blood vibrated at fifteen ohms, Italian blood at twelve ohms, Jewish blood at seven ohms . . . etc.

A December 1933 photo of two grinning couples on the clubhouse porch, highball glasses raised in the air, under the headline PROHIBITION OVER, SPIRITS RETURN TO WEST HEART. The gleeful tone of the article, sprinkled with wry innuendo, made it clear that in truth the spirits had never really left.

A July 1938 article headlined LINDBERGH, FORD AT WEST HEART. The accompanying photo of a man greeting the two famous guests, squinting in the sunlight, was captioned: *Dr. Theodore Blake greets American heroes Charles Lindbergh and Henry Ford, on the occasion of their address to the Club, speaking on the current political moment and the situation in Europe.* A second, smaller photo revealed Lindbergh bending over to shake the hand of a serious-looking young boy. I squinted; the boy seemed familiar . . .

I had only gotten past the first paragraph of this article—*a well-attended gathering with a supportive audience*—when I heard a floorboard creak.

Fred Shiflett, coffee mug in hand, was clearly pleased to have ambushed me. "You're up early." It sounded like an accusation.

"I do my best snooping early," I said.

Fred Shiflett sipped his coffee, taking his time. He was enjoying this. I stared right back at him, noticing the leathery skin and the closely cropped hair. Korea, probably, I thought.

"What are you doing here?" he asked.

"I was bored. Hunting books don't really do it for me, so I was just leafing through these instead. Something wrong with that?"

"Those are club books," said Fred Shiflett. "Not much interest to anyone else."

"I'm a curious guy," I said. "I'll read anything."

"You come here alone. You sneak upstairs. You poke around in the library. What would Mr. Garmond say if he knew?"

"Tell him and we'll find out," I said.

Fred Shiflett scowled. "I don't trust you," he said flatly.

"Then you're a good judge of character," I said. "But, honestly, I don't see why you care."

"I look after this place," said Fred Shiflett. "I live here, too. This is as much my home as theirs."

"Really? I saw a bunch of houses on the drive in, but I must have missed yours. Which one was it?" He stared back at me stonily. Not taking the bait, at least not yet. "They call them cabins, but really they're more like country mansions, aren't they? Where is your cabin? Deep in the woods, where it can't be seen? Where it won't embarrass the members?"

"You don't know anything about me," said Fred Shiflett.

"I know that you're taken for granted," I said. "That they ignore you until they need something. That they probably spend more money on booze than you make in a year. That when you're too old or too weak to carry wood or fix toilets they'll find someone who can and not give you another thought. Or am I wrong about them?"

"Right or wrong," he said, "I think you should leave."

"I get the sense of loyalty. It's commendable. But it has to run both ways. You've seen these people. You've seen what they have. Do you ever enter their homes when they're away? I would. See what they have, how they live. They think they're so clever, so good at hiding secrets. But they're not. That's why I'm here." I waited a beat. "If there's anything you think I should know, anything unusual, you can tell me."

"If I were you," Fred Shiflett said slowly, "I'd be care—"

He was interrupted by the roar of a truck outside, spewing gravel as it screeched to a stop, men yelling, cries of "Open the door, help him down, watch it, watch it—"

A final glare from Fred Shiflett—*To be continued*, it said—and then we both ran downstairs. A white-faced John Garmond was being helped through the door by his son, Ramsey, along with Duncan Mayer and Reginald Talbot. Garmond held a bloody rag pressed against his left shoulder. All the men wore thin canvas hunting vests, in deference to the warm weather, over Orvis field shirts (except for Ramsey, who wore a T-shirt) and khaki cargo pants.

"The kitchen," grunted Duncan Mayer. "The first-aid kit is in the kitchen." Reginald Talbot ran off.

The other two men lowered John Garmond onto a leather couch in the great hall.

"What happened?" I asked.

"I shot him, that's what," said Duncan Mayer, shakily wiping the blood from his hands onto his pants.

"Bad?" I asked.

"It's nothing," said John Garmond. "Really. It just nicked me."

"Let me see it," I said.

"What do you know about it?" asked Ramsey Garmond.

"This isn't the first gunshot wound I've seen," I said. "Let me look."

The bullet had torn off a small chunk of flesh from his shoulder, blood was everywhere, but John Garmond was right—it looked worse than it was.

"Stitches?" asked Ramsey Garmond.

"Definitely," I said. "But right now, we should clean it out."

Reginald Talbot returned with the first-aid kit, dropped it on the floor, and snapped open the white plastic lid. Duncan Mayer pulled out a brown bottle.

"What's that?" asked Reginald Talbot.

"Iodine," said Duncan Mayer. "You want me to use vodka instead?"

"If you're going to pour that on him, pull him off the good sofa," fretted Reginald Talbot. His face was so pale that I thought for a moment he might throw up. "No, not on the carpet, either. That was my mother's. She donated it to the club."

"Jesus Christ, Reg," said Duncan Mayer, glaring at the smaller man. He splashed the iodine messily over the wound. John Garmond groaned. "I know it stings. Sorry, John. Really. Sorry for everything. So stupid."

"It's all right," said John Garmond, through gritted teeth. "My fault. I shouldn't have just wandered off like that."

"Did you at least hit what you were shooting at?" asked Fred Shiflett, who had remained by the door. He gestured with his coffee mug at the man on the couch. "Assuming it wasn't him."

"I don't know," said Duncan Mayer.

"You don't know if you hit it, or you don't know if you were shooting at him?"

"Enough, Shiflett," snapped John Garmond.

"You want some coffee?" I asked him.

"God, yes. Water, too."

In the kitchen, the weekend's hired help were busy preparing for the big dinner at the bonfire. They stopped talking when I entered. I glanced inside the laundry room and saw a young woman shoving sheets into a washing machine. She stopped to stare at me. I shifted uncomfortably. Was that an accusing gaze? Or merely the whispers of a guilty conscience, a lingering gift or curse from the stern sisters at St. Thomas Academy of Brooklyn, New York?

Water, coffee, some bacon I grabbed off a rack. The color was returning to John Garmond's face.

"You should get him to the hospital," I said to his son.

"Maybe Dr. Blake could just . . . take care of it here?" asked Reginald Talbot.

I glanced at him sharply. "This man needs to go to the ER," I said.

"Fine, fine," said Reginald Talbot. "I'll help."

"Need another hand?" asked Duncan Mayer.

"No," said Ramsey Garmond.

They carried John Garmond out to the truck, leaving me alone in the great hall with Duncan Mayer. We stood there awkwardly, two strangers thrust into close company, like at a dinner party when the mutual acquaintances leave the table. Duncan Mayer was a serious-looking man in his late forties, tall, with a swimmer's broad shoulders and slate-blue eyes and dark hair going flint-gray. He wore an inscrutable expression now, but I remembered the snarling fury that had flashed across his face yesterday, when he confronted Alex Caldwell. The potential for violence flickered inside some men like a pilot light; Duncan Mayer might brood on his misfortunes for years, or even decades, I thought, before erupting into action.

"You all right?" I asked.

"Why wouldn't I be?" he asked warily.

"It's not every day that you shoot someone," I said. "Even by accident."

"So stupid," said Duncan Mayer. "It could have been so much worse. I'm lucky."

"So is John," I said.

"Of course."

"Unusual to be hunting deer," I said casually, "in the summer. Hunting season started early, I guess?"

Duncan Mayer stared at me coldly. "Maybe it did."

"I thought it usually began in October?"

"Look," said Duncan Mayer. "You're right. But this is a special case. As long as West Heart has existed, there's been a hunt on Independence Day weekend. Supposedly, Teddy Roosevelt came one year, though I don't really believe that. It's mainly a thing in the Garmond family, father to son. John's father took us both our first time. We were ten years old."

"Your father didn't take you?"

"No."

"But these hunts are illegal, are they not?"

"Technically."

"I've seen men sent to prison for technicalities," I said.

"Nobody cares what we do, out here, in the middle of nowhere," said Duncan Mayer. "And even if they did, there's no way for anyone to find out. We make our own rules."

"And on a property of this size," I added, "who is there to hear the distant sound of gunshots in the woods anyway?"

"Exactly."

"Your wife and son doing okay?"

Duncan Mayer stiffened. "What do you mean?"

"After yesterday. With the dog."

He relaxed. "That's right, you were here for that."

"They're doing okay?" I repeated.

"Fine. More or less," he said. "More less than more, honestly."

"Is that why he didn't go hunting with you?"

"Who?"

"Your son," I said. "Otto, is that his name?"

"Yes. Otto is not much of a hunter," said Duncan Mayer, deftly sidestepping the subject of his son's crippled leg. "Though few of us are, truth be told. We hunt up here for the same reason that we golf down in the city. A chance to be outdoors, get away from the wives. Drink at an hour that would be considered alarming in other contexts."

"Did you drink this morning?"

Duncan Mayer's jaw tightened. "You wouldn't be interrogating me, would you, Mr. McAnnis?"

"Not at all," I said. "Just making conversation."

He was looking down at something. I realized it was my hand, trembling at my side.

"Rough night?" he asked, eyebrows raised.

"Dinner at the Blake house," I said, stuffing my hands into my pockets. "Trying to keep up with Warren Burr."

"Good luck with that," muttered Duncan Mayer. "The man has a problem. I mean, we all do. But he *really* has a problem. Did she go after you?"

"Pardon?"

"His wife. Susan. She's not shy."

"No, she didn't," I said. "I guess I'm not her type."

Duncan Mayer looked as if he were about to say something, then stopped himself. "I suppose I'll see you later?" he asked, without much enthusiasm.

"At the bonfire? It sounds like quite a spectacle."

"It is," said Duncan Mayer. "If you have anything to sacrifice to the gods, bring it tonight."

×

McAnnis walks out to the grand porch of the clubhouse, listening to the emergency weather bulletin filtering up from the radio in the kitchen, unaware (of course) that you are being allowed to eavesdrop on his private thoughts as he argues with himself about whether he pushed too hard, revealed too much; unlike lawyers, who are taught never to ask a question to which they don't know the answer, detectives by disposition and necessity must speculate and provoke. At times, McAnnis is thinking, he feels like a foolish child poking a stick down into a burrow, not certain what sort of beast, if any, he will awake.

You are surprised, a bit, by this morning's display of self-pity from your protagonist, and you wonder if in truth he is simply suffering from hangovers of both the physical and spiritual varieties. Could McAnnis be struggling with the metaphysical weight of searching for weaknesses to exploit, trusts to betray, secrets to uncover and place, naked, obscene and wriggling, on the stage? Might he also be uneasy with his choice to suborn infidelity, hardly a capital offense, in this day and age, but nonetheless enough to induce a twinge of remorse?

These regrets, you decide, do him credit as a person, if not as a detective, and you find yourself feeling a bit sorry for him. Isn't that the risk that readers face in the first-person point of view? That you cannot help but identify with a Humbert Humbert as much as with a Huck Finn? And doesn't that leave you vulnerable to manipulation and misdirection?

You realize that McAnnis has returned his thoughts to the clubhouse library. Something is nagging at him. A detail or clue that he saw but didn't recognize. But what? The newsletters? The books? The wall of plaques?

He remembers now: a faint outline on the wall, at the end of the display of club president plaques. One had been removed. Its placement suggests that the missing plaque should have been the most recent, but the one above the outline is current—it reads *Reginald Talbot 1970–1975*. You begin to understand at the same time as McAnnis. The 1935–1940 plaque has been removed, recently, and each of the other plaques painstakingly moved into the place of its predecessor. An empty space in the middle of a display like this being more noticeable than one at the end.

Someone had gone to a lot of trouble over something very small. But who? And why?

Readers, like detectives, have nothing to go on but their own experience, and so, from the first sentence of this book, perhaps without even realizing it, you've been reviewing past fictions the way a sleuth might consult his case files for possible solutions or at least lines of inquiry. As a student of murder, you know that every crime initially presents with a virtually endless set of potential clues and story lines. But, properly pursued, every investigation takes on the shape of a funnel, ultimately narrowing to the motives that have driven men and women to kill for thousands of years—love, hate, fear, greed, jealousy—along with a panoply of lesser vices—lust, ambition, rage, vanity, shame, cowardice.

And so, like a forensic detective who seeks to match crime-scene fingerprints to a database of known criminals, you understand that the answers to this mystery may be found in the case files of your prior reading.

But to return to your protagonist: McAnnis is now walking back to the Blake house, tired and hungry and hungover, and thinking, as you are, that the honor of greeting guests as world-famous as Charles Lindbergh and Henry Ford would most likely fall to the club president.

✕

Case Study: The Guilty Detective

This difficult plot device has a long though tenuous tradition in Western culture, from Sophocles to Agatha Christie. We begin with *Oedipus Rex*, which, after two thousand years, remains a marvel of construction. The story, in brief: Oedipus has become king of the cursed city of Thebes, after fleeing Corinth to escape a prophecy that he will kill his father and marry his mother. The oracle reveals that the Thebes curse will be lifted only if Oedipus is able to find the murderer of the prior king, who had been killed by bandits at a crossroads. Oedipus remembers that he himself had killed a man in similar circumstances, but is reassured since his parents are, he believes, safe back in Corinth. He launches his murder investigation. A messenger arrives from Corinth and reveals that Oedipus was actually adopted; it's then exposed that his true father was the man he murdered and that the old king's widow is now, in fact, his wife, fulfilling the prophecy after all. In grief and despair, Oedipus stabs gold pins into his eyes and spends the rest of his days wandering in exile.

The particular genius of the Sophocles play is that Oedipus *doesn't know* that he is the man he seeks, which makes his obsessively focused investigation, leading to its inevitably tragic conclusion, all the more excruciating for the audience. In Kenneth Fearing's 1946 noir *The Big Clock*, the plot is reversed: the tension and dramatic irony derive from the protagonist's *knowing* that he's the culprit. George Stroud is secretly dating the girlfriend of his boss. One night, Stroud sees his boss walk into her apartment building. She is later found dead—murdered. The boss knows someone saw him enter the building; he assigns Stroud to find that witness, who of course is Stroud himself. Despite his best efforts to delay his own investigation, the walls begin to close in as Stroud's boss comes ever closer to learning the truth.

The premise of this conceit veers perilously close to melodrama, a risk highlighted by one real-life case so improbable that most writers would have dismissed it as too preposterous for fiction. Robert Ledru was a French detective of the Belle Époque era. In 1887, while on vacation, he was asked by local police to aid the investigation of a man found shot to death on the beach. Footprints in the sand revealed the killer was missing a big toe on his right foot; Ledru was also missing the same toe on the same foot. He had woken up that morning with wet socks and a bullet missing from his revolver, with no memory of the events of the previous night. Ballistics proved his gun had fired the fatal shot. Ledru, realizing he had killed the man while sleepwalking, confessed to his fellow police: "I have the killer and the evidence, but I lack the motive. It was I who killed Andre Monet." He was sent to prison and lived out the rest of his days under guard on a remote farm. (As unbelievable as this case may be, the legal and medical literature is filled with other stories of somnambulist homicide, in which spouses or children are often the victims; juries have tended not to believe, or accept, the claims of killers who resort to this defense in court.)

Devotees of Agatha Christie—is there a plot device she *didn't* try?—will recognize that she utilized a variant of this tactic in her final published Hercule Poirot novel, *Curtain*.

×

On the way back to the Blake house, I ran into Ralph Wakefield, Susan Burr's nephew, walking down the dirt road, binoculars hanging around his neck, clutching a thick book in his hands.

"What are you doing, Ralph?" I asked.

"Bird watching."

"Do you know a lot about birds?"

"Yes. A lot. Already today I've seen a wood thrush, a pine warbler, a woodcock, and a red-tailed hawk. I know most of them by sight, but if I don't, then I look it up in this book. That's why I have this book."

"Did your aunt suggest this?"

"Yes. She said she needed a break and that I should get out of the house."

I smiled. "Do you know where she is now?"

"I'm not sure. She said she might go to the lake."

"Thanks," I said. The boy fidgeted, one hand straying to the binoculars. "Can I ask you something else?"

"Sure," he said.

"But you have to tell the truth, okay?"

"Okay."

"Do you ever use your binoculars to look into people's homes, Ralph? Through their windows?"

"Sometimes," the boy admitted. "Is that bad?"

"Not necessarily," I said. "It depends on why you're doing it. Would you do me a favor, Ralph?"

"Sure."

"If you ever see something strange, something unusual, happening in one of these houses, will you let me know?"

"Is this for your detective case?" he asked eagerly.

"That's right."

"Okay," said Ralph. "I'll play detective for you. I'll find something strange and unusual."

"Good," I said. "But Ralph?"

"Yes?"

"Don't get caught."

×

The lake shimmered in the summer sun. Children diving from a rope swing. A beach filled with sunbathing women, lying on sand trucked in from miles away. Out on the water, a figure in a canoe paddled quietly toward the boathouse—a favorite setting, you recall, for scenes of discovered bodies. I was hoping to see Susan Burr, but Emma Blake was there instead, lying on a blanket in a yellow bikini, eyes hidden by oversized brown sunglasses.

"How'd you sleep?" I asked cautiously.

"Why do you ask?"

"Isn't that a thing people say?" I said. "How did you sleep? Did you sleep well?"

"I heard the yelling, if that's what you're asking," said Emma Blake. "Don't worry," she added. "I doubt anyone else heard. They all take sleeping pills." She studied me for a moment. "Do you do that every night?"

"Not every night."

"Most nights?"

"Some nights."

"Why?"

"I'm wrestling with the angels," I said.

"Whatever."

I indicated the space next to her. "Do you mind?"

"It's a free country," said Emma Blake. "Allegedly. They taught me otherwise in college."

"Vassar?"

She stuck out her tongue. "Smith."

I lay down, propped up on my elbows. Squinting in the sun, feeling faintly absurd in my guayabera and cutoff jean shorts. Watching the children splash in the shallows. Emma Blake turning her body, slightly, toward me. Dragonflies hovering across the face of the water.

"Sleep is a curious thing, isn't it, when you think about it?" said Emma Blake. "We all decide to tuck ourselves into beds like little babies, to stop thinking anything, to stop doing anything. To stop *living*, essentially. It's creepy. What are we at three a.m. but a nation of corpses, waiting to be reborn in the morning?"

"The only thing I know about sleep," I said, "is that I don't get enough of it."

"That's your own fault," said Emma Blake. "Like last night. Was it as good for you as it was for her?"

"I don't know what you mean."

"I think you do."

"I'm ignoring that." I shaded my eyes with my hand, squinting in the sunlight. "Christ, it's bright."

"Look at me," said Emma Blake.

She took off her sunglasses to study my eyes. Hers were clear and blue-gray. When I looked away, she grabbed my chin and ordered me to stay still.

"Your pupils are dilated," she said finally, putting her sunglasses back on. "Whatever you're on, be careful. I don't think you'd want my father to see."

Out on the floating dock in the middle of the lake, a group of boys was playing King of the Hill. They looked identical: bare-chested, long-haired, absurdly skinny, and already as brown as hazelnuts. One boy slipped on the slick wood and crashed to the deck with a slap that was audible from the beach. The others laughed. One began to sing in an intentionally off-key falsetto, "O say can you see . . ."

"It's been a long time since I've seen this much red-white-and-blue," I said. "The flags on every cabin, the bunting at the clubhouse."

"The good people of West Heart can't help but love America," said Emma Blake. "It's more or less required."

"Love it or leave it."

"Exactly."

"If only," I said, "there was a way to love America and leave it at the same time."

One by one, the boys were diving off the floating dock and swimming in long easy strokes back toward the shore. The last time I saw Emma Blake, she'd probably been their age. Casually, I asked her about growing up at West Heart. As I'd hoped, she began telling stories about the club. The island in the lake where children would play Tom Sawyer battling the pirates. The lean-to by the dam, home to lost virginities. The cliff trail named for the old woman who hiked it every day until she fell to her death. The teenage daughter who disappeared for nine months, and when she returned, the family announced they'd adopted a distant relative's baby. The late-night poker games after which ashen-faced men would toss empty wallets onto nightstands and slide into bed next to their wives in the bleakness of a gray dawn.

The club, Emma Blake continued, consisted of seven thousand acres that, while technically part of the incorporated hamlet of Middleton, in practice operated as its own independent fiefdom. The northern side of the club abutted the hills cascading down from the mountains like the last rumblings of an argument, pockmarked with caves and littered with massive granite boulders left by retreating glaciers. The club had two lakes on the property; in years past, both had been clear and swimmable, but of late one had become choked with lily pads and bulrushes and the muck of fallen trees.

"We're just a decade or two from it becoming a swamp," said Emma Blake.

The dam at the end of Heart Lake was a spot for mischief: during the day, it might be shivering younger kids daring each other to brave the thirty-foot drop into the pool on the other side; after nightfall, it was teenagers sharing illicit vices that evolved over the years from cigarettes and booze to barbiturates and hallucinogens. A hundred miles of trails looped around the property, not all of them marked; one path, which wound behind the homes in the central part of the club, was known as "Lovers' Lane," a clandestine pathway for late-night adulterers seeking to avoid the main gravel road. There was a story, too good to be true, of two husbands who stumbled into each other while en route to midnight trysts with each other's wives, and who exchanged nothing more bitter than a terse *Good evening*.

The southern end of the club, which constituted the bulk of the property, was given over to hunting. The area seemed wild and unkempt, at least compared with the rest of the club, the forest so thick in spots that it was virtually impassable—but it was in fact a manicured killing ground. Decades of caretakers had planted and pruned the wilderness to maximize the hunters' returns, cultivating food plots with salt licks and clover and radishes for the deer, and strawberries and oats and chicory for the bears. Visitors to West Heart walking through the southern trails would often remark on what appeared to be pleasant fields of wild blueberry and currant and mint, but which were, in truth, carefully tended death traps.

"We used to stock the lake, too, with fish, but we stopped a few years ago."

"Why?"

"Don't know. Cost too much, probably."

Bald eagles could be seen along the river, occasionally warring with the crows and ravens amid the treetops. In the marshy back-woods, you might stumble upon an occasional blue heron. Emma Blake recalled surprising one in its nest: it struggled into flight like a prehistoric creature, laboriously flapping its immense wings, squawking in fury and defecating in midair as it made slow passes through the trees, trying to frighten her off.

"We have company," I said, nodding.

Otto Mayer was limping through the sand toward an Adirondack chair. A long scar ran up his left thigh and disappeared under his swim trunks.

"What happened to his leg?" I asked.

"That information," said Emma Blake, "is going to cost you. Where did you go last night?"

"When?"

"Midnight is not very late," she said. "It's almost an insult to have a rendezvous at that hour."

"I assumed no one would care."

"We don't. But we do. People here like to know everything about everybody. So tell me," she said, "do you enjoy women that old?"

"She's not that old," I said.

"To me, *you're* old," said Emma Blake. "She's ancient. So tell me. Women that old: Are they 'experienced'? Do they 'know what they like'?"

"Actually, yes."

"Fascinating. And that makes up for the sagging tits, that thing on the neck, what do you call it?"

"That's enough, Emma."

"The wattle?"

"You know her. Is that what she looks like?"

"No." She pretended to pout. "Unfortunately. You know that you're not unique, right?"

"I'm aware."

"Where'd she take you? Room 302?"

That stung.

"Pretty detailed information," I said. "You should be a detective."

"The maid likes me. Mary. I give her Quaaludes sometimes," said Emma Blake.

"So what happened to Otto Mayer's leg?"

Emma Blake frowned and picked up a magazine. "Car accident," she said tersely. "Very sad."

"Because of a bum leg?"

"He wasn't alone in the car. The other guy didn't make it."

"The other guy?"

"Alex Caldwell's son. Trip."

A brief image of a man kneeling on the ground over a dead dog—*You wanted to find a way to hurt to me, to hurt Claudia and Otto, and now you did.*

"Is that why—"

I was interrupted by a loud buzzing overhead. A biplane was flying low over the lake. It dipped its wings in greeting to the swimmers below, who waved back, then banked away toward what I supposed was the local airport.

"I wonder if that's John Garmond," said Emma Blake.

"Why do you say that?"

"Because he's an amateur pilot. I flew with him once, when I was little. He told me he's been obsessed with aviation since he was a kid."

I squinted up. "Don't think it's him."

"Why?"

"Because he was shot today."

I described the scene at the clubhouse that morning, watching her carefully to see if she had any reaction to the shooting. She did not. But it did get her talking about hunting, and then about guns. West Heart, it seemed, was bristling with weaponry.

"What's happening there?" Emma Blake asked abruptly, pointing toward the beach.

A knot of children who had been whispering conspiratorially set off abruptly at a sprint toward the boathouse. Their mothers sat up, confused, craning their necks from their beach chairs as the kids raced down to cluster around something at the water's edge. Even from this distance, I could see little faces twisting around nervously to look back at the adults on the beach.

"Something's not right," said Emma Blake.

"No, it's not," I said. "I'll go take a look."

There is something particularly awful about horror in broad daylight. As I crossed the beach, I felt the eyes of the mothers following me from behind dark sunglasses. I could hear insects buzzing on the lake. As I got closer, I realized the kids were eerily quiet, aside from some jostling—*to get a better look*, I thought.

"Let me through," I said.

A little girl was standing closest, the lake licking at her toes. She gazed up at me, blue eyes inscrutable and unblinking, then turned back and pointed.

The body was bobbing gently in just a few inches of water, facedown, snagged on a fallen branch. The small current trying to tug it away every few seconds. A woman, wearing a thick housecoat. Her hair splayed out on the water. A shock of white.

Claudia Mayer.

×

A delicate moment for every murder story: the first corpse. It is, you think, the moment for which the mystery was made, as when a match lying in a drawer for ages is finally fired into brilliant incandescence, so bright it hurts to look at, before immediately beginning to consume itself. In these opening pages, you've been savoring the anticipation, the slow buildup of potential energy, the meticulous plotting that sets the stage for what's to come. But once the body is found, there is no going back. The mystery will race ahead according to its own inexorable logic, posing an entirely new set of questions. Will the killer make a mistake? Who will emerge as a suspect? Which false clues will beguile the detective? Which false solutions? And of course—will the killer strike again?

While you enjoy the thrills of the middle act, you can't help but feel a certain wistful longing or even nostalgia for the beginning, the way a lover, in the months afterward, might fondly recall the start of an affair. But here at West Heart, the ceremonies of death have begun. Word has spread. A crowd is gathering. And so you return to the page, curious to discover what twists will follow this first inevitable death, a moment you've seen some writers play as tragedy, others as farce.

Emergency vehicles parked on the grass behind the boathouse.

An ambulance, a sheriff's 4x4, a deputy's cruiser.

Yellow tape.

Otto Mayer insisting on seeing the body.

Led away, pale and dazed, by Ramsey Garmond.

Emma Blake trying to shoo away the children.

John Garmond, bandage visible beneath his polo shirt.

Conferring gravely with the sheriff.

Heads turning as Duncan Mayer's truck rolls to a stop.

Eyes rimmed red.

"Where is she?"

Voice hoarse.

John Garmond places a hand on his shoulder.

Duncan Mayer shrugs it off.

Walks leadenly to the ambulance.

Climbs into the back.

The paramedic lifts a sheet.

Duncan Mayer drops his head.

The paramedic drops the sheet.

People turn away, out of respect.

All but two.

The sheriff watching the bereaved husband.

And Adam McAnnis watching the sheriff.

×

My first body was a woman who'd been shot by her husband after a night of drinking. I was on a ride-along with my father and his partner. It was the first time he'd brought me to work. I sat in the back of their black 1948 Plymouth Deluxe, listening to profane banter that I couldn't understand, barely tall enough to see out the window. All day, I was quietly terrified that if they arrested a criminal I'd have to sit next to him. My father was a different man than he was at home—bigger, meaner. That morning, he'd brought me into the station, placed his thick hands on my shoulders.

"This is my boy," he said.

"Your old man's a hard-ass, kid," said another detective. "Are you a hard-ass, too?" I shrugged. They laughed.

"Send him down to Vice," another detective said. "Pop his cherry."

They wore suits and fedoras and smoked cigarettes end to end. They were casual and quick and didn't seem to care what anyone thought—except each other. Apex predators in a city of carrion. One detective was already sweating through his shirt, jacket off, sleeves rolled up, tapping at the keys on a black typewriter that seemed absurdly small for a man his size, swearing every time he made a mistake. "Fuck my mother," he exclaimed. The others laughed.

When the call came, my father got serious—"Keep your mouth shut and your eyes open," he told me. I nodded. "Want some coffee before we go?" I shook my head.

The murder was in a fifth-floor walk-up in Hell's Kitchen. The halls were dark; broken glass crunched underfoot. The photographer was already there, loudly smacking his Wrigley's. He arched an eyebrow when I walked in, glanced at my father, then shrugged. A uniformed cop was in the hall, talking to the super.

I hadn't known that people could live like that. Flies buzzing around dishes piled high in the sink. Bottles of liquor everywhere. A filthy couch polka-dotted with singed holes from cigarettes. A giant withered plant in the corner; my father said later that the killer had taken to urinating in its pot when he was too drunk or lazy to make it to the toilet.

"H.B., look," said my father to his partner. His name was Horatio Brown, but no one—except me, years later—ever called him that. My father lifted a chain that had been draped over the top of the mirror, from which dangled dog tags and a shriveled human ear. "You bring home any of these?"

H.B. grunted. "Marines sold them for five bucks a pair in Midway. Ten bucks in Hawaii."

The body was in the bedroom. She was fully dressed. Black hair, red lipstick. A single white high-heel pump hung precariously from her left foot. Her torso was a mass of blood.

"How many shots?"

"Too messy to tell."

"Must have emptied the chamber."

"Where's the gun?"

H.B. nodded at the open window.

"We'll check the alley in a minute," said my father. "Where's the perp?"

"Sleeping it off in the precinct hotbox."

"We'll hit him after lunch." My father shot me an impassive look. "You okay?"

I nodded.

"Bickford's?" asked my father.

"Lindy's?" countered his partner.

"I can't eat that shit anymore," said my father.

They settled on George's Cafe on West Thirty-third, my first lunch in Manhattan. I had a chocolate milkshake. My father had a steak, rare. "You're not hungry?" he asked, blood pooling on the white diner plate.

My first body. Not the last. Booby-trapped corpses left in the jungle to rot. Zipped-up bags enclosing teenagers with tags on their toes, waiting for transport home. Villages of the dead that you'd smell before they came into view. And later: called to the morgue by my father's old colleagues to identify a naked woman on the slab. *She had your card in her purse, imagine that. Care to tell us what this is about?* Or: the irresolute end to a missing-persons case, a college dropout who turned up dead on the abandoned docks where hustlers would go to turn tricks. *When we said where we'd found him*, the homicide dick told me, *the parents said you should ID him . . .*

And, of course, the body of my father itself. An open coffin, an Irish wake, a bar closed to the public and filled with men I'd worshipped as a child, now old and fat, waiting for their own heart attacks. Disabled off the force, or retired, or still somehow wearily tagging evidence from yet another victim in yet another stinking apartment. My father's friends stared at me with distaste, like I'd betrayed some higher calling: they did not like private detectives. H.B. by then was too sick to attend, which perhaps was just as well.

My mother returned to County Clare afterward, as if America were just a dream she'd fallen into as a girl, who had awoken years later as an old woman in an empty house. She lived now in the stone cottage where she'd been born, writing me occasional letters of matters so foreign that they seemed written by, or to, a stranger: stories of stillborn sheep and fungus in the barley and drunken priests and teenage boys who left in the night to die shooting AR-18s on the blood-wet cobblestone streets of Belfast . . .

. . . and you're enjoying these little morsels of biography, you're not the type who wants a total cipher as your detective, you want some history. Not too much—this tale is not about him—but just enough to make you care, just enough so you understand how he's different from the last detective you read. Are you also, perhaps, reflecting on your own first corpse? Was it someone you knew? Someone you loved? Did you understand, then, the cold, brute reality of death: that it's defined by absence? The magic is gone. A drab curtain falls in a shabby theater and the conjurer is wearily packing his mail-order tricks backstage into a scuffed suitcase, bus ticket sticking out of his blazer pocket. In the end, you think, all that's left is a mechanic's diagnosis of what went wrong: a malfunctioning valve, a loss of fluid, a spark that failed to ignite.

Claudia Mayer was a suicide. Any fool could see that. I knew she was off when we spoke, the chimes tinkling over our heads. There were no overt signs of violence on the body. Her housecoat was weighted down with stones in the pockets. I heard the whispers from the crowd: *She seemed even worse lately . . . I knew she was depressed, but I never thought . . . I'd heard she was drinking . . .*

And yet. The sheriff had studied Duncan Mayer closely, too closely. He'd walked through the dark corners of the boathouse like a man searching for something. A brief interrogation with the haggard new widower, sitting in the driver's seat of his truck. *No, there wasn't a note*, Duncan Mayer appeared to say. Then the sheriff left, heading down a side road away from the clubhouse.

"Toward Alex Caldwell's place," said Emma Blake. She'd removed her sunglasses. Her eyes were puffy.

"That sheriff . . ." I said.

"What about him?"

"I heard him say to John Garmond, 'You people have a problem with July Fourth.'"

"Yes."

"What did he mean by that?"

Emma Blake sighed.

"I told you about the car accident. Otto Mayer and Trip Caldwell. Trip died. It was five years ago, on this holiday weekend. A year later, to the day, his mother, Amanda Caldwell, committed suicide."

"How did she do it?" I asked, though I'd already guessed.

"She drowned herself in the lake," said Emma Blake.

×

Not my case. A dead woman in a lake. All signs pointing to suicide. She'd been depressed, drinking, taking pills. Nothing to do with anything. Not my case. Not my problem.

I wanted that to be true. But the client was interested in "anything unusual." A dead woman in a lake. Two, as a matter of fact. Years apart. Linked by tragedy and grief and anger. Both suicides? Neither? By now, the client had probably learned of this death, would be curious about whether I was curious, and if not, why not. Questions, I concluded, had to be asked.

I was still on the beach. The emergency vehicles were gone. Some kids had torn away pieces of the yellow CAUTION tape from the lakeside crime scene and were wrapping it around their heads and wrists, laughing, admiring their reflections in the boathouse windows. They reminded me of the gang members I'd seen in the city who wore police hats and badges, God knows where or how they got them, flaunting the gear on street corners like trophies from a vanquished enemy. Sometimes you'd even hear the crackling of a CB radio tuned to the local precinct. I was regarded in my neighborhood as a curiosity: not-quite-a-cop but definitely not someone who belonged, a throwback or relic, the kind of person who probably should have moved off the block a long time ago.

Ramsey Garmond was talking to Emma Blake, explaining that he'd just come from the Mayer house. They were all of a generation, I thought. Emma, Ramsey, Otto . . . the dead kid, Trip. A decade younger than me. Watching coverage of the JFK assassination on black-and-white TVs, pimply-faced, confused, not a little frightened. Their first assassination, but not their last.

Ramsey Garmond's face clouded over when he saw me. He probably thought I was bad luck. First the dog, then his father's shooting, now Claudia Mayer. Yesterday he'd been a prince, blond hair shining in the sunlight. Now his carefree smile had slipped.

"How's Otto?" asked Emma Blake.

"A mess," said Ramsey Garmond. "Even more than usual."

"To be expected," I said, joining them.

"Yes."

"Your dad seems okay," Emma Blake said tentatively.

"He's fine," said Ramsey Garmond. "Just a few stitches."

"How was the ER?" I asked.

"Fine."

He needed to be pushed. "An emergency room is like a prison," I said.

"How so?" Ramsey Garmond asked warily.

"It's a mirror of the community," I said. "For better or worse. Ever been to Bellevue?"

"No."

"I recommend two a.m. on a Saturday night for the first-timer. It's the purest experience. Shootings. Knifings. Addicts who've had too much or too little of their favorite drug. Bowery boozers dying of dehydration. Prostitutes clutching their ribs and coughing up blood sitting next to pimps who were annoyed at themselves for misjudging that final kick. Once, I saw a circus performer, still in costume, who'd been mauled by some sort of animal. He was scared to tell me which one did it."

"Scared of what?" asked Emma Blake.

"Losing his job."

"What were you there for?" asked Ramsey Garmond.

"I was on a case," I said. "So I imagine this ER was nothing like that?"

"Of course not," said Ramsey Garmond. "There was a drunk who'd wrecked his car. A woman who'd fallen down her stairs. Some poor kid who lost a couple fingers to fireworks."

"Did they call a cop to come talk to you?" I asked.

"A deputy, yes," said Ramsey Garmond. "How did you know?"

"Standard procedure whenever there's a shooting," I said. "Even an accident."

For the first time that day, a cloud passed across the face of the sun. A gust of wind momentarily stirred the surface of the lake, a hint of the storm to come. Emma Blake shivered.

"Did the deputy seem interested?" I asked.

"Not particularly," answered Ramsey Garmond.

"Did he want to talk to Duncan Mayer?"

"No."

"So you didn't tell him that Duncan fired the shot?"

"Listen," said Ramsey Garmond, with a quick glance at Emma Blake. "We didn't tell the deputy what happened. Not really."

"Because the hunt was illegal."

"Outsiders wouldn't understand. It's a family tradition. Father to son. Half the time, we don't even shoot anything."

"So you said what?"

"My father said he was cleaning his gun and it went off."

"The deputy wasn't suspicious?"

"No," Ramsey Garmond said impatiently. "Look, the people up here, the people who matter, they know my dad. When he said it was an accident, they believed him."

"Do you?"

"Do I what?"

"Do you believe him?"

Ramsey Garmond stiffened. His fists clenched. I started thinking about how hard to hit back if I managed to dodge the first blow. "What's wrong with you?" he asked finally.

It was the type of question I'd long ago stopped trying to answer.

×

Emma Blake watched as Ramsey Garmond plodded across the sand toward the clubhouse. Then she spun around and shoved me in exasperation.

"Your bedside manner is awful," she said.

"Must be why I'm not a doctor."

"Ramsey didn't deserve that."

"Didn't he?"

"We grew up together," said Emma Blake. "Ramsey and Otto and me."

"And Trip Caldwell," I said.

She put her sunglasses back on. "Yes."

Emma Blake turned back toward the lake. A few children had resumed swinging off the rope, diving into the water, laughing.

"Should they be doing that?" she asked.

"Why not?" I said. "You think the water is contaminated some-how?"

"No. It just seems . . . disrespectful."

"They're kids, leave them alone. How long has it been since you swung into the lake off a rope?"

"Years."

"Maybe that's your problem."

We watched them laughing and splashing in the water. Earlier, when the ambulance with Claudia Mayer's body left, a few of the children had run after it, singing some kind of twisted nursery rhyme:

> Touch your toes
> Touch your nose
> Never go in one of those
> Hold your collar
> Do not swallow
> Until you see a dog

"I'm going for a walk," I said.

"Where?"

"Anywhere."

"Want company?" asked Emma Blake.

"No," I said, not unkindly. "But I'll find you later."

I set off down the same side road that the sheriff had pursued earlier, retrieving Ralph Wakefield's map from my shorts pocket to make sure I was on the right track. I followed the sounds of chopping wood echoing through the trees. Soon I came across Alex Caldwell, ax in hand, a pile of split wood at his feet, catching his breath.

×

Adam McAnnis is beginning his interrogation of Alex Caldwell, but your thoughts have returned to Emma Blake and her offer to accompany the detective, not for his sake, you suspect, but for her own. A desire not to be alone. You sense that she is shaken, unnerved, perhaps, by a premonition of the toll that decades at West Heart, living among these people, could exact on a woman's spirit. And, in fact, the women of this mystery, as in many mysteries, all seem to be victims, of life if not murder. Emma Blake pilfering Quaaludes from her parents' medicine cabinet, sharing them furtively with a maid from town. The anxiety and depression medications prescribed to her mother. The loneliness of Susan Burr. The sadness of Room 302. The deaths of Amanda Caldwell and Claudia Mayer. Whatever secrets may or may not be hiding behind the wary glances of Jane Garmond.

There is, you think, a desperation here, women trapped by age and class into roles they never wanted and now don't know how to escape, stuck in amber as the world beyond West Heart evolves. It feels dangerous . . .

. . . and by now the introductions have been made, McAnnis has explained his presence, and Alex Caldwell is talking, talking. He's a lean, gaunt man, hollow-cheeked, all tendon and sinew, coiled with tension like a spring. He looks as if he'd been sanded down to the absolute minimum. He looks like a man whose wife and son are dead.

"So you're here because you're a stranger," said Alex Caldwell. "Unafraid of being seen with the village pariah."

"What do you mean?" I asked.

"No one else will talk to me. They think I'm a killer."

"Of dogs or of people?"

Alex Caldwell paused. "Is this the part where I say I didn't kill Claudia Mayer?"

"It is."

"I didn't kill Claudia Mayer," he said.

"Did the sheriff ask you that?"

"He did."

"And what did you tell him?"

"That I'm sure she committed suicide," said Alex Caldwell. "Something I am acquainted with."

"I've heard about that," I said. "And you have my condolences. But that is precisely why they suspect you. It's curious that your wife and Claudia Mayer killed themselves in the same way, in the same place, on virtually the same day, just a few years apart."

"She must have had her reasons."

"Yes, but we don't know them," I said. "The police say she didn't leave a note. Most suicides do."

"Mine didn't," Alex Caldwell said flatly.

"And that can be painful," I said. "When they don't, it's usually because the reason is clear. The death of your son, for example. But sometimes the suicides don't leave a note because the reason, the real reason, is a secret or a shame that they want to take to their grave."

"And you think that's the case here?"

"I don't think anything. Not yet."

"So you're investigating this?"

"The Claudia Mayer case is in the good hands of the Stafford County Sheriff's Department," I said. "But I'm an inquisitive man. I ask questions. Sometimes people answer. I can't help myself."

"I'm surprised you were invited up here."

"Why?" I asked.

"A man in your profession is not a welcome thing. So many secrets. So many lies. To each other and to ourselves. This goddamn place," Alex Caldwell said savagely. He put another log on the stump and hacked it in half with one strong, clean swing. "We should have left years ago."

"Why don't you leave now?"

"Honestly? I'm waiting out the sale. If I'm going to leave, I might as well do so with a good payout. Get something out of my great-grandfather's investment."

"So you support the sale?" I asked.

"Yes."

"Would you say most other members do as well?"

"I have no idea," said Alex Caldwell. "I'm the outcast, remember?"

"One last question," I said. "That has to be asked."

"Go ahead," Alex Caldwell said warily.

"You say you didn't kill Claudia Mayer. But that's not what I was getting at."

Alex Caldwell stared at me a long time. Unconsciously shifting the grip on his ax. Finally, he said: "No one has ever asked me that. Except you."

"I'm sorry."

"But no," he said. "I also did not kill my wife."

×

And it's now, in this brief interlude, between the release of one breath and the intake of another, that you stop to consider a problem that's been vexing you since the opening paragraphs of the novel: you have sensed other characters lurking at the edges of these pages, like shades in purgatory. After all, didn't James Blake say that three dozen families belonged to the club? If so, where are they? Didn't the detective glimpse children, other families, down at the beach? Wasn't there said to be a crowd on the porch, for the Thursday night Sixer? Yet only a few were named. Who were the rest? Who was gathered at the scene of Claudia Mayer's suicide?

You sense that the author is caught between the demands of the rules of the genre (limiting the characters to a reasonable number), and the demands of verisimilitude (the probable size of a hunting club like this, the population on a holiday weekend, etc.). It doesn't really matter in the end, you reflect, as long as he plays fair, as long as he doesn't cheat by producing a killer in the final act who was not introduced in the first.

These preoccupations momentarily distract you from the story as it moves relentlessly toward the principal set piece of this second day—the bonfire—and a new set of questions. What is a bonfire before it burns? (What is a dancer before the dance?) Nothing but a junk pile, a heap of wood. All potential energy and expectation, the fever dreams of an ephemeral performance, the delight of knowing that what you're seeing exists only in this moment, never to be repeated exactly like this ever again . . . You've been anticipating the bonfire for many pages now, and, indeed, that evening, when McAnnis arrives at the site, in the midst of a vast grassy field near an abandoned barn, you are pleased to find that West Heart's July Fourth bonfire is enormous—some fifty feet in diameter, half that height in the center, not yet lit so you can see the base of firewood but also the flotsam and jetsam of discarded lives: dilapidated chairs, bureaus, broken picture frames, wooden pallets, a child's sled, the wreckage of a picnic table, what looks like part of a rowboat . . . The capstone to the whole surreal scene, topping the heap like a star or an angel on a Christmas tree, is what's left of an upright piano, legs removed or broken off, missing a good portion of its black and white keys, sagging at a slight angle at the peak of the pile, totally incongruous, like a battleship in a cornfield.

"I told Shiflett to put it there with one of the logging tractors," Dr. Blake said, beaming in satisfaction. "Been out of tune for years. Mice had been at it."

"Impressive," I said, and meant it. "Is it always like this?"

"First time with a piano. We had an old surrey one year. But, generally speaking, yes."

"Have you seen *Wicker Man*, doc?" I asked, eyeing the tower of kindling.

Dr. Blake grinned crookedly. "I'm sorry, Adam. But you've stumbled upon our secret. We lured you here to burn you alive in our annual sacrifice. Designed to ensure a good harvest of annuities and carried interest. Do you play piano?"

"Not really."

"Too bad. Because that would be a lovely way to go. Playing your own funeral mass on the way out. Or maybe a jaunty ragtime number. The second line of a jazz funeral." Dr. Blake abruptly adopted a somber expression; he must have remembered he was supposed to care about his neighbor's tragic demise. "I suppose it's not right to joke, after what happened today."

I hesitated. "It's complicated," I said finally.

"John thought about calling it off," said Dr. Blake. "But I insisted we proceed. What would we do, just sit around in our homes, alone? Better to be together. Except for Duncan and Otto Mayer, of course."

"Can I ask you a question?"

"Sure."

"How heavy were the stones in her housecoat?"

The doctor sighed. "Heavy enough, if that's what you're asking. Though I suspect, knowing Claudia, and having seen a fair number of suicides in my time, that pills and alcohol were involved, too."

"She was troubled?"

"Aren't we all?" he asked. "But yes."

"Marriage problems?"

Dr. Blake shrugged. "It's human nature to look for explanations. Underlying meaning. But I don't think there are always reasons for this sort of thing. *Motives*, to use your language. Sometimes people think. And sometimes they just *do*. There could be no reason at all. Or there could be a million, which amounts to the same thing."

The far end of the field had been designated as a parking lot and was filling up: McAnnis spotted Range Rovers, Harvester Scouts, Land Cruisers, Jeep Wagoneers, Ford Broncos, one AMC Javelin, and what looked like a fully restored Willys MB. Linda Ronstadt was on the radio. Little kids were running around with sparklers. An older boy clutched a quiver of bottle rockets. The first stars of evening were beginning to wink into life, and the sky as yet betrayed no sign of the incoming storm.

"By the way," I said. "I want to thank you for your hospitality."

"It's our pleasure, of course," said Dr. Blake.

"Not everyone is so happy to have a private eye in the house."

"We have nothing to hide," Dr. Blake said dismissively. "And anyway, I was curious about you. I was surprised when James said you were coming. It had been so long . . ."

I could feel the question hanging in the air, but as long as it remained unasked, I wasn't going to answer it.

×

Dinner was set on outdoor tables, wheeled in by the kitchen staff I'd glimpsed that morning. Trays covered in tinfoil, peeled back to reveal still-steaming offerings of beef Stroganoff, mac and cheese, broccoli . . . scattered bowls of popcorn for the kids, along with a giant quivering Jell-O with what appeared to be apricots, plums, and strawberries suspended inside like butterflies trapped under glass.

For the adults, bottles of wine and a painter's bucket full of something pink and frothy.

"Dr. Blake's rum punch," said John Garmond, grinning. "Be vigilant."

Among the staff was the maid I'd seen earlier at the clubhouse. Plain-looking, hair pulled back in a bun, wearing a cook's smock. A young person doing an old person's job. I waited until dinner was laid out, and she was alone, before making my move.

"Mary, isn't it?"

"That's right," she said warily.

"You're friends with Emma?"

"She told you that?"

"It came up somehow, I forget how." I gestured toward the dinner buffet. "You did a great job tonight. Not that anyone here would notice."

"Thank you."

"I bet you haven't gotten a single compliment from any of these people."

"No," she said. "No, I haven't. Not that I care what they think, anyway."

"That's right. A job is just a job," I said. "Have you worked here a long time?"

"A couple years. Not long."

"Still, I bet you've seen some . . . interesting things."

She looked at me in a way I'd come to recognize. "Are you a cop?"

"No."

"You talk like a cop."

"My father was in the police," I said. "Maybe some of it rubbed off on me."

"I don't like cops."

"Me neither," I said. "That's why I'm not one. Can you imagine being a teenager with a cop as a father? Anyway, sorry if that's how I come across. Let me make it up to you."

"How?"

"I was just about to go smoke a joint. I'd love some company."

Mary was still skittish. "If you're a narc, don't you have to tell me if I ask you?"

"I think that's what the law says, yes."

"Are you a narc?"

"I swear to you, I'm not a narc." I pulled out the joint. "Come on."

The cars were all parked on the grass at the other end of the field. Behind a truck, mostly hidden from view, we passed the joint back and forth, exhaling smoke into the thick summer air. Coughing and laughing. Talking to the help: a well-worn tactic, and for good reason. Intimacy, resentment, a tongue loosened by drugs or alcohol—it's a reliable combination when it comes to digging up dirt.

"Is the clubhouse always so empty upstairs?" I asked.

"Usually. Sometimes club members book rooms for weddings and parties and that sort of thing. We usually have lots of relatives come in around the holidays, too. Thanksgiving. Christmas. There's a big party at New Year's."

"What about the rest of the time?"

She smirked. "Are you asking if people use those rooms to cheat on their husbands and wives?"

"I suppose I am."

"The answer is yes. Of course. Where else would they go?"

"A hotel is the customary choice."

"The nearest 'no tell' motel is twenty miles away. And it's a dump. These people are too snobby for that. Anyway, the clubhouse is convenient. You can slip out, do your thing, and be back before anyone's awake." Mary pausing for another toke. "Room 302 gets the most action. Mrs. Burr. Have you met her?"

"Yes."

"Were you there last night?"

"Pardon?"

"Sorry, just asking," said Mary. "Someone was. Messier than usual. Also, Room 312, down the hall."

"Does that one get much use?" I asked.

"Sometimes. It has a window facing the creek; I imagine people like that."

"People?"

"I don't know who uses that one. I only know about Mrs. Burr because she left a hair clip one time. I recognized it because I'd seen her wearing it earlier."

"Did you give it back to her?"

"No," said Mary, touching the clip in her hair—a gold snake with emerald eyes.

"You kept it?" I asked, surprised.

"Why not?" said Mary. "She wouldn't dare to ask for it back. And her husband certainly wouldn't notice. I've thought that maybe some of the other women have recognized it, but no one's said anything. Probably scared that I'd be wearing some of their clothing next."

"So just those two rooms—302 and 312?"

"Those are the only ones that seem regular, if you know what I mean. Other rooms get used, but not as often."

I ventured a few more questions on other subjects—Emma Blake, drugs, club finances, new members—but didn't get much else out of her.

"Nice talking to you, Mary," I said. "Get home safe. There's a storm coming."

In fact, the storm was on everyone's lips when I returned to the still-unlit bonfire—the weather being a safer topic, no doubt, than suicide. Emma Blake was sitting alone in a teal-and-white woven plastic lawn chair just beyond the gathering crowd.

"You've been smoking weed again," she said accusingly.

"I went looking for you first," I protested. "You weren't around."

"So you found someone else?"

"A friend of yours. Mary."

"Grilling the servants? Isn't that a bit cliché?"

"The old tricks work the best," I said.

"I suppose," said Emma Blake. "You know, I'm not sure you picked the best weekend."

"Why is that?"

"Sounds like this storm tonight is going to be bad."

"We'll be a Locked Room," I said.

"What's that?"

"Strictly speaking, it's when a murder victim is found alone in a room, usually locked from the inside, windows sealed shut, that sort of thing. But I was using it in the more expansive sense of any isolated location—an island, a train trapped by snow, a country manor on the moors . . ."

"A remote hunting club?"

"Exactly."

"There are only two roads in and out of West Heart. It wouldn't take much for those to become impassable," said Emma Blake. "One is just a muddy track, and the other goes over the old bridge across the kill."

"The what?" I asked.

"The kill. You drove over it on the way here. The creek under the bridge. West Heart Kill. It's an old Dutch word," she explained, seeing my confusion. "Meaning *stream* or *creek*."

"I always wondered."

"I've heard there was a New Year's blizzard a couple decades ago," Emma Blake continued, "that trapped people here for over a week."

"Did they start eating each other?"

"Metaphorically speaking, maybe," she said. "Strange flesh."

"Excuse me?"

"That's what Shakespeare's Caesar accuses Mark Antony of eating during an ill-fated passage over the Alps."

"Strange flesh," I said. "I like that. Other men?"

"Presumably."

"Isn't it a bit counterrevolutionary to read Shakespeare these days?"

Emma Blake gazed at him flatly. "Your Shakespeare," she said, "is not the same as my Shakespeare."

×

Case Study: The Locked Room

The Locked Room is the most famous plot device in the entire canon. Variants are endless, but as a general rule, all include a victim found in a room locked from the inside, and which, the reader is assured, no one would have been able to access. The victims are alive before entering the room; upon discovery, they are dead. It is a puzzle that tends to evoke the supernatural—the phrase *locked from the inside*, uttered in pallid horror by a butler or constable, can chill the spine—but which usually runs aground on a disappointing, more mundane explanation. This is because, in a word, the Locked Room is *hard*. The best that Poe and Conan Doyle could do was concoct beasts (orangutan, snake) to enter the room in ways impossible for any human. Other writers have resorted to increasingly baroque, implausible solutions that frankly insult the discerning reader: air gun, poison blow darts, a pistol tied to a balloon, a bullet made of ice that melts inside the body after being fired . . .

One real-life Locked Room puzzle epitomizes such over-the-top solutions: In 1936, a woman was found dead, of an apparent bullet wound, lying in front of her coal furnace. No one else had been seen entering or leaving the premises. No gun was found at the scene. A scientist studying the death discovered the "bullet" was actually a copper projectile broken off a detonator cap used for blasting tunnels in mines. He surmised that it had been accidentally left in the delivery of coal to the poor woman's furnace, exploding into her chest once the heat rose, a staggeringly improbable but wholly accidental death.

Of the few acceptable solutions in fiction, special attention must be paid to the first person who enters the room. He or she is often the murderer, in this fashion: the victim is actually still alive (but comatose, perhaps via drugging) when the would-be rescuers burst open the locked door; the killer then coolly murders the victim in full view of everyone standing by, gaping at the spectacle of what they presume is already a corpse. This type of crime is best perpetrated by a doctor, coroner, or veterinarian; it must feel logical, without raising suspicion, that they would be the first to examine the body. A knowledge of anatomy is also required to kill deftly without notice, crouching over the victim, shielding others from view—an ice pick inserted through the ear, into the brain, would do nicely. The most clever weapon is an item that is not out of place inside that particular Locked Room, but which the murderer secreted away earlier: a favorite letter opener, perhaps, a thin silver stiletto kept by the colonel as a memento of some unfortunate colonial adventure, and now slipped through the left armpit, straight into the heart . . . the murderer pretending to check for signs of life with one hand while surreptitiously ending it with the other.

The most dedicated practitioner and explicator of the Locked Room was John Dickson Carr, whose novels almost exclusively centered on this device. In 1935's *The Hollow Man* (published in the United States as *The Three Coffins*), Carr devoted an entire chapter to the famous "Locked Room Lecture," in which his sleuth, Dr. Gideon Fell, outlines seven possible categories of solutions, each with endless variations. The lecture created a sensation in the mystery game; just a few years later, the novelist and critic Anthony Boucher had the baffled police lieutenant in his *Nine Times Nine* (1940) study Carr's book in hopes of finding an explanation for his own "real life" Locked Room murder. The lieutenant eventually decides that none of the solutions fit his case, though the discerning reader of Boucher's novel will recognize the hint in number five: "It is a murder which derives its problem from illusion and impersonation . . ."

A footnote: Among his many other pursuits, Anthony Boucher was an enthusiastic promoter of detective fiction from around the world. He was fluent in several languages, including Spanish. It's perhaps not surprising, then, that for a special "All Nations" issue of *Ellery Queen's Mystery Magazine*, Boucher convinced the editors to publish his translation of an Argentine poet and essayist hardly known within the United States. Thus, in that fateful *EQMM* August 1948 issue, beneath a typically garish cover showing a black-gloved woman being shot in the back by a woman in a green evening dress, alongside stories with titles like "Killer in Khaki" and "Being a Murderer Myself," readers would find a surreal tale of detection called "The Garden of Forking Paths"—Jorge Luis Borges published in English for the very first time.

×

Dusk was beginning to settle across the field. Fireflies blinked in and out of existence, chased by laughing children. The egg toss had concluded; a man I didn't recognize was crowned winner amid rumors that he'd cheated by hard-boiling his projectiles. Cheers erupted when he proved the skeptics wrong by smashing an egg against his head, downing a celebratory flute of champagne with yolk running down his temple.

I had some questions for Reginald Talbot, the treasurer, so I went looking for him. I found him stationed by the bucket of Dr. Blake's punch, looking anxious.

"Anything wrong?" I asked.

"What?" he said, startled. "No. Why do you ask?"

"You seemed . . . troubled."

"That's just my face."

"Tough to be a treasurer," I said, "with a declining treasury."

"What do you know about it?" he asked suspiciously.

"I heard some talk at dinner last night," I said. "I gather the club investments haven't exactly been hitting pay dirt."

"It's the economy," said Reginald Talbot. "Nothing's working. All the returns are small, or worse. Puts a hell of a stress on the club finances. Everyone wants to keep the same amenities, but no one wants to pay more dues."

"I feel it, too," I said. "The economy, I mean."

"Really?"

"A detective is a luxury item," I said. "Let's face it. Nobody *needs* a detective. When money is tight, either you learn to live with your suspicions or you take care of them yourself."

"How so?"

"Shooting or strangling, mostly," I said. "Poison, too. Husbands strangle their wives. Wives poison their husbands. Everybody shoots everybody else. Considered from a certain angle, detectives perform a valuable service for society."

"What's that?"

"We get in the way."

"I'll drink to that," said Reginald Talbot, hoisting a plastic cup full of punch. We stood in silence a moment. Watched children throwing sticks onto the woodpile. Heard the loud *pop!* of a champagne cork. *Not exactly a nun's fart*, I thought.

"There is a solution, you know," said Reginald Talbot.

"To what?"

"The club finances. The economy."

"Sell?"

"Well, yes, but there's more to it than that," said Reginald Talbot. "You have to find the right buyer. Have you ever been to a casino?"

"Sure."

"Good business model?"

"Seems like it."

"It's the *perfect* business model," said Reginald Talbot, eyelids fluttering with excitement. "They mint money. For every good gambler, like myself, there are hundreds of chumps lining up practically begging to donate their cash. No matter what happens to them in their jobs, no matter how terrible the economy, these dupes will be there, getting off buses, wallets in hand. That's a hundred-percent certainty. And in business, that's invaluable."

"Makes sense," I said. "I suppose. I'm not much of a businessman."

"Where did you go?" asked Reginald Talbot.

"Sorry?"

"When you went to the casino, where did you go?"

"Las Vegas, obviously."

"The point being, that was your only choice."

"I'm not sure I understand what you're getting at."

"That's the only gambling town in the country. Ninety-nine-point-ninety-nine percent of the population lives outside of a hundred-mile radius of Las Vegas. People have to travel there, plan big trips. But what if I told you"—Reginald Talbot now really warming to his subject—"that, instead of bringing the people to the casinos, you could bring the casinos to the people?"

"By rail or by truck?"

"I'm serious. There's a referendum to legalize gambling in New Jersey on the ballot for November, it might pass this time. But there's a better option. Have you ever heard of the Seminole tribe in Florida?"

"The Indians?"

"Yes, the Indians. I have a friend in the tax bureau down there. He says in just a few years, the Seminole tribe is going to open *their own casino* on their own reservation. Don't you get it?" he asked. "It's their tribal land. They have sovereignty. United States laws don't apply."

"I'm not sure that's true," I said carefully.

"It's complicated, but, anyway, on this point I am one hundred percent positive. The Indians are going to open their own casino. And it won't stop there. Once that happens, every Indian tribe in the country is going to try to get in on the act. Mark. My. Words."

The rum punch had stained his lips pink. Reginald Talbot, though he didn't know it, was contributing to my club dossier: confirming some details, adding others, including some, I thought, that my client would perhaps have preferred me not to know.

"Can I tell you a secret?" he asked.

"Certainly," I said.

"This property, West Heart property, is Indian land."

"No shit."

"No shit indeed. When the Patriarchs first created this place—"

"Patriarchs?"

"Like in the Bible. That's what we call them. The founding families. Blake, Garmond, Talbot, Burr. When they bought this land, it was part of the original Oneida territory."

"Never heard of it."

"It was sort of a patchwork thing. Lands scattered all over the state that were considered part of the Oneida reservation. More distant parts, like here, they didn't mind selling off."

"For twenty dollars' worth of beads?"

"Not quite. But not far off. The point being, the Oneida could, in theory, buy back the land, then offer a ninety-nine-year lease to someone—namely, us—to run a business."

"A casino?"

"Exactly."

"Seems a bit far-fetched."

"Trust me," Reginald Talbot said fervently. "In twenty years, all of the woods in New England will be filled with casinos owned by Indian tribes you've never heard of. The ones who get there first will get the biggest jackpot."

"And that will solve all your problems?"

"Most of them," he said.

"And the rest?" I asked.

He raised a cup of Dr. Blake's rum punch and drank.

×

John Garmond lit a flare, red sparks crackling and hissing in his hand, then tossed it into what I suspected, from the way the flames immediately licked into life, was a gasoline-drenched patch of timber. In just a few minutes, the flames had spread across the entirety of the exposed wood.

Suddenly there was a quick series of explosions—*POP POP POP POP!* As the bystanders ducked and shrieked, my hand instinctively reached under my shirt for the gun that was lying useless in a drawer beneath a pile of underwear.

"M-80s," cursed John Garmond. "Stupid kids. I warned them not to do that this year."

"Dangerous," I said.

"A few years ago, some idiot buried a couple of three-inch shells deep inside the pile. Wood shards went everywhere. We were lucky no one was killed."

The flames had licked their way to the piano at the top of the pile, and the strings began to creak and stretch in the heat. There was a loud, violent twang as a string snapped; people around the fire jerked back involuntarily. Then another string snapped, and another. I felt like I was watching an animal die.

Across the fire, a woman's voice lifted in song. Opera, full-throated. Jane Garmond.

"She was an understudy at the Met," her husband said quietly. "Before we got married."

"Puccini," explained Meredith Blake next to me. "*Madame Butterfly.*"

"I've never seen it," I said. "Never seen any opera."

"It's the one where the geisha, Butterfly, marries an American naval officer named Pinkerton."

"Like the detective agency."

"If you say so," Meredith Blake said dubiously. She continued: "After the wedding, Pinkerton leaves Japan for three years. During that time, Butterfly bears his son. When Pinkerton returns, he is accompanied by his new American wife, who has agreed to adopt the child. Faced with the loss of both her husband and her son, Butterfly commits suicide."

"So—a happy ending."

"By opera standards."

We listened to the aria. I couldn't understand the words, but I recognized the famous melody, the tone of longing and love and ill fate. On the outskirts of the fire, I saw Susan Burr slip away from her husband's side and walk toward the trees at the edge of the field. A few moments later—not enough, probably, to avoid suspicion, but I was impatient—I followed her.

×

"Midnight?" I asked. "Room 302?"

"I'd love to," said Susan Burr. "But we better not. There's a big storm coming in. We don't want to get trapped there."

"Don't we?"

We'd been making out like teenagers against a tree. Here, just inside the tree line, the murmur of the crowd and the crackle of the fire were far enough away that we could hear the sounds of the forest at night: crickets, wind in the treetops, the rustle of unseen creatures on the branches overhead.

"'Heavy petting' is what they called this when I was a kid," said Susan Burr. "It's been ages."

"A lost art," I said.

"We now prefer our gratifications to be instant," she said. "At least, I do."

"Me, too."

"But when everything is permitted, something is lost. Anticipation. The pleasure of delayed pleasure. The slow buildup of suspense."

"Want a joint?" I asked.

We passed it back and forth. From our vantage point, the West Heart members were just silhouettes against the bonfire.

"A lot of unhappiness here," I observed.

"Here, there, everywhere," said Susan Burr. "It's all the same.

The Age of Sadness, maybe the historians will call this. The Age of Intoxication. The Age of Quiet Weeping Desperation."

"Were you surprised today?"

"By Claudia? I suppose so. I didn't know her very well. She was a quiet woman, in her own head. The kind with too many thoughts, too much of the time."

"Did you and Duncan Mayer ever . . . ?"

A few moments of silence. The glowing red tip of the joint flaring, then receding.

"No," she said.

"For lack of opportunity or lack of interest?"

"Let's just say he was spoken for," said Susan Burr. "Now it's my turn to ask the questions."

"Go ahead."

"Who hired you?"

"Who says anyone hired me?"

"Don't be coy," said Susan Burr. "Everyone here talks, you know. You've been asking questions all over the club."

"It's just my nature."

"Bullshit. But fine," she said. "What about me? Was seducing me part of your plan?"

"I seduced you?" I said. "And here I thought you had seduced me."

"Do you have your eyes set on anyone else?" she asked.

"At West Heart?"

"Yes."

"No," I said.

"What about Emma Blake?"

"Who?"

"Isn't she the type to tempt an older man?"

Instead of answering, I kissed her again.

A few minutes later, when we needed a break to ease the temptation of returning to Room 302, Susan Burr resumed her interrogation.

"So what's your story, Adam McAnnis of the late, once-great city of New York?"

"What do you mean?"

"Where do you come from?" asked Susan Burr. "Who are you? How'd you become a detective?"

"You're looking for an origin story? What if I don't have one?"

"Make it up."

"Fine," I said. "My father was a cop. A homicide detective. He wanted me to enter the family business—"

"The family business being murder?"

"Exactly," I said. "But I went to college instead."

"Great."

"Then I dropped out."

"To do what?"

"I didn't know at first. I knocked around a bit. Then I enlisted in the army and shipped off to Vietnam."

"Why did you do that?" Susan Burr asked incredulously.

I looked at her in the dark. "What's the dumbest thing you ever did?"

"I don't know," she said. "I'd have to think about it."

"Well," I said, "I don't have to think about it."

"Why did you lie about it last night?" she asked. "At dinner."

I shrugged. "I'm used to it."

"Used to lying?"

"Yes."

"About the war?"

"And other things. But yes, the war. I don't need or want the grief. I'm a hero. I'm a war criminal. I'm an imperialist. I'm a freedom fighter. I should have fled to Canada. I should have served another tour."

"The sons of West Heart," said Susan Burr, "were not on the front lines."

"No," I said. "I don't imagine they were."

"What did you do after Vietnam?"

"I needed a job, so I joined up with my father's former partner, who by then was running his own private-detective agency. My dad never forgave him. That was where I spent my apprenticeship."

"Learning the trade."

"That's right. Hours and hours of sitting in parked cars. Standing miserably in the rain, watching silhouettes in an apartment window break their marriage vows. Contested wills. Embezzled partners. Missing persons. A husband disappears: I find him, years later, with a new family. A lady vanishes: her parents think, correctly, that the husband killed her."

"What was your boss like? Your mentor?"

"His name was Horatio Brown. A throwback," I said, smiling at the memory. "The type who kept a bottle of whiskey in his desk. Smoked three packs a day. Would occasionally flip through a thick file of his favorite dirty photos that he'd snapped on the job. Believed, as a physical rule of the universe, that every client was lying to him. In that, I've found, he was not necessarily wrong."

"What happened to him?"

"A stroke. After he died, I struck out on my own."

"What did you study in college?"

"Philosophy."

"Really?" she asked.

"Really."

"Has that been"—trying not to laugh—"helpful to you?"

"Inasmuch as it's a study of how people *ought* to live, in theory, not at all," I said. "But it's useful in thinking about how people actually *do* behave, and why. Whether we really know what we think we know. How our minds trick us into forging false connections between unrelated events. What does 'truth' really mean, anyway? And what definitions should we use for things like knowledge, guilt, innocence . . . ?"

"Why, Adam McAnnis, you surprise me," Susan Burr said mockingly.

"How so?"

"Metaphysics are for the young," she said. "Only the foolish cling to it as we age."

"It's an occupational hazard," I said. "All those hours alone, locked inside your own head. Thoughts chasing one another, around and around and around. Contemplating the deceits and dead ends of the cosmos. Hoping the cheating lovers hurry up so you can take a piss."

"You fret so much about whether truth exists," continued Susan Burr, "but isn't it your job to find it?"

"I took a case once from a woman whose husband had been convicted of murder," I said. "She was convinced he was innocent."

"Was he?"

"My findings were inconclusive. I discovered nothing new, aside from witnesses who were even less reliable, years later, than they were at the time of the murder. There was no physical evidence linking the husband to the crime. No alibi. No smoking gun either way. No other suspects. What the police had was thin but made a certain amount of sense, at least in theory. The DA took his shot with the jury and won. That was it. Messy and unsatisfying. I had no answers, but a man was still in prison for life and his wife was left alone, wondering if she really knew him like she thought she did."

"And how much did you charge her for that?"

"A gentleman never tells."

The truth is, I hadn't charged her anything. Brown always said I was too soft to be a detective.

×

Definition

Mystery: mist(ə)rē, from the Greek, *mystērion* (μυστήριον). The fabled seventy translators of the first Greek Bible, the Septuagint, used the word to express a divine secret that could be glimpsed only by revelation. The same word was used in a pagan context to describe the esoteric rituals of the mystery cults of ancient Greece. Centuries later, actors in the "mystery plays" of medieval England acted out key scenes from the Bible, from the Creation to the Last

Judgment (scholars say these plays influenced Shakespeare and his contemporaries; for example, *Macbeth*'s porter scene purportedly evokes the demon porters pathetically trying to stop Christ in *The Harrowing of Hell*). In premodern English, the word was also associated with *craft* or *art;* many of the mystery plays were performed by an associated guild (the shipwrights might act out the Noah's Ark story; the vintners, Christ turning water into wine; the goldsmiths, the gifts of the Magi, etc.). These medieval guilds took a cue from the ancient Greek mystery cults, protecting their members with secret gestures and tokens that allowed guildsmen to covertly recognize fellow adepts.

Scholars know that the word *mystery* has always been associated with the occult, with the uncovering or revelation of that which has been, or perhaps should be, hidden. It has obvious connections to mystics and mysticism, a link that no doubt enriched the many séances of that noted Spiritualist Sir Arthur Conan Doyle.

×

John Garmond was checking his watch, conferring with Reginald Talbot, both men looking nervously back through the woods toward the lake.

"What's going on?" I asked James Blake.

"It's time for the fireworks," he said. "Past time, actually."

"Who's handling them?"

"Fred Shiflett, over at the beach. Been doing it for years. He's become a pyrotechnics expert."

I'd left the forest several minutes after Susan Burr, trying to act casual but feeling faintly ridiculous as I rejoined the crowd around the bonfire. Emma Blake gave me a look, which I ignored.

The crowd was waiting, waiting. It began to feel like something was wrong. I wondered about Fred Shiflett, imagining his corpse crumpled on the beach—could you kill a man with a firework, if you had to?—but then we heard the distant *oomf!* of a launch, a couple seconds of nothing; if I narrowed my eyes I could maybe,

maybe, make out the tiny dot streaking against the night sky, and then the radiating blast of red and gold and green . . .

And as the West Heart members mingle around the flames, enjoying the heat pulsing on their cheeks, you think that a clever writer could exploit this bonfire for purposes of plot. A killer with a theatrical disposition might enjoy the private joke of secretly burning his evidence in full view of a crowd, knowing the final bit of proof needed to prove his guilt had been immolated before a hundred clueless witnesses. Or perhaps it's a matter not of bravado but of necessity, the murderer having had no opportunity to dispose of the evidence beforehand: if, for example, someone needed to burn a suicide note that the police had been told didn't exist.

You are also thinking, as the detective and the others watch the nighttime display, heads tilted back, explosions reflected off eyeglasses and the windshields of the cars parked at the end of the field, that fireworks would be good cover for a shooting. After all, you reason, wouldn't the sound of a gunshot be camouflaged by the general cacophony of the evening's entertainment? Could you, in fact, time your bullet into the back of the head to coincide precisely with a rocket's detonation? The victim slumping to the ground, unnoticed, as you toss the weapon into the inferno so convenient and so close. Has anyone in this crowd thought about that? Planned for it? Do they have the nerve?

That's how you would do it if you were a murderer, or a mystery writer. But that does not appear to be the plan here. Instead, you recognize the telltale signs of an episode that novelists or critics deem necessary for *pacing*, or *rhythm*, the relaxation of tension before the next turn of the screw, in this case, the literal calm before the storm . . . And in these sentences the characters seem more forlorn, lost in thought, faces lifted to the sky, remembering how, when they were kids, each explosion would elicit gasps of wonder and delight, a feeling impossible to recapture now: fireworks, past childhood, are a melancholy enterprise. You feel, now, the story pausing for breath. John Garmond has taken Jane Garmond's hand. Susan Burr stands alone. James Blake refills Ramsey Garmond's plastic cup. Warren

Burr mutters something to Reginald Talbot. Jonathan Gold is with Emma Blake, gesturing at the heavens. Adam McAnnis is in the back, alone, watching, watching . . .

You understand that you are being permitted a final glimpse of each potential murderer or victim before the crime.

The night air has become electric, thick with foreboding. Smoke from the last firework is drifting across the trees when, in the distance, a bolt of lightning illuminates the sky, crackling across the undersides of the gathering clouds. A few seconds later, the thunder follows.

A drop of rain. Then another.

"We'd better get out of here," says John Garmond.

Within minutes, amid a steadily increasing rainfall, the entire field has been emptied. The tables left for retrieval the next day, or the day after. Trash bags filled with empty wine bottles and uneaten trays of food abandoned. People running toward cars, jackets over their heads. Tires already sinking into the softening earth. High beams cutting through the gloom—you wouldn't want to run over anyone, by accident, in the dark and the rain . . .

Left behind, with no one to watch it, is a kind of miracle. The bonfire still burns amid the deluge, a raging fury so hot that it seems untouched by the storm. But if there is a message in this moment of transcendence, there is no one to receive it: the men and women toweling off inside their cars are as oblivious to the bonfire burning through the rain as bystanders in the Icarus legend ignoring a boy falling from the sky. People hunger for epiphany, you think, they clamor for it, but, given a chance, who among us would actually recognize it? Or, having seen it, would choose to act?

×

And now: the final moments of a person's life. In these closing paragraphs of the day, the perspective shifts, transparently mimicking the language of film, a camera's omniscient, pitiless eye roving around West Heart to reveal the effects of the storm. Torrents of water gushing into the clubhouse basement. A power line down in the road, hissing sparks, twisting and coiling like a snake. A tennis court swamped, the net half submerged. The camera roving down a muddy channel that used to be a road to zero in on a massive ancient oak that is beginning to lean for the first time in centuries of life, betrayed not by wind but by water, loosening its clutch on the soil. And then the tree is falling, falling, a great and calamitous crashing across the road.

The camera now arrives at an old wooden bridge. The kill below has been transformed into a tumultuous river, surging over its banks. The bridge begins to sag on one side. Planks of sodden, rotted timber break off. Slowly, then all at once, like an aging beast whose exhausted legs crumple beneath it, the bridge slides into the water.

The camera is now in front of the clubhouse, observing from the gravel parking lot. And then—there! The briefest flash in a downstairs window. And then it's gone.

Lightning. The roar of thunder. And the relentless falling rain.

Amid such bedlam, who would possibly register the sharp snare-drum crack of a solitary gunshot in the night?

×

Questionnaire

1) Do you believe that Claudia Mayer's death was a suicide?

YES

NO

2) Do you believe that the death of the Mayer family dog was an accident?

YES

NO

3) Circle the names of the probable murder victim(s).
   Select all that apply.

   A. JANE GARMOND

   B. JOHN GARMOND

   C. DUNCAN MAYER

   D. ALEX CALDWELL

   E. SUSAN BURR

   F. WARREN BURR

   G. EMMA BLAKE

   H. DR. ROGER BLAKE

   I. REGINALD TALBOT

   J. JONATHAN GOLD

   K. ADAM McANNIS

4) Circle the names of the probable murderer(s). Select all
   that apply.

   A. JANE GARMOND

   B. JOHN GARMOND

   C. DUNCAN MAYER

   D. ALEX CALDWELL

   E. SUSAN BURR

   F. WARREN BURR

   G. EMMA BLAKE

   H. DR. ROGER BLAKE

   I. REGINALD TALBOT

   J. JONATHAN GOLD

   K. ADAM McANNIS

5) Who hired the detective? And why?

   _____

   _____

6) Do you believe that our cultural fascination with murder is reflective of an innate, perhaps evolutionary propensity for violence? And that compulsively reading about the act of killing is a way to indulge those passions in a manner that civil society can tolerate?

YES

NO

7) What emotion would be most likely to drive you to kill? (Select only one.)

LOVE

HATE

8) Do you ever look at your spouse or lover, during moments when they're unaware of your gaze—reading a book like this one, perhaps—and calculate the sum of your regrets? Do you ever imagine a life without them, and consider what you'd be willing to do to make that happen? Do you ever wonder if they're thinking the same about you?

×

. . . a mob of Watsons, all watching with round eyes like owls . . .

SATURDAY

The rain was still falling when we woke, an older nation, not know-ing, yet, that the roads were blocked, not realizing, yet, that one of us was a murderer. Did he or she spend a sleepless night in bed, kept awake by the fury of the storm and the dread of the morn-ing's inevitable discovery of the corpse? Did they practice their part? Rehearse how surprise and dismay disfigure the features of the innocent? Examine their alibi for holes?

Truth be told, the innocent likely slept as poorly as the guilty, in this storm, amid the thunder and the lightning and the shocking silence when the power cut out. A few precious seconds of noth-ing but the rain outside falling, falling, before the clicks that sig-naled the generators rumbling into gear and, one by one, the sounds of the house—the ambient hum of the fridge, the ticking of the kitchen clock, the language of the lifeless objects that we take for granted—all coming back like breath returning to a body.

On mornings like this, we would normally call around for gossip, the delights of misfortune when it's not your own—seeking to know whose basement flooded, whose roof was cratered by a tree—but this morning we couldn't. Hands lifted receivers to find no dial tone: the phone lines were out. So we put on galoshes and rain jackets and ventured out into the rain. Jane Garmond was found stumbling down the muddy track. One question was all it took—*I don't know where he is, I haven't seen him since last night*—and then the search began in earnest.

Meredith and Emma Blake were the ones to find him, sprawled out in the great hall of the clubhouse, in front of the bare gray hearth. His eyes open, fixed on nothing. A pool of congealed blood, nearly black, beneath his head. And the wretched detail that, once we understood it, haunted us the most: a smear where some vermin—a rat, perhaps, from the cellar—had streaked though the still-wet blood, leaving ghastly splotches in a trail to the kitchen.

And you're imagining this rat, smeared with John Garmond's blood, dragging its belly across the stores in the pantry, while reflecting on this new gambit by the author, shifting to the "we" of the first-person plural, a form you've seldom encountered in murder mysteries, and for good reason, since the "we" effectively obscures the "who"—which, you realize, might be the reason to tack in this direction now, when the "who" moves to the heart of the story, a ploy allowing the murderer's individual identity to be concealed in the "we" like a leaf hidden in a forest, or a body on a battlefield. You sense, too, that the first-person plural is meant to evoke a Greek chorus, as well as, perhaps, the collective guilt of the not-quite-innocent, the voice of a dramatis personae in which everyone is either a victim or a suspect.

×

"Anyone have a shortwave radio? No? Then, until the roads are cleared and phone service is restored, we are alone. Time is the enemy, if we are to discover the killer. Right now the pulse of the murderer is racing. He didn't sleep, his thoughts are scattered. But soon he may collect himself, review his alibi, patch the holes in his story, and successfully pass himself off as an innocent man. I say *man* simply for convenience," added Adam McAnnis, "but of course the murderer may be a woman as well. I propose we begin investigating right away. Any disagreement?"

We were gathered in the parlor next to the great hall, inside of which John Garmond's body still lay, covered by a sheet. Fred Shiflett, in his 4x4, had driven in the rain down both West Heart Road and Greenfield Road to confirm our isolation. There was some bickering about the old West Heart Kill bridge—hadn't we talked for years about its decay? But no one had ever wanted to spend the money to fix it. Which then led, briefly, to the old arguments about failed investments and raising dues, before Dr. Blake shamed us with a reminder of the corpse in the next room.

Meredith Blake quite sensibly had said that we needed some coffee—*Or something stronger,* Warren Burr had growled, predictably—and with her son's help had brought a couple of trays from the kitchen with coffee and Entenmann's. Until they returned, we'd sat in silence, afraid to speak, measuring with sideways glances the depths of each other's hangovers, a familiar state compounded by lack of sleep and the bleak reality, still only just settling in, that West Heart had become a crime scene. We warily eyed the detective.

"Why should we listen to you?" asked Warren Burr.

McAnnis crossed his arms, studying each of us in turn as we squirmed on the mahogany leather couches and wingback chairs of the parlor. "Because John Garmond hired me," he said.

A murmur of surprise swept across the room. Glances were exchanged. We tried to decipher the shock or alarm we read in one another's eyes: Was it mere surprise, or mutual suspicion, or something else entirely? Who was now recalculating how much poor John may have suspected? Which of us was now wondering, *How much does this detective know?*

Dr. Blake broke the silence. "Why would John do that?"

"He had reason to believe he was in danger," said McAnnis. "I was supposed to keep my eyes and ears open for any sort of threat."

"If your job was to protect him," pointed out Meredith Blake, "then you failed. Obviously."

"I was not hired to be a bodyguard," explained McAnnis. "John thought he was capable of safeguarding himself and his family. He wanted me to corroborate or refute his suspicions."

"And did you?"

"I found there was a threat, yes."

"Would you care to explain?" demanded Warren Burr.

"I don't think that would be wise."

Silence again. The ticking of the mantel clock. Outside, the steady rain.

"Look here," said Reginald Talbot. "I don't care what you say about the scope of your investigation. The fact is, your client is dead. Why, then, should we trust you to pursue this inquiry?"

"Because," said McAnnis, "I'm the only person in this room who is not a suspect."

We stayed quiet, trying to adjust to this new calculus. Paranoia hung thick in the air of the stuffy room, windows closed against the rain. We were also keenly aware that objecting to this inquiry could itself be viewed with suspicion.

"So what do you propose?" Meredith Blake asked finally.

"I question each of you individually, one by one. Alone. That includes Duncan Mayer."

"He's grieving. Can't we leave him out of this?"

"Unfortunately not," said McAnnis. "I will also need to talk to Jane Garmond. She's back at her house, I assume?"

"Yes, with Emma," said Meredith Blake. "Is it really necessary, so soon after . . . ?"

"Yes. I'm sorry." McAnnis surveyed the room. "And the other guest. Jonathan Gold. Where is he staying?"

"In the empty cabin next to the Talbots."

"Could you ask him to come down here? Thank you," said McAnnis. "It's probably also wise to review the club financial records. Mr. Talbot, could you please provide the books?"

"I'm not sure that would be appropriate—"

"Both sets of books, please."

Silence.

Meredith Blake: "Reginald, what is he talking about?"

"Nothing." Reginald Talbot was blinking furiously.

"I'm also interested in that question," said Dr. Blake. "What did he mean, Reg? Both sets of books?"

"He doesn't mean anything," said Reginald Talbot. "He doesn't know what he's talking about."

"I have been given to understand that there are two sets of records for West Heart," said McAnnis. "Perhaps this practice predates you as treasurer—I don't know. Though I suspect others do. Money can be a powerful motive for murder. I need to look at those books."

"Reg—" said Dr. Blake.

"Fine," Reginald Talbot said. "I'll get you the books. And I'd like to know who the hell you've been talking to."

McAnnis ignored him. "All right, everyone. It's best to get started immediately."

"What do we do about . . . ?" Susan Burr, who had been silent up to now, asked softly, gesturing toward the great hall.

"We can't leave him there, obviously. It could be days. Anyone have a camera? James? Please, go get it. Let's take as many photographs of the scene as we can." McAnnis paused for what he knew would be an unsettling proposal. "Then, if you agree, Dr. Blake, we'll need to move him to the kitchen freezer."

Meredith Blake gasped. Susan Burr strangled a sob. The blood drained from James Blake's face. So much shock and suspicion, each of us a potential suspect or witness, absorbing the aftershock of murder: the awful truth of how swiftly a living, laughing, loving, breathing human being can become a corpse.

"I think that would be best," Dr. Blake said gravely.

×

Adam McAnnis stood over the body with Dr. Blake and James Blake. Blood had seeped through the white sheet in a great splotch under the head. We'd left them alone with poor John, shuddering as we passed the great hall, each of us relieved to be spared the unpleasant tasks they faced. After all, there were breakfasts to be made, hang-overs to be tended, dogs to be fed. Life, we thought, goes on. The secret shame-filled triumph of the living over the dead.

McAnnis held one corner of the sheet, Dr. Blake the other. With a nod, they slowly pulled the sheet off the body in what felt like a macabre parody of a statue's unveiling to the public.

"Jesus," said James Blake.

"You okay?" asked his father.

"Yes."

"You don't have to stay," said McAnnis.

"It's not my first body," said James Blake. Adding, in response to McAnnis's arched eyebrows: "I was the one who found Trip Caldwell and Otto Mayer in the car."

The three men studied the corpse at their feet. There was a gap-ing hole in the back of John Garmond's head, hair matted by coagu-lated blood. His skin was ashen; his lips were pulled back from the teeth in a terrible rictus.

"Did he die in pain?" asked James Blake.

"That grimace comes from the skin tightening during rigor mortis," said his father. "It's a myth that the rictus comes from a violent death. Also not true, needless to say, is the claim that a final image of the murderer can be captured on the pupils of the victim."

"What camera do you have?" asked McAnnis. "Polaroid? Perfect. Let's get this over with."

"Take pictures of everything?"

"Everything."

The men fell quiet, the silence interrupted only by the click and whir of the Polaroid. James Blake passed the photos to McAnnis, who flapped each for a few seconds before laying them out on the fireplace hearth, where the images bloomed to life like half-finished sculptures emerging from a block of marble.

"Shot in the back of the head," observed James Blake. "The killer surprised him."

"Not necessarily," said McAnnis. "The killer could have ordered him, at gunpoint, to turn around. Perhaps because the killer didn't want to look him in the eyes when he—or she—pulled the trigger. That would be telling. Or maybe John realized the killer was about to shoot and he tried to flee. Or he simply turned away instinctually. Or—he trusted the killer and turned his back, never suspecting he'd be shot."

James Blake stopped clicking.

"I'm out," he said. "No more film."

"We have enough photos," said McAnnis. "Doctor?"

Dr. Blake sank to his knees to examine the body, first gently closing the eyelids. "Nothing under his fingernails," he said, delicately lowering the dead man's hands to his sides. "Nothing defensive. It's likely John never touched his murderer."

"And the gunshot?" asked McAnnis.

"Your guess is as good as mine. But fairly close range, I would think. Not right against the head, but not the far side of the room, either."

"Time of death?"

"I'm not a coroner, obviously. I would be cautious about using my conclusions for anything more than general guidance."

"Understood."

"Fine. It's just after ten o'clock now," Dr. Blake said, glancing at his watch. "Rigor mortis is not quite complete, although it's close. I'd say between midnight and two a.m."

"Makes sense. The jacket and boots are dry, too."

"I would know more precisely if I checked the body temperature," said Dr. Blake. "But, quite honestly, I don't think I'm prepared to do that."

"Of course," said McAnnis. "I'm done here, if you are, doctor."

"Now what?" asked James Blake.

"Now we move him," said McAnnis. The putrid smell of feces and urine had filled the room, and he gestured toward the closest window. "Open that, will you?"

The men were sweating. James Blake slid the window up, and the sound of the downpour, muted before, filled the hall, along with a wave of cooler air.

They spread the sheet next to the body and then paused uncertainly.

"Lift him up?"

"Maybe best to just roll him over."

Once the body was on the sheet, they grabbed the corners, the Blakes at one end, McAnnis at the other.

"Should have kept a fourth man," said McAnnis. "Ready? One, two, three—"

They lifted, grunting from the strain, then began to shuffle clumsily across the room.

"Christ, look underneath," said the detective. Blood was oozing from the gaping hole in the head, dribbling through the sheet and onto the floor. "He's going to drip the whole way if we carry him like this."

"There's a big food cart in the kitchen," said James Blake. "Put him down. I'll go get it."

He returned with the cart and a blue tarp that the club used for clambakes. McAnnis, clearly annoyed with himself, said: "Should have thought of that to begin with. Okay, ready? Again. One, two, three—"

They lifted the corpse onto the cart and wrapped it in the tarp. You pause to think about this surreal scene as they wheel through the silent halls of the clubhouse, sweating from the heat and the strain, hungover, reflecting on the macabre comedy of this moment, the awkward farce of moving a body. Do we delight in these episodes because they allow us to confront the uncomfortable truths of our bodies: how we begin, how we end? Do we laugh at the bungling men moving a body because it mirrors more mundane tasks: the flopping weight of a mattress, the cursing strain of a refrigerator being shoved up three impossible steps? Is a corpse so different, really, from a piece of furniture? These questions, you think, all lead back to the ineffable enigma of the moment of death, a transition as imprecise but absolute as the moment when a child turns her face to the leaden sky, realizing that the rain has turned to snow.

The men hesitated in front of the kitchen's walk-in freezer.

"Is this really the right thing to do?" asked James Blake.

"It's about seventy-five degrees right now," said his father. "If we don't do this, the situation will get unpleasant very quickly. And the roads could be blocked for days."

"Should we put up a sign, at least?" asked James Blake. "We don't want people accidentally opening the freezer."

"And what would it say?" McAnnis asked testily. "'Keep Out—Murder Victim Inside'?"

"Children have been known to sneak in here, looking for ice cream," Dr. Blake said.

"If I was a kid, a sign like that would make me *more* likely to open the door," said McAnnis, remembering the crowd of children at the lake, ogling Claudia Mayer's body. "Let's get him inside and then worry about everything else."

It was not a large freezer and they had to spend several minutes rearranging boxes to make room. Several packages of steaks found a home beneath the cart. In the end, they decided on a simple DO NOT ENTER sign, taped to the freezer door.

"Should we say a few words?" asked James Blake.

"Should we have a drink?" asked McAnnis.

×

Methods

Shooting. Stabbing. Drowning. Burning. Blunt object. Poison. Fists. Feet. Teeth. Strangulation. Asphyxiation. Defenestration. Explosion. What the Romans called *damnatio ad bestias* ("condemned to the beasts"). Also, less direct methods: denying medication, inducing a heart attack, inducing a seizure, inducing a suicide . . .

The human body is a feeble thing, and there are many ways to die.

Murder mysteries tend to be coy about the actual moment of death: a clean and simple stabbing, a single gunshot wound, or, best of all, an elegant poison that leaves no garish mark upon the body—these are the preferred techniques of the genteel detective novel, a tradition that continued through the hard-boiled fiction of later decades. But mystery's cousins are seldom so blood-shy. The narrator of Edgar Allan Poe's "The Tell-Tale Heart" murders an old man and then hides the corpse beneath the room floorboards, above which he conducts that final, ruinous conversation with police ("tear up the planks!—here, here!—it is the beating of his hideous heart!"). In Roald Dahl's "Lamb to the Slaughter," a wife kills her husband by bashing him over the head with a frozen leg of lamb and then serves it for dinner to police investigating the case, effectively making them accomplices in the elimination of the murder weapon. In Patricia Highsmith's "Slowly, Slowly in the Wind," a farmer murders a neighbor and then hides the body by disguising it as a scarecrow in his field, where it is later discovered by children on Halloween.

Agatha Christie's notebooks offer a veritable forensic murder workshop, with multiple methods proposed, evaluated for novelty and effectiveness, and then accepted or dismissed. Christie at one time worked as a pharmacist; it's not surprising, then, that poison was among her preferred methods. In America, the FBI produces a regular report on homicidal techniques, filled with endless tables of grisly statistics that read like a catalogue of cruelty ("Other" being a particularly hair-raising survey of misanthropic inventiveness). The FBI statistics confirm what Christie knew intuitively—that poison is, by and large, a woman's method of murder. The statistics also demonstrate a companion point: that strangulation is a distressingly common way for women to die (most often, at the hands of a husband or lover). The discrepancy between these two dry facts speaks to the brutal realities of gender, power, and physical violence in domestic life, the harsh secrets of the closed doors behind which men have loved and hated and killed women for centuries.

The most poetic murder in the detective canon may come courtesy of Dorothy Sayers, who discovered an ingenious way to kill using nothing but the tolling of the bells, bells, bells . . .

×

After breakfast came the interrogations. We were summoned to the clubhouse, one by one, to meet with the detective, ensconced in the library, surrounded by books and artifacts of West Heart's past. Since the phones were out, we had no way to commiserate but by slipping on our galoshes and raincoats and braving the dreary wet afterthought of the storm—*Just thought I'd stop in for coffee, do you mind? It's been such a terrible twenty-four hours*—but, of course, really stopping by to ask: *How was it? What did he ask? What did you tell him?* Each of us maintaining the fiction that the person we were talking to couldn't be the murderer, of course not, it had to be someone else—and, of course, everyone else thinking the same.

Jane Garmond was first.

×

Jane Garmond

Q: I'm so sorry about this.

A: [. . .]

Q: When was the last time you saw your husband alive?

A: Around midnight. He got a phone call and said he had to go to the clubhouse.

Q: Who was it?

A: I don't know. He didn't say.

Q: You didn't ask?

A: No.

Q: The storm was in full force by then. Did you think it was odd for John to be going out at that time?

A: He said there was something wrong at the clubhouse that he had to take a look at. I thought maybe there was flooding, or a tree had fallen, something like that.

Q: And he never returned?

A: No. I went to sleep shortly after he left.

Q: What did you do when you woke up and realized John wasn't there?

A: I was worried, obviously. I went out looking for him.

Q: Your son was in the house, too, correct? He didn't go with you?

A: Ramsey was still asleep—I didn't want to wake him, although I should have. I wasn't thinking clearly, I guess.

Q: Where did you go?

A: All over.

Q: Did you come here? To the clubhouse?

A: Yes.

Q: You did? But you didn't see . . . anything?

A: No. From our house, the closest door to the clubhouse is in the back. Near the kitchen, away from the great hall.

Q: You searched the clubhouse?

A: Yes.

Q: But never looked in the great hall?

A: No.

Q: Were you . . . Did you look in the rooms on the third floor?

A: Yes.

Q: Because you thought he might be there?

A: Yes.

Q: Were there any rooms in particular that you checked?

A: I checked all the rooms.

Q: The call that John got—was it from a man or a woman?

A: I don't know.

Q: I'm sorry, but I have to ask these questions.

A: I understand.

Q: Did you not wake your son to go look for John

because you thought he might have been with another woman?

A: That was part of it, yes.

Q: Who?

A: [. . .]

Q: Who did you suspect was the other woman? Again, I'm only asking because it's important.

A: I think we're at the point in the interview where I invoke my rights, as a grieving new widow, to kindly ask you to please just fucking move on.

Q: Understood. Of course. Can I get you anything? Water?

A: I would take some coffee.

Q: Anything in it?

A: The strongest thing you have.

Q: . . . discussion about West Heart?

A: No, he didn't talk about club duties much. Like I told you before, there's not much to it. Paperwork. Meetings.

Q: Did he do anything, as club president, to rub anyone the wrong way?

A: No one was going to kill John because he vetoed a new hiking trail.

Q: Of course. But there may have been other tensions? Concerning, for example, this question of selling the club?

A: I'd be lying if I said there wasn't some bad blood. Not everyone has managed their money so well. They need the cash.

Q: I find that interesting.

A: I'm sure you do.

Q: Everyone here seems so . . . comfortable.

A: This whole place is a Potemkin village. Nothing is real. People talk and act like they're rich while secretly selling off their grandmothers' jewelry.

Q: I take it you and John are doing fine?

A: We're frugal. Smarter. Or, at least, more risk-averse. We don't invest in dubious concerns. We don't gamble.

Q: Do people gamble here at West Heart?

A: Certainly.

Q: Who?

A: There are poker games, late at night. High stakes, from what I understand. Just the men, though I suspect Susan might attend from time to time.

Q: Does your brother gamble?

A: Why do you ask?

Q: We were talking about it. He has some ideas, in this regard, for West Heart.

A: I've heard them.

Q: And?

A: Reg thinks a lot. Too much. I believe he just sees how much money they make in Las Vegas and thinks, Why not me?

Q: Does he go there often?

A: He goes. I don't know if it's what you would call "often" or not.

Q: And does Reginald invest in "dubious concerns" as well?

A: How is any of this relevant?

Q: I'm sure it's not. Forgive me.

Q: Did John seem worried by anything recently? Had he been acting differently?

A: No.

Q: What did he tell you about the hunting accident?

A: He was a bit shaken, of course. He'd been shot, after all. And of course Duncan felt awful.

Q: Did you go with him to the hospital?

A: Yes, both Ramsey and I took him to the ER over

in Middleton. I drove. Eight stitches, was all. But it took forever. And of course it's stupid, not to mention illegal, to be hunting at this time of the year at all. It's some sort of Garmond tradition. Of course, when John said it was nothing to worry about, the deputy believed him.

Q: Did John bear any ill will toward Duncan?

A: No. Why should he? It was an accident.

Q: He and Duncan were friends?

A: Yes, very close. Their whole lives, basically. They grew up going here.

Q: As did you.

A: [. . . ?]

Q: The scar.

A: Of course. I'd forgotten I'd told you.

Q: Do you mind if I ask you about Claudia Mayer?

A: No. Though I don't see what that has to do with what happened to John.

Q: Probably nothing. But I'm suspicious of coincidences. Two tragedies, so close together—it's worth examining.

A: Of course.

Q: How well did you know Claudia Mayer?

A: Decently well, I would say. We've known each other for years, since their wedding, though really we only saw each other during summers and holidays.

Q: Were you surprised by her suicide?

A: [. . .]

Q: I'm sorry, but I have to ask.

A: I suppose I wasn't surprised. Not really.

Q: Why?

A: It made sense. The whole thing with the Caldwells—Claudia never really got over it. And of course, seeing her son limp about, every day, like a permanent reminder. That only made it worse. And . . .

Q: Yes?

A: She had problems with pills and booze. Like we all do.

Q: How was her marriage?

A: No better or worse than anyone else's, probably.

Q: How was your marriage?

A: [. . .]

A: We shift to the past tense rather quickly, do we not?

Q: I'm sorry.

A: I loved John, if that's what you're asking.

Q: That's not the same thing.

A: No, it's not. We had our troubles, too, over the years. But we always got through it.

Q: Can I ask about Ramsey?

A: What about him?

Q: Did he stay up later than you did? Or did he go to sleep at the same time as you say you did?

A: Is this your way of asking if my son can corroborate my alibi in the murder of my husband?

Q: If you like.

A: Why don't you ask him yourself?

Q: I will have to, of course. Also: where were you Thursday night?

A: Nowhere. Home.

Q: All night?

A: Yes.

Q: One last thing—

A: Yes?

Q: Last night, at the bonfire . . . the singing. That was beautiful.

A: Thank you. I don't do it often, anymore.

Q: So why did you last night?

A: I don't honestly know. The mood took me. Perhaps I was inspired by the fire. The impending storm.

Q: The morning's tragedy at the lake?

A: Yes. That, too.

Q: Puccini, wasn't it?

A: Yes. The aria was "Un Bel Dì." Meaning "One Fine Day."

Q: Why did you choose that particular song?

A: Why does anyone do anything? My heart moved me to do it, and so I did.

Q: That will be all, Mrs. Garmond.

×

Reginald Talbot

A: Here you go.

Q: What are these?

A: The accounting ledgers. The books. Both sets.

Q: What am I supposed to do with this?

A: You asked for them!

Q: I'm not an accountant. I can't read these. It would be gibberish to me.

A: Then why did you ask for them?

Q: I didn't need to actually *see* the secret books. I just needed you to confirm that they existed.

A: [. . .]

Q: What's that?

A: You're a bastard, you know that?

Q: Let's start with the hunting incident. You were there, right?

A: Yes, myself, Ramsey Garmond, and Duncan Mayer.

Q: Were you with John?

A: I was nearby. I heard the shot, then some yelling.

Q: Yelling or screaming?

A: I think I know what you mean. Yelling. Not

panicked or anything. I'm not sure. I was distracted—I'd just nearly picked off a buck myself.

Q: Is it always the same pairings, or do people mix it up?

A: We mix it up, depending on who is around. It changes from year to year. John is always there, obviously. Ramsey if he's around.

Q: And that day? Who chose the pairings?

A: What do you mean?

Q: I mean—did Duncan ask John to pair off?

A: Are you suggesting that Duncan plotted to be with John so he could shoot him? Wouldn't that be a little obvious?

Q: Hunting is a dangerous sport. Accidents must happen all the time. So, did Duncan ask him?

A: I don't remember. I think so. Yes.

Q: Is Duncan a good shot?

A: We all are. This is a hunting club.

Q: Let me put it this way. Would you say that he normally hits what he aims at?

A: I suppose so, yes.

Q: What does John Garmond look like?

A: Excuse me?

Q: Does he look like a deer?

A: For Christ's sake—

Q: Or a bear?

A: No, he doesn't.

Q: Does it not seem quite a coincidence that the same man is shot twice on successive days?

A: Obviously, yes.

Q: Perhaps a novice killer would need a "practice" day, to learn what it tastes like, to test his own nerve, before committing himself to the fatal shot?

A: I don't know. That's your area of expertise. But I

don't think Duncan Mayer is the type to plot to kill a man in cold blood.

Q: So he might do it in the heat of the moment? Driven by passion? Rifle in hand, if his enemy just happens to walk into his sights?

A: I don't know.

Q: Another scenario. Perhaps the murder was a crime of opportunity by a killer who recognized that the first shooting would create an immediate suspect for the second? And that Duncan Mayer would, quite possibly, be blamed?

A: So ruin an innocent man's life? That's terrible.

Q: So is murder. But, obviously, only a fool would secretly kill a man after publicly failing to kill him the day before. Unless he is so desperate that he takes the risk. If Duncan Mayer is not the murderer, then I doubt the true killer expected this plotline to hold. But it does create confusion.

Q: Where did you go last night after the fireworks?

A: I went home. I was there all night.

Q: You're married, correct?

A: Yes. But Julia isn't here. She's at her mother's for the weekend. Probably the last visit before the baby.

Q: So there's no one who can confirm your whereabouts?

A: I suppose not. Is that a problem?

Q: Not necessarily.

A: I didn't kill John Garmond.

Q: I didn't ask if you had. The cabin next door is currently vacant?

A: Yes.

Q: But Mr. Gold is staying there this weekend.

A: Yes. It's not unusual, for prospective members. At

any given time, there are usually a few empty homes on the property. People move, people sell, et cetera.

Q: Did you see anything unusual from his cabin last night?

A: No.

Q: Would you have noticed if he had left at any point?

A: I don't think so. I didn't spend a lot of time looking out the windows—there was nothing to see. The storm was pretty bad by that point.

Q: That will be all, Mr. Talbot. For now. And on second thought, I think it would be best if you left the books with me.

×

Duncan Mayer

Q: Thank you for doing this. I can't imagine how difficult all this is for you.

A: It's fine.

Q: To lose your wife and your best friend the same weekend—so tragic. An almost unbelievable coincidence.

A: Are you saying you don't believe it?

Q: I'm saying that not everyone would have the strength to talk to me today.

A: Did I have a choice?

Q: We all have choices, Mr. Mayer.

A: Do we? If I had refused to come here, how would that have looked? What would Jane have thought? Or Ramsey? Or Otto?

Q: I don't know. What would they have thought?

A: Ask your questions, detective.

Q: Let's start with yesterday morning.

A: But John was killed last night.

Q: I'm just trying to understand everyone's movements leading up to the murder.

A: [. . .]

Q: How did the day begin for you?

A: I woke up early, before dawn. To go hunting, as you know.

Q: You didn't notice that your wife wasn't in bed?

A: We sleep in separate rooms.

Q: How long has that been going on?

A: Not long.

Q: Days? Weeks? Years?

A: Just a few months.

Q: And why did it start?

A: [. . .]

Q: [. . .]

A: I don't know.

Q: I think you do.

A: Have you ever been married?

Q: No.

A: You can be married for a long time, and still not know the other person. Not really.

Q: You told the sheriff that you didn't find a suicide note.

A: Yes.

Q: Was that the truth?

A: Yes.

Q: Forgive me, but—were you surprised?

A: I was shocked but not surprised.

Q: And why was that?

A: Claudia was always . . . troubled.

Q: Emotionally.

A: Yes. I didn't really understand that until Otto was born. She was unable to take care of him. She didn't hold him, she didn't feed him. She cried all the time, more than he did. For months.

Q: That must have been difficult.

A: Of course. Claudia got better, eventually. We never really talked about it. But, later, she would have these bouts of— I don't know how to describe them. She would become catatonic. It might last a few hours or a few days. It was like that year after year, Otto's whole life. But it got worse after the accident.

Q: The accident in which Trip Caldwell died.

A: Yes. And then Amanda's death . . . Obviously, it was too much.

Q: Did she ever seek help?

A: She saw lots of psychiatrists. Took pills, so many pills. Even found religion, for a while. Nothing helped. In the end, she just drank.

Q: It must have been tough on your son. When he was young.

A: He had a vague sense that his mom wasn't like other moms. But kids are incredibly self-absorbed. They don't think of their parents as real people. It wasn't until after college, after the accident, that he understood how dire her situation was. On the other hand, he and I were always close. I suppose that was the one good thing to come out of it.

Q: Had Claudia ever talked about . . . ending things?

A: No.

Q: That's surprising.

A: Is it?

Q: People who do this . . . tend to think about it for a long time, beforehand. They obsess about it. Even though the decision, when it comes, can be very abrupt.

A: You're asking a lot of questions about a suicide for a man who's supposed to be investigating a murder.

Q: When Claudia got religion, what religion did she get?

A: She went back to being a Catholic. It's how she was

raised. She liked the gravity of the rituals. It's all rather somber and esoteric, and that suited her, I think.

Q: If your wife had become a Buddhist, she might have become acquainted with the parable of the blind men and the elephant. Each man puts his hand on a different part of the elephant—the trunk, the flank, the tail, and so on. Of course, they each describe a different beast.

A: Meaning what?

Q: Meaning that any detective could be deceived if his investigation only touches on one part of the mystery.

A: And that's why you're asking me about Claudia?

Q: When was the last time you saw her alive?

A: The night before. I went to bed early, because I had to be up. She was on the porch.

Q: What was she doing?

A: Drinking. And looking down at the lake.

Q: You were home all night?

A: Yes.

Q: Where was your son?

A: Not sure. Out somewhere. On holiday weekends like this, there's always a late party or card game in one house or another.

Q: Do you think it's possible that this wasn't a suicide?

A: Why would you ask that?

Q: I have to ask everything. I know about the Caldwells. The car accident, the tragedy with the wife. I saw the incident with Alex Caldwell and your dog. He has good reason to hate you and your wife, does he not?

A: Yes. But . . . I can't see it. I really can't.

Q: Let's get back to yesterday morning. Hunting. Please describe everything that happened before I saw you at the clubhouse.

A: We met by the bridge.

Q: The four of you.

A: Yes. Myself, John, Ramsey, and Reg. About a

quarter of a mile back in the woods from the bridge are fields full of berries. The club planted them there, years ago, to attract bears and deer. We paired off and then hiked in.

Q: How were the pairs decided?

A: I don't remember.

Q: Go ahead.

A: John stopped at a deer stand, and I decided to loop around the edge of the field. About twenty minutes later, I saw something moving in the brush and . . .

Q: You fired.

A: Yes.

Q: When did you realize that it was John?

A: Almost immediately. He was yelling. I came running. A minute later, the two others showed up. We helped him back to the truck and then raced back to the clubhouse. That's when we saw you.

Q: Why not straight to the hospital?

A: It's far. Over twenty miles away. He needed some immediate first aid. And I could tell it wasn't bad, that he was going to be okay. John kept apologizing.

Q: For what?

A: He left the stand without any kind of signal. Then wandered out into the target area, looking for me.

Q: You were lucky that you were unlucky.

A: Absolutely.

Q: So was John. Lucky, that is. At least for a few more hours. You're certain that you fired that shot?

A: Yes.

Q: Is it possible one of the other two men fired?

A: Not sure. I don't think so.

Q: You didn't hear another shot?

A: I don't remember.

Q: Where were you last night?

A: At home with Otto.

Q: Just the two of you?

A: Yes. People had stopped by earlier. John and Jane. Meredith Blake. A few others. They brought food. Offered their condolences. Eventually, I asked them all to leave.

Q: What did you do all evening?

A: What is there to do? Otto and I talked for a bit. We drank and cried. Everyone else was at the bonfire. After a while, we couldn't bear even to be with each other and we went to our rooms. And then the storm came.

Q: You were home all night?

A: Yes.

Q: Did you make any phone calls? Before the power went out?

A: No.

Q: Can you think of any reason why someone would want to kill John Garmond?

A: No.

Q: Did you kill him?

A: No.

Q: Did you kill your wife?

A: No.

×

Alex Caldwell

Q: You didn't go to the bonfire last night.

A: No.

Q: Where were you?

A: At home.

Q: Can anyone corroborate that?

A: I live alone. As you know.

Q: Of course. And the prior night?

A: Thursday? I went to Middleton. Jake's Tavern.

Q: What for?

A: I didn't feel like drinking alone.

Q: What time did you leave?

A: Midnight.

Q: Can anyone confirm that?

A: Jake, probably. Why are you asking about Thursday night? John was killed last night.

Q: Claudia Mayer most likely died sometime Thursday night.

A: [. . .]

A: Anyone who would kill a dog would also kill a person. Is that it?

Q: Did you resent the Mayers, after the accident?

A: Yes.

Q: Did you blame them for your son's death?

A: I blamed Otto. He was driving.

Q: And who was to blame for your wife's suicide?

A: She was. I was. They were. The whole goddamn human race, as far as I'm concerned. Can I go now? Is there anything else?

Q: Just a few more questions. Back to John Garmond. Can you think of any reason why someone would want to kill him?

A: Maybe something about the club sale. If he opposed it, and others wanted it, or needed it. Or maybe it was a jealous husband.

Q: John was having an affair?

A: That's a grandiose way of putting it. Probably. I don't have any direct knowledge.

Q: You don't mind so casually slandering the dead?

A: I liked John. He was never anything but straight with me. But he was infected with the spirit of the age, too, like all of us. We've pulled up our anchors. We're just drifting now, aimlessly. And now the storm has come, hasn't it?

×

We saw the detective on the porch around midday, shielded from the rain by the overhang, smoking a cigarette between interrogations. Passing by, each of us greeted him with a hesitant wave; we compared notes later. How did he look? Troubled? Confident? Emma Blake was the only one to interrupt his solitude, brazenly bumming a cigarette.

"Not exactly what you bargained for, is it?" she asked.

"What do you mean?"

"When James invited you up here."

"No," said McAnnis. "It's not."

"You don't have to do it, you know. Not really."

"Someone has to."

"You?"

"Someone."

"Do you really think that one of us is a murderer?"

"It seems that it would have to be that way, yes. Perhaps a murderer twice over."

"You mean Claudia? And it's somehow linked to John?"

"It's possible."

"Have you been learning anything?" asked Emma Blake.

"Yes. I think so," said McAnnis. "The facts accumulate. Certain clues pull together like magnets. Others resist explanation. The picture remains opaque. You have to be wary, I've found, of creating false connections. Sometimes a coincidence is just a coincidence. The human mind yearns for order, even to the point of inventing it where, in truth, there's just chaos. And even when all the facts are known, separating the guilty from the innocent can be difficult."

"What do you mean?"

"I have an old puzzle for you," said McAnnis. "It's a parable of sorts."

"A parable?" Emma Blake said skeptically. "What are you, a priest?"

"Just an amateur or a recovering philosopher," said McAnnis. "But listen. Consider the case of White, who is about to trek across a desert. His enemy, Black, poisons the water bottle in his satchel. Another enemy, Blue, later steals the water bottle, not knowing that it's poisoned. You with me?"

"I'm with you."

"White is deep into the desert before he discovers the theft. He dies of thirst. The question: Who is guilty of killing White? Is it Blue? Is it Black? Both? Or neither?"

"It has to be Blue," said Emma Blake. "He stole the water bottle. White died of thirst."

"But didn't Blue actually *delay* White's death? If he hadn't swiped the bottle, wouldn't White have surely sipped Black's poisoned water much earlier, and died from that?"

"Then it's Black."

"Black's method of murder was poison; White died of thirst."

"So neither?"

"Let's consider. Black's link to the death was severed by Blue's theft. As for Blue—how can *preventing* someone from drinking poison be an act of murder?"

"Yet both meant to kill him."

"Indeed. But *attempted* murder implies failure," said McAnnis. "A survivor of the deed. Yet White is dead."

"So who killed White?"

"That's the riddle. We have a murder but no murderer."

Emma Blake thought a moment. "I know who killed White," she said finally, exhaling smoke.

"Who?"

"White himself. It's his fault, for having so many enemies!"

McAnnis smiled wearily. "I'll submit that solution to the academy."

Emma Blake stubbed out her cigarette on the porch railing. Through the trees and the rain, they could see a children's playground, seesaw and swings and slide all half submerged, and beyond that, West Heart Kill, still restless and tumbling, a quiet creek awakened to clamor. They listened to the rain drumming against the leaves and the sharp pinging of drops against the metal lids of the garbage bins out back.

"This parable of yours is entertaining but very abstract," Emma Blake said finally. "Real life is different. In the end, *someone* shot John Garmond. And if you're right, *someone* drowned Claudia Mayer."

"We'll see," said McAnnis.

×

Dashiell Hammett's "Flitcraft Parable"

Halfway through *The Maltese Falcon*, Dashiell Hammett interrupts the action to have Sam Spade tell an odd little story to the novel's femme fatale, Brigid O'Shaughnessy, which has become known as the "Flitcraft Parable." In brief: A woman hires Spade to find her husband, Charles Flitcraft, who disappeared five years earlier, after walking out of his Tacoma real-estate office. He left behind a wife, two children, and a successful business. He had no financial troubles and no extramarital vices. Flitcraft had been, in a very American way, happy. Hammett writes: *"He went like that," Spade said, "like a fist when you open your hand."* The detective eventually finds Flitcraft living in Spokane with a new wife, a new baby, a new business, and a new name: Charles Pierce. Spade confronts him; Flitcraft explains that one day, in Tacoma, he was nearly killed by a falling beam at a construction site. His brush with death sparked a revelation: Flitcraft understood that life, which he had thought was logical and orderly, was in fact entirely governed by chance. He loved his family, but could no longer continue in the life he'd been living, pretending that the universe was not random and meaningless. Flitcraft considered this to be a reasonable decision. He wandered around the Pacific coast for several years, before finally settling in Spokane and sliding back into the same groove he had occupied before. Hammett writes, in the voice of Spade: *". . . that's the part of it I always liked. He adjusted himself to beams falling, and then no more of them fell, and he adjusted himself to them not falling."*

This story is important to Sam Spade. He tells it precisely, repeating certain details to get them right, without any preamble, and without any explanation for why the story might be relevant. After he's concluded, neither he nor Brigid O'Shaughnessy ever mentions it again.

Commentators have speculated on what kind of message, if any, Spade was trying to send to his femme fatale; others have pondered possible nods to the work of the philosopher Charles *Peirce;* stylists have appreciated the flat, fatalist tone and its pitch-perfect details (with its frankly interchangeable midsized Washington towns); literary critics have endeavored to show how the story echoes or foreshadows other plot twists in the novel. Nothing satisfies. It may be that we don't credit the answers because the wrong questions are being asked.

The mystery of the parable is not why it mattered so much to Sam Spade. The mystery is why it mattered so much to Dashiell Hammett.

In 1930, when he published *The Maltese Falcon,* Hammett's career as a novelist was nearly over. He had spent years drinking, his health already shattered by a bout of tuberculosis contracted in Europe when he was an ambulance driver during the Great War, which left him too frail to return to work as a Pinkerton detective. His formal education ended at age thirteen. He would later spend five months in jail for connections to communists. An irredeemable womanizer prone to recurrent infections of gonorrhea, Hammett spent the last decades of his life in a tempestuous affair (they never married) with the playwright Lillian Hellman (of whom Mary McCarthy famously sniffed, ". . . every word she writes is a lie, including 'and' and 'the'"). His last book, 1934's *The Thin Man,* is about a husband-and-wife sleuthing team whose predominant features are wit and a casual, devastating addiction to alcohol (Hammett soon drank himself into impotence). He lingered on for years, impoverished, at one point living in a cabin in rural New York. He was finally killed by lung cancer in 1961 at the age of sixty-six.

None of this, obviously, was known to Hammett when he invented Charles Flitcraft. But he must have had premonitions of his fate. He'd already rejected the life that Flitcraft was born into, and to which he returned. And Hammett already knew the lessons—from his ordeals of war, disease, and detection—that Flitcraft learned from the falling beam.

Hammett devised this parable, one may conjecture, to justify himself. Charles Flitcraft is a critique of everything Hammett had rejected in his life and work. Flitcraft's casual and cruel abandonment of his family, and the equally casual and cruel creation of a new family, is Hammett's judgment on those outwardly contented human beings, endlessly retracing their own steps from home to work to home and back again, that he observed from the tavern window every day.

This explanation is serviceable, as far as it goes. But it feels incomplete. And so here we must venture deeper into speculation and propose that this story was a mystery even to Dashiell Hammett himself. Charles Flitcraft fascinated him for reasons he couldn't understand. A pulse of longing throbs beneath the parable: Hammett writing about a man who glimpsed the terrifying indifference of the universe, its cosmic mockery of petty human lives, but who over time was able to return to happiness. And this heartache, from a writer already sick and old and doomed in just his fourth decade of life, is what gives the parable its power.

There are no answers for this sort of mystery—only questions. Ultimately, we are left wondering: did Dashiell Hammett invent Charles Flitcraft not out of anger or spite, but out of envy?

×

Adam McAnnis is walking down the silent, empty hall of the clubhouse's third floor, smoking a joint, pushing open doors as he goes. He pauses inside Room 302, staring at the bed, now cleaned, changed, tucked, and turned down by Mary the maid. He takes a toke and proceeds down the hall, sidestepping a drip of water from the ceiling pooling on the carpet—the roof must be leaking—and stops at Room 312. The window looks out on the kill, normally just a trickle but now a muddy mess. This bed reveals nothing as well. What is he looking for? You don't know and neither, it seems, does he . . . idly opening drawers, peeking in the wastebasket, pulling back the shower curtain . . . Whoever was here Thursday night left no clues behind, or else they did, and Mary the maid has a new item in her wardrobe; perhaps also, you think, a new weapon of blackmail.

The detective is stretching his legs and clearing his mind after a morning of interrogations, puzzling over the case. So far, the best thing he's got, you think, is the midnight call to John Garmond. The caller was presumably the killer, or the killer's accomplice, luring him to the clubhouse. And this person had to be confident that John wouldn't tell his wife who was calling. That implies some shared secret. Find that, and you find the murderer.

Or: There never was a phone call, and Jane Garmond is lying. In which case, why did she lie? And why, then, did John Garmond go to the clubhouse? Did his wife somehow trick him into leaving, at that hour, in the middle of the storm? Or did she invent some urgent errand that required them both? You can imagine the scene: John Garmond walking into the great hall, not finding whatever it is that he expected to find; puzzled, he begins to turn, but the bullet blows apart the back of his head; he dies not knowing that his wife pulled the trigger . . .

Or: Jane Garmond waits until her husband has left, flashlight in hand, to trudge through the rain, then picks up the phone. *He's on his way*, she might say. *Don't lose your nerve.*

Or:

Or:

Or:

And: There is the matter of Claudia Mayer. Was it suicide or murder? Did her husband kill her, for reasons unknown? It would not have been difficult. Everybody knew that she popped too many pills and drank too much booze; Duncan Mayer could have waited for her to pass out, then carried her unconscious body to his truck and driven in the dark to the boathouse on the lake, where a pile of stones lay waiting, filled the pockets of her housecoat, pushed her gently out into the soft current pulling toward the dam . . . Or, if he was made of sterner stuff, he might have held her head underwater first, just to be sure.

Or: Alex Caldwell killed her, out of grief and revenge. The logistics are more complex. He would have had to entice her to a nighttime rendezvous at the lake, perhaps with a promise of rapprochement, healing old wounds—would that have been enough? And how could he have ensured that Claudia would not tell her husband?

Or: Claudia Mayer committed suicide over some as-yet-unrevealed outrage.

Or: Claudia Mayer killed herself for the familiar but incomprehensible reasons that have driven suicides for millennia—depression, sadness, hopelessness, despair.

Or:

Or:

Or:

This is the part of the mystery, you know, when all the little seedlings begin to sprout and flower: let a thousand motives bloom . . .

It's a lot to track. You imagine that older readers might scribble notes in the margins, or even keep a separate journal of clues and predictions. You're not that kind of reader. But you enjoy the puzzle. It's a commonplace that mystery novels are only read once, but that's not true for you. The second reading offers its own pleasures and pitfalls: knowing recognition at the artfully planted clue, surprise at an item you missed the first time, belated disappointment at the too-obvious hint or innuendo. Of course, there is another possible emotion: the irritation, halfway through a book you've picked up at a beach house or airport, at realizing that you've read the novel before, but have no memory as to the *who, what, how,* and *why*—only that it is likely to be Colonel This or Professor That but never, ever, the butler.

Adam McAnnis has wandered downstairs into the empty kitchen. You think he is looking for clues, but then he begins to pull items out of a fridge. He is pouring a glass of lemonade, making himself a sandwich—you suppress a shiver—with the corpse, by now frozen solid in the walk-in freezer, just steps away.

He is eating alone, sitting on a stool at the kitchen's metal worktable. He glances at his watch. Drains the lemonade in one gulp. Quickly finishes his lunch. The next round of interrogations must be about to begin.

×

Susan Burr

A: Is this awkward for you?

Q: I was about to ask you the same thing. Are you okay?

A: Yes. No. Not really. It's a shock, obviously.

Q: That there was a murder, or that the victim was John Garmond, specifically?

A: Both.

Q: John was well liked?

A: I would say that's true.

Q: You joked to me, two nights ago, about your husband being a murderer. But maybe it wasn't a joke.

A: I was just saying it to be . . . to make things feel more dangerous. To heighten the pleasure.

Q: It worked.

A: This is crazy, but—

Q: But what?

A: The clubhouse is empty, right?

Q: We can't.

A: I know. But still.

Q: We really can't. But I understand the feeling. I feel it, too. Death does that. Once, at a wake, I opened the door to what I thought was the bathroom and found the widow on top of the caterer.

A: I'm not the widow.

Q: Of course. The point is, the psychological reasons for why that happens are well understood.

A: Death makes us horny, is what you're saying.

Q: Yes. But we've wandered off the path here.

A: Sorry.

Q: Where were you last night?

A: At home. All night. Warren and I.

Q: In the same bed?

A: Yes.

Q: What time did you fall asleep?

A: Not sure. Maybe around one a.m.? We had a couple of drinks when we got home, after the fireworks.

Q: Are you a light sleeper?

A: Would I have known if Warren got out of bed, crept to the clubhouse, and murdered John? Is that what you're asking?

Q: [. . .]

A: You may have noticed, with your keen powers of observation, that my husband is a drunkard. There is little difference, for him, between falling asleep and passing out. And when he does, it tends to be for a long time. Thank God.

Q: Let's talk about Claudia Mayer. I'm now forced to consider whether her death was really a suicide.

A: I'm sure it was.

Q: Why?

A: I don't . . . I'm not sure. It just makes sense.

Q: Did Claudia Mayer have a poetic or dramatic temperament?

A: What do you mean?

Q: Her friend Amanda Caldwell committed suicide by drowning herself in the lake. It's a romantic way to do it, as these things go. But it's even more romantic to kill yourself in the same way, on the exact same day, years later.

A: Claudia was a bit like that, yes.

Q: Did she feel guilt over her friend's pain? That her son survived the car accident while Amanda's son died? And that Amanda couldn't live with the grief?

A: Of course.

Q: Enough guilt to kill herself?

A: I don't know. Yes. I suppose so. Maybe. With everything else.

Q: Everything else? Like what?

A: I don't know. Life. Aging. Money. Marriage. Politics. The economy. Everything going to shit, basically. That everything else.

Q: Let's circle back to consider the other possibility. That it wasn't suicide.

A: Is that what you think?

Q: I don't think anything. Not yet.

A: Claudia was harmless. I can't imagine that she had any enemies.

Q: That's the question we often ask—*did she have any enemies?* But it's not really the right question. What we really mean is—*was there any reason someone might want to kill her?* It's not the same thing.

A: Are you asking that now?

Q: Yes.

A: I can't think of any reason.

Q: Was she an inconvenience to anyone? Was she in the way? Financially? Sexually?

A: Again, I don't know.

Q: When you lack motive, you focus on method. Is it possible that someone who knew Claudia, who knew her history and her temperament, would realize that her committing suicide on this date, when her friend and her friend's son both died, would *make sense*, as you say? That it would *feel right*?

A: I suppose it's possible. We all know each other pretty well up here.

Q: Well enough to build a murder plot?

A: I don't know.

Q: In a faked suicide, the murderer is almost always a spouse. Or some other loved one.

A: I don't think Duncan Mayer killed his wife.

Q: I just find it odd that, of the two deaths here in the last twenty-four hours, Duncan Mayer is linked to both.

A: What's the link to John?

Q: Duncan Mayer shot him in the shoulder yesterday morning. A hunting accident, supposedly.

A: Oh. That. I heard about that.

Q: Did you think I meant something else?

A: No, not at all.

Q: But you don't think it's significant.

A: These men up here are mediocre woodsmen, I must say. I suspect these hunting trips are just another excuse to drink. Bullets are probably flying every which way, some mornings.

Q: Last night, you told me that Duncan Mayer was "spoken for."

A: I did?

Q: Yes. Spoken for by whom?

A: [. . .]

Q: It could be important.

A: I feel like we've wandered off the path again.

Q: You seemed upset this morning.

A: When?

Q: At the clubhouse.

A: Of course. A man was murdered.

Q: What was your relationship with John Garmond?

A: Was he my lover, is that what you're asking?

Q: Yes.

A: He was.

Q: [. . .]

Q: [. . .]

Q: For how long?

A: It's difficult to answer that question. These things ebb and flow, especially as you get older. The first time, years ago. After that, occasionally. When the mood struck us. We were both adults. You of all people should understand.

Q: And recently?

A: More often.

Q: Any particular reason?

A: Not really. We're just billiard balls spinning around, aren't we? Every now and then we clack together. It all feels very random.

Q: Does your husband know?

A: I don't know. Probably. He doesn't ask. And neither do I.

Q: Does Warren have affairs?

A: I would assume so. Again, we don't talk about it. But he travels, sometimes, for work. He returns to the city alone, often, while I'm left here.

Q: Anyone at West Heart?

A: Not that I know of.

Q: Did John love his wife? And vice versa?

A: Honestly, I'm not equipped to answer or even understand the question.

Q: Did John ever talk about club business? Finances, anything like that?

A: God, no. And if he tried, I wouldn't have allowed it. Life is too short. I hear enough financial misery from my husband. You're supposed to be spared that with your lover.

Q: You've been very forthright.

A: Are you jealous?

Q: No. Should I be?

A: Of course not.

Q: Can you please tell your husband to come down? He's after the doctor.

×

Dr. Roger Blake

Q: Thanks for your help earlier.

A: Of course. It was my duty. I've been worrying about the body temperature, that it could be important. I wish I'd felt up to handling it.

Q: It's quite all right.

A: The way you do it properly is either rectally or by slicing a hole in the abdomen and sliding the thermometer in that way. Neither seemed . . .

Q: Respectful?

A: I'm a materialist, I don't have romantic ideas about bodies, even those of my friends. But still. I just couldn't.

Q: I'm sorry. You'd known John Garmond for a long time?

A: His whole life. He was much younger than me. I remember, when I went off to medical school, he was still just a scrawny kid, swinging off the rope into the lake. Him and Jane Talbot and Duncan Mayer—they were inseparable.

Q: Good friends?

A: Yes.

Q: Something more than friends?

A: [. . .]

Q: It could be important, doctor.

A: During their high-school years—college, too, I think—a sort of triangle developed. Jane dated John, then Duncan, then neither. Then maybe both, I don't know.

Q: But she married John.

A: Yes.

Q: And John and Duncan remained friends.

A: Yes.

Q: *Yes*? Or *yes, but* . . . ?

A: *Yes, but*, I suppose. It's been hard. Twenty-five, thirty years have passed? But I don't know that you ever get over your first love. Don't you agree?

Q: You may not be a romantic, but as a private detective I'm more or less obligated to be one. Of the hard-nosed-exterior type, of course. And I agree with you. Although a later love that feels like a first love has its own merits . . . Were you ever a club president? Like your father?

A: My father was never club president.

Q: I'm sorry. I must have been confused. And you?

A: Yes, I took a turn. About fifteen years ago.

Q: How is the office chosen?

A: Election. One vote per household.

Q: And is it just a matter of passing the conch around the fire?

A: What does that mean?

Q: Not important. How would you describe the job?

A: A bunch of chores, really. Pretty mundane stuff. The president handles process. And he has veto power for certain things, though it's rarely used.

Q: What sort of things?

A: New member applications. Opening land to logging. The disposition of the club.

Q: Meaning whether to sell or not?

A: I think so. Yes.

Q: On this question of selling the club, John was not supportive, is that correct?

A: That's right.

Q: But what about the rest of the members?

A: I suspect a majority would back the sale. Some think this whole place is out of date. Some need the money.

Q: Would he have used his veto to block the sale? Even if a majority wanted it?

A: I don't know.

Q: Will Jonathan Gold be accepted as a member?

A: I think so.

Q: Even though he is Jewish?

A: No one cares about that sort of thing anymore.

Q: Did they use to?

A: No more than anyone else.

Q: Would you say the members are political?

A: They vote, if that's what you mean. They talk about elections and taxes.

Q: Most are conservative, correct?

A: I think that's a fair description.

Q: Nixon, Reagan, Buckley? That crowd?

A: Correct.

Q: Has it always been that way?

A: I believe so.

Q: Anticommunist, obviously?

A: Of course.

Q: And before the war? Opposed to FDR, the New Deal?

A: Probably.

Q: Intervention in Europe?

A: I'm not sure. Why does that matter?

Q: It probably doesn't. Thank you, doctor.

×

Warren Burr

A: So you questioned my wife?

Q: Yes. I'm talking to everyone.

A: I'm sure you were . . . thorough.

Q: Shall we start with last night?

A: Certainly.

Q: Where were you between the hours of midnight and two a.m.?

A: Drunk.

Q: That's not a location.

A: On the contrary. It's a nation-state with its own laws and traditions. Well populated. I've been a citizen in good standing for years.

Q: You were at your house?

A: Yes. As I'm sure Susan told you.

Q: She did. She said that you . . . went to sleep after a few cocktails.

A: I passed out, is what she said.

Q: It creates a bit of an awkward situation. She is your alibi, but you cannot be hers.

A: How inconvenient for her. I certainly hope she didn't do something foolish like shoot a man in the back of the head, then.

Q: You were not a fan?

A: My feelings for John Garmond were no better or worse than my feelings for anyone else.

Q: So you had no special reason to dislike him?

A: Do I have any special reason to dislike you?

Q: [. . .]

Q: What kind of business are you in?

A: Is that relevant?

Q: Potentially.

A: I'm in the transportation business.

Q: I was under the impression you were in finance.

A: I transport wealth from point A to point B.

Q: That's a service people need?

A: Anyone can store money. It's moving the money that requires real expertise. Especially if you want to avoid undue attention.

Q: And business is good?

A: Good enough.

Q: I understand that you're keen on selling West Heart. Most others who feel similarly need the money, I think.

A: *Needing* money and *wanting* money are different things.

Q: The Burrs were one of the founding families. No qualms about ending the tradition?

A: Qualmless.

Q: Do you own a gun, Mr. Burr?

A: Of course.

Q: More than one?

A: It's a hunting club.

Q: When was the last time you fired a gun?

A: I don't remember.

Q: So if, after the storm ends, the authorities were to test your firearms, they would find that none had been fired recently?

A: Be my guest.

Q: Are you a violent man?

A: Why do you ask?

Q: You threatened me the other night. And a man who makes threats without the will to back them up is a fool. You don't strike me as a fool.

A: Whatever I may have said, I've already forgotten . . . I say a lot of things to a lot of people.

Q: You said a mouth like mine could land me in trouble.

A: That's true, isn't it? I bet you've said things before, in your work, that led to—what? A thug pulls a knife on you? A gun? A man in the back room of a bar decides to send some muscle to "teach you a lesson"?

Q: Is that what you would do?

A: Of course not. I'm a businessman, that's all.

Q: If West Heart isn't sold, would you welcome Jonathan Gold as a member?

A: Sure. Why not?

Q: What do you think of him?

A: I don't think anything.

Q: You didn't know him before his application?

A: No. I've only met him a couple times, on his membership visits up here. Why he would want to join, I have no idea. But a new face, new money—that would be welcome.

Q: As I said, Susan is your alibi. But you're not hers. Did she have any reason to dislike John Garmond?

A: Had he moved on, is that what you're asking?

Q: So you knew?

A: Knew what?

Q: It didn't bother you?

A: You were asking, detective, if John had moved on.

Q: Yes.

A: You were asking if Susan was a woman scorned.

Q: Was she?

A: If you knew Susan like I know Susan . . .

A: [. . .]

A: [. . .]

Q: Is something funny?

A: Not at all. But Susan is not a romantic woman. She has no illusions about anybody or anything. When she tires of her trinkets, she's more than happy to toss them away and find something new. Have you ever been married, Mr. McAnnis?

Q: No.

A: Then you certainly won't understand. But I'll explain it anyway. Every marriage is an isolated universe, with its own laws of physics. At the center is a black hole. From the outside, you can't make sense of it. You can't see into it. Light doesn't escape it. And the forces inside can tear you apart.

Q: Another threat?

A: As you like.

Q: [. . .]

A: Making headway, are you?

Q: Some. But I have confidence. As they say—murder will out.

A: How interesting. Is that what they say?

×

Definition

Murder: mər-dər, of Teutonic Germanic origin. Archaic forms include **morþor, murthur,** and **mourdre.** The *OED* cites *Beowulf* (circa 750) as the earliest usage; among the passages that include it are the lines describing "God's adversary" Grendel and his dam: "morðres scyldig ond his módor éac" ("guilty of murder, and his mother, too"). Several centuries later, Chaucer's "The Nun's Priest's Tale" (circa 1386) offers "Mordre wol out, that se we day by day" ("Murder will out, that we see day by day"—apparently the source for the expression "murder will out," meaning that the crime will eventually come to light).

Of relevance also is the *OED* citation for "the murder game," also called "playing the murders," dating from the 1930s, both as an actual parlor or dinner-party game in which someone played "the corpse" and someone else "the murderer," and the reference to such games in mystery novels by the likes of Ngaio Marsh and Cecil

Day-Lewis. These were clearly inspired by the gamelike nature of the "puzzle mystery," and the next logical step for some novelists was to forgo the novel, so to speak, and focus just on the puzzle. In his magisterial study of the genre, *Bloody Murder*, Julian Symons notes that one writer began producing "murder dossiers" instead of novels, each essentially a box filled with clues: "hair, matches, poison pills . . . photographs of the characters . . . telegrams, letters . . ." etc. Enthusiasts (they were no longer quite "readers") were expected to sift through the clues and piece together a solution. From there, obviously, it was a short jump to board games like Clue, devised in 1943 by a musician who was inspired, he said, by watching aristocrats "play the murders" at weekend getaways for which he was hired to perform.

The *OED* also contains an entry for the delightfully morbid "murder of crows" ("morther of crowys," circa 1475), which was purportedly inspired by the propensity of crows to feast on the dead, particularly on battlefields. But, sadly, there is ample evidence that collective phrases like this were merely fanciful inventions concocted for medieval glossaries like *The Book of Saint Albans* from 1486 and revived, centuries later, by James Lipton in his *An Exaltation of Larks* from 1968. Logophiles may, of course, exercise poetic license in continuing to indulge in such treats as "a skulk of thieves," "a poverty of pipers," and "the unkindness of ravens."

×

How were we supposed to entertain ourselves on a day of rain after a murder? What was expected of us? We sat in our cabins, smoking, reading, trying to read, accepting an invitation for an afternoon of cards, regretting it almost instantly, inventing excuses, then deciding to go after all . . .

It was difficult to trust the time: the clocks seemed scarcely to move, and it hardly seemed possible that less than a minute had passed since you'd last looked. The light, such as it was, seemed unchanging from morning to afternoon to evening. We turned our faces away from bedroom doors, behind which some of us might be heard to weep, tears for the victims or, more likely, for ourselves.

It was amid such morose tedium that an idea took hold, an idea that, once contemplated, could not be released, an idea that batted aside such moral qualms as *But is it respectful?* and moved directly to more practical considerations of *Where shall it be held?* For we had fixed on a Sixer as the solution, the sole remedy for such dire solitude. In other words, we were all badly in need of a drink.

Certain houses being obviously off-limits, we settled on the Blake house as our *lieu de fête;* not ideal, certainly, since it also doubled as the temporary home for our visiting detective, whose relentless inquisitiveness had grown tiresome (for most) and threatening (for some). But it would serve for the matter of an hour or two—the occasion, if nothing else, to toast the memory of poor old John.

These next few paragraphs are, oddly, spent surveying the history of drinking at the club: infamous Sixers, New Year's parties best forgotten, bloody noses and broken hearts, West Heart's brief but illustrious role as a way station on the "Prohibition Road" transporting Canadian whiskey down to New York City and points south . . . all of which only vaguely interests you, giving you space and time to contemplate the lies uncovered so far, lies built upon lies, like the miracle of compound interest upon which these old money families undoubtedly rely for their fortunes. How do you separate the mortal from the mundane? Reginald Talbot lying about the club finances. Warren Burr lying about whether he knew Jonathan Gold (*I try to avoid my husband's associates,* Susan Burr had said). Dr. Blake lying about whether his father was club president. (How could that possibly matter?) And of course Someone, or several Someones, lying about being at home the last two nights. Who was in Room 312? Who was in the hall just outside the door? Who fired the bullet that killed John Garmond?

×

Adam McAnnis returned from a smoke on the porch to find Jonathan Gold sitting on a leather sofa in the library, paging idly through a thick book.

"*West Heart: The First 50 Years*," he said, flipping back to the cover. "It's a nice touch, that *First*. A certain . . . almost childlike naïveté. Boundless optimism. Because of course there will be another fifty. And another fifty after that. Because we are not the kind of people to whom bad things happen." Jonathan Gold closed the book. "Charming."

"We should have a formal interview," said McAnnis. "About the murder."

"I think not."

Jonathan Gold stood and walked along the bookshelves, fingertips brushing the spines. Almost delicately, he teased a book out from its spot and watched as it teetered on the edge of the shelf, before letting it crash to the floor. Then he did it again. And again.

McAnnis said nothing.

"So the dead man hired you?" Jonathan Gold said finally.

"I had to say something," answered McAnnis.

"Very clever."

"Bought me some time."

"Indeed. I appreciate the artistry. The dead man was not there to refute you. Yet it seemed eminently plausible. And no doubt there was more than one person in that room who had reason to worry that you were hired to investigate *them*." Jonathan Gold crossed his arms. "I didn't think you had it in you."

"I appreciate the vote of confidence," McAnnis said dryly.

"Expressing confidence is not why I'm here," said Jonathan Gold. "These recent unfortunate events have intruded upon our enterprise."

"I've made progress."

"Have you?"

"I have some accounts for you to review."

"Ah, yes. The famous two sets of books. I'll look at them, of course. But numbers can be made to tell any story you'd like. I have magicians who can make whole properties appear and disappear, just by changing the symbols on a page."

"Is that how you know Warren Burr?"

Jonathan Gold forced a thin bloodless smile across his face. "Very good, Mr. McAnnis," he said. "Perhaps I have underestimated you after all."

"Lucky guess."

"I won't bother to ask you how you know that. I'm certain my associate would not have revealed as much, even if he was deep in his cups, as he often is. A weakness," said Jonathan Gold, "that enemies might try to exploit."

"Does he have enemies? Do you?"

The other man waved his hand dismissively. "Enemies, friends, it can be hard to distinguish between the two. Sometimes a man can be both at the same time." He stared at McAnnis. "I hope these tragedies haven't been too much of a distraction from your real assignment."

"On the contrary," said McAnnis. "They might be linked."

"How so?"

"You know how investigations are. Right now, I see through a glass darkly. But soon . . ."

"I'm skeptical," said Jonathan Gold. "I do like to permit my dogs some leash. But quote unquote solving the murder may be the easy part."

"What do you mean?"

"Guilt is a tricky thing. Do you know the story of David and Bathsheba?"

"Only vaguely. The sisters of St. Thomas were prudes about the juicy parts of the Bible."

"I'll fill in the gaps of your education, then," said Jonathan Gold. "David is on his palace rooftop when he sees the beautiful Bathsheba sunbathing in the nude. He exercises a king's prerogative and summons her for sex. But she's married; when she becomes pregnant, therefore, David fears exposure of his adultery. So he concocts a plan to put her husband at the front of the siege lines, where the fighting is fiercest. The plan works; Bathsheba's husband is killed in battle, and David takes her as his wife."

"And they lived happily ever after."

"We'll get to that. From a legal point of view, it would be difficult to make a criminal case against David. It was an enemy sword that struck down the husband. The struggle was a legitimate battle that would have been fought anyway. And David was miles away at the time. Legally, then, David was innocent."

"But?"

"But while that might be man's judgment, it is not the judgment of God. To rebuke David, God sends a prophet who tells a parable about a rich man stealing and slaughtering a poor man's sheep. David is outraged by the rich man's crime and sentences him to die; the prophet reveals the culprit to be none other than David himself. 'You are that man!' the prophet screams at David, in what I must confess seemed like a very dramatic moment to a young boy in Brooklyn who everyone *knew* would grow up to be a rabbi just like his father."

Jonathan Gold paused to indulge this memory with a private, sardonic smile. McAnnis remained silent.

"The prophet also makes it clear," Jonathan Gold continued, "that God doesn't accept David's attempt to distance himself from his crime by arranging for the husband to be killed by foreign hands. Murder is murder. God curses David's house, and his reign crumbles amid his family's incest, rape, fratricide, and civil war."

"What's the point?"

"The point is, without God we are left to rely upon the law. And the law is a crude tool for seeking justice. I say that as a lawyer. Intuitively, we know that David is guilty; in conversation, we might go so far as to say David *killed* him or even *murdered* Bathsheba's husband. Yet the law says he is innocent."

"And?"

"And nothing," said Jonathan Gold. "I'm just setting expectations."

There was the creak of a door downstairs, footsteps on the floorboards. And then a voice crying, "Hello? Hello?" The voice of a child.

McAnnis cocked his head at the lawyer.

"Don't let me keep you from your inquiries," said Jonathan Gold. "All of them."

"Don't forget the books."

"Of course not," said Jonathan Gold, scooping up the ledgers left by Reginald Talbot. "We'll talk again soon."

McAnnis found Ralph Wakefield downstairs in the doorway of the great hall, trying not to look at the inkblot stain by the hearth. He was wearing a child's bright-yellow rain jacket and boots, dripping water onto the floor. His binoculars hung around his neck.

"Yes, Ralph?"

"You told me to look for anything strange and unusual."

"Yes."

"I found something strange and unusual. A cabin in the woods."

McAnnis sighed. "There are lots of cabins in these woods, Ralph."

"But I saw a man inside. He was hiding something in the floor."

"Who was it?"

"The man whose house we were at for dinner."

"Dr. Blake?"

"Yes."

×

The cabin was about a half mile back in the woods. A little far to walk, this late in the day, but McAnnis certainly couldn't ask James or Emma Blake for a ride. So they walked, the boy and the detective, in the rain.

"Where are your mom and dad, Ralph?"

"I don't know."

"Europe?"

"Yes," said Ralph. "Mom is in Paris and Dad is in Rome."

"I thought you said you didn't know."

"I just say that when I don't want to answer."

McAnnis grinned. "Adults do the same thing."

McAnnis wore fireman boots that he'd bought at a thrift store near his apartment, but he didn't have any other rain gear besides a poncho he'd swiped from the clubhouse closet. His pants were soaked. The tree canopy provided some shelter from the rain, but at this time of summer the ferns were prehistorically large, waist-high on McAnnis, neck-high on the boy, and they were soon soaked as they bushwhacked through a trail so overgrown that it was hard to see.

"You sure you know where you're going?"

"I'm a West Heart expert," Ralph said proudly. "I've walked all over."

"I don't suppose you know another way out of here," muttered McAnnis.

"Sure I do."

McAnnis stopped. "What? Really?"

"Maybe. I've seen the dirty man—what's his name?"

"The caretaker? Fred Shiflett?"

"Yes. I've seen him drive down a track near his cabin, and come back with grocery bags."

"You sure?"

"I had my binoculars."

"Where's his cabin?"

"Deep in the woods, away from the others."

"You tell anyone about this?"

"No. Should I have? Did I do something wrong?"

"You haven't done anything wrong, Ralph. You're doing great." They walked for another few minutes in silence, and then McAnnis asked: "Were you walking around the other night, the night we met? Maybe after the dinner party?"

"After dinner it's my bedtime," insisted Ralph.

"Sure. Of course," said McAnnis. "But when I was a boy, I hated bedtime. I hated it so much, in fact, that sometimes I stayed awake in bed, waiting until my parents went to sleep, and then I snuck out of the house. You ever do that sort of thing, Ralph?"

"I don't know."

"I would sneak out and wander all over the neighborhood. I lived in the city, so it's not like here. One time I climbed right underneath this giant bridge, the Brooklyn Bridge, and wrote my name on a piece of brick where no one would ever see it. No one but me would ever know it was there."

"Is it still there now?"

"I'm not sure. I'm too old to go back there now. Maybe some other kid's name is there now. Maybe your name."

"I've never been to the Brooklyn Bridge!"

"There are lots of Ralphs in the world. Lots of Adams, too."

"Who's Adam?"

"That's me."

"My uncle called you something else," said Ralph. "A bad name."

"I bet he did," said McAnnis. "Did your aunt ever call me anything?"

"No."

"So, anyway, Ralph," McAnnis continued, "if you were like me, and maybe you snuck out at night, and maybe you saw something, and didn't know who to tell about it . . . well, you could tell me."

The boy was quiet a moment, then said: "I saw the man with the bad leg."

"Which man? The younger man?"

"He looks old to me. The man who limps."

"Where did you see him? Was it near the clubhouse?"

"No, it was in the woods. On a trail."

"What time?"

"Late."

"Did he see you?"

"No."

"Did you see anyone else? The lady with the streak of white in her hair?"

"No."

The forest gloom was settling onto them like a blanket. McAnnis hadn't brought a flashlight. This probably should have waited until morning.

"You know that a man was murdered last night, right, Ralph?" McAnnis asked gently.

"Yes."

"He was one of the men at dinner."

"I know him. My aunt knows him," said Ralph. "You're trying to find out who did it?"

"That's right."

"It was someone here? Someone I know?"

"I'm afraid so," said McAnnis. "Are you scared, Ralph?"

"I don't know."

The cabin was smaller than McAnnis had expected, almost a shed compared with the homes back in the main part of the club. A large tree limb had fallen on the slanted roof during the storm. The windows were dark. Cobwebs hung beneath the eaves. Dangling from hooks on the porch were some rusty tools—a hacksaw, several knives of varying length, one particularly evil-looking hooked blade—that McAnnis realized must be used to butcher a kill. He knocked, waited a moment, then tested the doorknob. It opened.

McAnnis and the boy stepped inside and across the rough-hewn wood floor. There was just one room, containing a bare card table, chairs, a propane lantern, and a dirty cooler in the corner. He didn't see a sink or any light switches—no electricity or running water. Over the fireplace hung a deer skull with a sweeping eight-point antler rack. On the mantel there was a photo of Dr. Blake and a teenage James, before McAnnis knew him, crouched over the body of a deer. Also: a photo of a younger Dr. Blake with his arm around a man that McAnnis recognized, from the old West Heart clippings, as his father.

"Where is it?" asked McAnnis.

Ralph pointed at a braided rug next to the card table. McAnnis pulled it back to expose the faint outline of a hatch. The boy silently offered McAnnis a Boy Scout knife from a clip on his waist.

"Thanks."

Inside the hatch there was a metal box, the type you might pick up at an army-navy surplus store. With a glance at Ralph—should he let the kid stick around for whatever this might be?—McAnnis popped the latch and opened the lid.

Newspaper clippings, bits of paper, fabric. He sifted through the contents with his fingers. A patch bearing an iron cross. Another with the lightning-bolt letters *SS*. A metal pin with an eagle clutching a wreath surrounding a swastika.

"What is all that stuff?" asked Ralph.

"I'm not sure," said McAnnis. "Mementos of war."

The newspaper articles, yellowed and crumbling in his hands, were all in German. But one article, from 1933, included a photo. It showed a man McAnnis recognized as Dr. Theodore Blake standing next to a smiling fat dignitary in uniform. The caption included a location, Berlin, and a name: "Reichsstatthalter Hermann Göring."

"Was I right to come get you?" asked Ralph. "Is it anything unusual?"

"Yes," said McAnnis. "It's unusual."

The detective tilted the box. A metallic click. McAnnis pulled out a pistol.

"What is that?" asked Ralph.

"A Luger."

"Is that German?"

"Yes. From the war."

"Vietnam?"

"No, a different one."

"How did it get here?"

"That, Ralph, is a very good question."

McAnnis sniffed the barrel but couldn't tell if it had been recently fired. He put everything back as he had found it, closed the hatch, replaced the rug. He glanced around. Nothing else of interest.

"What now?"

"Now," said McAnnis, "we go back to the Blake house. You hungry?"

"Starving."

They walked back through the woods in silence. McAnnis was surprised when, without asking, Ralph silently took his hand.

And as man and boy step through the fern-filled forest, you wonder for the first time about the inevitable John Garmond autopsy, and what type of bullet the medical examiners will extract from the back of his head. Will they be able to tell, for example, if the bullet came from a foreign gun, received as a gift decades ago from a new important friend? Or perhaps it was bought at a pawnshop, the sort of store where the truly esoteric souvenirs of hate and violence are kept in a back room, for the connoisseur to savor in private? You wonder, also, whether a man like that would be pleased that this gun, with its secret personal significance, was at hand for his first foray into murder.

×

We were gathered at the Blake house for the Sixer. It had seemed like a good idea in the solitude of the dreary afternoon drizzle but less so in the claustrophobic lamplight of evening. We stood in small knots, clutching our drinks like life preservers, furtively noting the red-rimmed eyes, the pallid skin, cigarette ash falling on the carpet, trembling hands, each of us in the private well of our own suffering beginning to wonder: *My God, do I look as bad as that?*

The detective arrived late, with that boy in tow. The one staying at the Burr house. We'd seen him all summer, alone, traipsing around the club. We thought of saying something to Susan, but to what end? He was not her child, and children were not her thing. But we had to admit that it bothered us, all that exploring—the *snooping*, it was described as, more than once. The binoculars, we suspected, were stolen from the hunting gallery of the clubhouse, the display case where one might find a few old compasses, an ancient blood-stained bear trap, a flute made from a stag's antlers . . . an irresistible set of temptations for a young boy's wandering hands. What, really, was there to do about it? Besides, wasn't there something a little bit *off* about young Ralph Wakefield?

"I feel like the skunk at a garden party," said McAnnis. He'd finally acquired a drink, a gin and tonic, and was talking to the doctor, for whom, some of us noticed, he'd seemed to be searching as soon as he walked through the door.

"Surely it's not so bad as that?"

"Everywhere I look, I see a suspect," the detective muttered into his drink.

"In theory, I suppose," said Dr. Blake. "But aren't some more likely than others?"

"Don't talk to me about theories," said McAnnis. "All I have are theories. But even the false ones can be helpful."

"How is that?"

"It's a problem of verisimilitude."

"I'm afraid you'll have to explain."

"In fiction, it's the struggle to give the story an appearance of reality. But in philosophy, it's quite different. Verisimilitude is the idea that some false theories can be closer to the truth than other false theories, and explaining how you make that distinction."

"As a doctor, that is to say, as a man of science," said Dr. Blake, "I think that sounds ridiculous. Either something is true or it's not."

"It's more of a spectrum, is the thinking," said McAnnis. "We can never actually arrive at the truth, *per se*, but our failed attempts still provide some insights."

"So philosophers would say that even false theories can be useful."

"So would detectives."

The two men fell silent, to drink, as if by mutual assent. Then McAnnis nonchalantly, as if deliberately pivoting to a lighter stream of conversation, asked: "Any famous people ever come to West Heart?"

"Celebrities? Here? Sure," said Dr. Blake with a laugh. "Warren

Beatty and Faye Dunaway dropped by a Sixer just the other day. Jack Nicholson took a dip in the lake. He's an avid swimmer—not many people know that. Pacino likes to hunt. He's a crack shot. Took down the bear you see at the clubhouse."

"What about in the past?"

"Why do you ask?"

"I saw in one of the old records in that library that Henry Ford and Charles Lindbergh visited once. Ages ago. In the 1930s, I think."

"Really? I don't remember that at all. Of course, I was young."

"They met your father."

"I must not have been there. Probably away at medical school."

"He never talked about it? They were two of the most famous Americans of their day. You don't know why they came?"

"Sorry, no idea."

"Did your father inspire you to get into medicine?"

"I suppose so. He was in general practice. Kids, mostly. Rashes and runny noses." He sniffed. "I'm a cardiologist."

"Where did he get his degree?"

"He was a Harvard man," said Dr. Blake. "Like me."

"Did he ever study abroad?"

"No, I don't think so."

"I found some sort of diploma tucked away in my bedroom closet. It was in German, so I couldn't make heads or tails of it, but I did see that his name was on it."

"Probably some sort of honorary degree." Dr. Blake shrugged. "He had a few of those. You found it packed away in a box, you said?"

"Did he ever travel abroad? Maybe before the war?"

Dr. Blake smiled in a way meant to suggest amiable confusion. "What is this about, Mr. McAnnis?"

"Nothing."

The detective held up his empty glass in the universally understood gesture of *Excuse me, I need a refill,* and headed to the bar, feeling as he did so the doctor's eyes lingering on his back.

McAnnis lingered alone by the bar long enough to finish the

next gin-and-tonic and pour himself another. No one, he noticed, seemed eager to talk to him. He stepped outside for some fresh air and found Emma Blake, sitting underneath the low overhang of the roof that covered part of the terrace, smoking a hand-rolled cigarette of a not unfamiliar nature.

"You've been holding out on me," lectured McAnnis. "If you were well stocked this whole time, why did you keep pestering me for it?"

"A girl never buys her own drink or smokes from her own stash," said Emma Blake. "Not if she can help it."

"Does a girl share?"

"This one does."

She passed him the joint. McAnnis coughed; she laughed. Emma Blake's weed was stronger—better—than what he was used to, down on the Lower East Side.

"I saw you interrogating my father."

"Making conversation," said McAnnis, eyes still watering.

"Please," said Emma Blake. "So is he the murderer?"

"Doubtful."

"What, then?"

"I was curious about your grandfather."

"That rotten old man? Really?"

"You didn't like him?"

"Nobody did."

"Why?"

"He had breath like a dead animal. Yellow crooked teeth. I once saw him take some food out of his beard and eat it. Did you know he was a children's doctor? Can you imagine the nightmares that man caused?"

"Some fairly shallow reasons for hate, Emma."

"He was also unkind. And embarrassing."

"To the club?"

"So I gathered, though I don't really know the details. He died when I was still a kid."

" 'I was so much older then,' " quoted McAnnis. " 'I'm younger than that now.' "

"Excuse me?"

"Dylan."

"Who?"

"You're kidding."

"Only vaguely. You ever listen to Fleetwood Mac?"

The rain had stopped, though no one inside seemed to have noticed. From the terrace, McAnnis could see a figure on the road, breathing the red tip of a cigarette in and out. Then the figure took a few halting steps, and the detective knew who was down there lurking in the night, and why he wouldn't come up to the house.

"I'll be right back," he told Emma Blake.

Another cigarette had been lit by the time McAnnis made it to the road.

"I hear you've been asking questions about my mom," said Otto Mayer.

"The club asked me to investigate."

"The police already came," said Otto Mayer. "What's your angle?"

"I'm just asking questions. As much to rule things out as to rule them in."

Otto Mayer kicked at the gravel. "Did you ask my dad if he killed her?"

"I did."

"What did he say?"

"He said he didn't."

"I think he believes that."

"Do you?"

"Depends," said Otto Mayer, "on how you define it."

"I understand she'd been . . . not well for a long time."

"Her whole life. Or at least, my whole life. It would get better, then worse, and so on, year after year."

"It must have been painful."

"It was."

"Do you think she committed suicide?"

"Of course."

"If I may ask—why so sure?"

"She was having another spell . . . That's what she called them. Her *spells*. The last few years had been very bad."

"Since the accident."

Otto Mayer nodded. "Yes. And so much worse after Amanda Caldwell . . ."

"I've heard the story."

"I feel guilty about it, of course. Though maybe I shouldn't. Maybe it's just that Trip was unlucky. I could easily have died, too. And it's not like I escaped unscathed," he said, tapping his leg.

"You don't have to convince me," said McAnnis. "I'm not here to judge your guilt or innocence."

"My understanding," said Otto Mayer, "is that's exactly what you're here to do."

McAnnis shook his head. "At the end of a case, I provide a report with facts and figures. Dates. Accounts of who said what. That's all."

"You forgot about the manila folders with all the dirty photos."

McAnnis ignored that. "Did she know about your father?"

"Yes. Some of it. All of it, by the end."

"Did you know?"

"Not everything. Not until yesterday." Otto Mayer lit another cigarette. He was smoking them end to end, lighting each from the nub of its predecessor and grinding them into the mud. McAnnis noticed that his fingers were trembling slightly. "Did you know she went missing last month?"

"I did not. Your father didn't mention it."

"She was gone for two weeks."

"Where did she go?"

"We don't know."

"Friends?" suggested McAnnis. "Family?"

"Neither. We called hospitals, hotels. Filed a missing person's report. The police asked if we wanted teams with dogs searching the woods. Searching West Heart."

"Did you?"

"We did not."

"When did she return?"

"Just a few days ago."

"Did she say anything?"

"No," said Otto Mayer. "And my father didn't ask her."

"Did you think that was peculiar?"

"Yes. Until yesterday."

The lake. The sun's glare off the water so brilliant it made everything seem like a dream. The buzz of a biplane, flying low, banking its wings in greeting to the swimmers below. Emma Blake, eyes hidden by dark sunglasses, flirting. The splash of a child off the rope swing. And then the cold fist in his stomach as McAnnis walked to the water's edge to find the corpse bobbing in the gentle tide. Turning around to see this younger man back at the beach struggle to his feet, everything in his form and figure suggesting, somehow, that he knew.

"I'm sorry."

"I had to see her, to be sure," said Otto Mayer.

"Not everyone would have been willing to do it."

Floaters being among the worst category of bodies to identify. Especially in fresh water. By the time McAnnis saw her, the fish had been at her face.

"Emma took me home."

"Was your father there?"

"No, he'd gone fishing by the bridge. Emma sent someone to get him. I made her leave. I went into my mom's bedroom. That's when I found it."

McAnnis looked at the paper, folded in half, that Otto Mayer pulled from the pocket of his rain jacket. He'd guessed, but hadn't wanted to press.

"When my dad asked me, I said I'd found nothing."

"And that's what he told the sheriff," said McAnnis. "That could complicate things."

"I'll explain, if I have to," said Otto Mayer. "Do you want to see it?"

"Yes."

The glow from the Blake terrace didn't quite reach the road, so McAnnis pulled out his lighter to read the note in the dark. Faint, spindly handwriting. Written in pencil, like the homework of a child.

"And you didn't know this?" asked McAnnis, after he'd read the note twice.

"No."

"Your father must have told her. Recently, most likely. That's why she went missing."

"I assume so."

"Why are you giving me this?"

"My mother's case is closed," said Otto Mayer. "Or at least I consider it closed. But the John Garmond case is open."

"It could be connected."

"Maybe."

"If anything, this note casts a shadow on your father."

"I'm aware," said Otto Mayer. "But I don't think he killed John. Do you?"

McAnnis avoided the younger man's eyes, carefully refolding the piece of paper. "Mind if I keep the note?"

"It's yours. I don't want it anymore." Otto Mayer watched the detective tuck the note into his pocket, then asked: "Are you going to tell Ramsey?"

"I think that," McAnnis said slowly, "is not my place."

"What, then?"

"I need to talk to Jane Garmond," he said. "And to your father."

Otto Mayer nodded, then turned to limp away. By the time McAnnis got back to the terrace, Emma Blake was gone.

×

The Disappearance of Agatha Christie

On the night of December 4, 1926, Agatha Christie abruptly disappeared from her home. She was found on December 15, unharmed, at a Yorkshire hotel spa. Those missing eleven days transfixed the British public and sparked a media sensation; every twist and turn in the case was breathlessly covered on the front pages of all the major newspapers. In the years since, her disappearance has inspired scores of books, several documentaries, at least two films, and one *Doctor Who* episode. But the mystery remains unexplained.

By the end of 1926, Christie was on the verge of stardom; her new best-selling novel, *The Murder of Roger Ackroyd*, had upended the genre and ignited controversy. She was married, unhappily, to Colonel Archibald Christie, who was having an affair with a woman named Nancy Neele. On December 4, she kissed her seven-year-old daughter good night and left their home. Her car was found the next morning, abandoned, in a picturesque spot named Newlands Corner.

Over the next eleven days, a nationwide hunt was launched. Thousands of volunteers organized search parties in local woods. Divers searched the bottom of the nearby (and purportedly bottomless) "Silent Pool." Sir Arthur Conan Doyle consulted his favorite medium in a bid to find Christie (and published his findings in *The Morning Post*).

Theories proliferated:

She had amnesia.

She was perpetrating a publicity stunt to gin up book sales.

She'd killed herself.

She'd been murdered.

Christie's fellow mystery novelist Dorothy Sayers herself inspected the scene of the disappearance, on assignment for *The Daily News*, and succinctly summarized the scenarios: "In any problem of this kind there are four possible solutions: loss of memory, foul play, suicide or voluntary disappearance."

The days passed; the speculation intensified; one lead after another fizzled. The public's focus turned, inevitably, to her husband. At the time, the newspapers reported that Christie had left three letters behind prior to her disappearance: one to her secretary (purportedly containing scheduling information), one to her brother-in-law, and one to her husband. Intriguingly, the latter two were both burned after being read; a newspaper reported that Archie claimed, "There was nothing in it having any possible bearing on his wife's whereabouts."

The search finally ended when a band member at the Harrogate Hydro hotel in Yorkshire recognized Christie (one biographer claims that she'd been dancing the Charleston nightly to "Yes! We Have No Bananas"). Newspapers reported that, as had been widely assumed, she had been suffering from amnesia. These front-page articles also noted that she had checked into the hotel under the name of Teresa Neele, but failed to register the most important clue: that the supposedly amnesiac Christie had used the last name of her husband's mistress.

Just over a year later, after months of speculation and criticism, Christie broke her silence in an extraordinary interview with the *Daily Mail*. She described a botched suicide attempt sparked by despondency after the death of her mother and "a number of private troubles, into which I would rather not enter." She said she deliberately drove her car toward a quarry; in the resulting accident, she hit her head on the steering wheel and lost her memory; she wandered in a daze for twenty-four hours, during which time she somehow made her way to London and then to Yorkshire. At the hotel, Christie said, she became convinced she was someone else: "I had now become in my mind Mrs Tessa Neele of South Africa." Christie said she believed she was a widow and added that, while reading about the famous novelist's disappearance in the newspaper, "I regarded her as having acted stupidly."

It was the only time Christie commented publicly on the disappearance. Her memoir doesn't mention the incident at all.

In the decades since, the theories expanded:

She was in a "fugue state."

She was solving a real-life murder.

She was committing a real-life murder.

She realized she was being poisoned by Archie and fled to recuperate.

She was faking her death to pin the blame on Archie.

She staged her disappearance to disrupt Archie's planned weekend getaway with his mistress (the factually plausible yet psychologically unsatisfying and dramatically unfulfilling conclusion of a 1999 biography).

Whatever the truth, the dramatic possibilities inherent to a mystery novelist's mystery have resonated for decades . . .

Curious literary fact 1: Patricia Highsmith adapted the Christie disappearance for her novel *A Suspension of Mercy*, but in her version, the novelist is the dastardly husband, not the vanishing wife. The additional twist is that, with their marriage in tatters, the husband has been writing a fantastical account of how he might kill the wife—an account that implicates him with the police when she disappears without leaving a trace.

Curious literary fact 2: Christie's disappearance inspired a publicity stunt that began the following year and ran for decades; the editors at the *News Chronicle* published the photo of a man dubbed "Lobby Ludd," who, they claimed, had vanished mysteriously but was thought to be wandering between various seaside resorts (the newspapers hired actors to play the role). A cash prize of ten pounds was offered. Readers who spotted the man could claim their reward by accosting him with the phrase "You are Mr Lobby Ludd and I claim my ten pounds." Graham Greene dramatized this gimmick for a key plot device in his novel *Brighton Rock*.

Curious literary fact 3: In the 1993 TV adaptation of Christie's "The Jewel Robbery at the Grand Metropolitan," the screenwriters added a comic detail not found in the original story—Hercule Poirot bears an uncanny resemblance to a version of "Lobby Ludd" called "Lucky Len." Throughout the episode, he is repeatedly stopped by tourists hoping to claim their reward, thereby inflicting on Christie's most famous invention a conceit inspired by her real-life disappearance decades earlier.

Postscript: Christie divorced her husband in 1928; he promptly married Nancy Neele. (The novelist later married the archaeologist Max Mallowan, with whom she stayed, happily, for the rest of her life.) After the divorce was finalized, Christie decided to take her first solo trip abroad; her destination was the Mideast. And so it was that, on one auspicious day in the autumn of 1928, Christie stepped on board the fabled Orient Express . . .

×

The Sixer—a subdued, desultory version of Thursday evening's—has wound down, and in these final pages of the day you see Adam McAnnis back in his room, alone. Sitting on the bed. He stands, crosses to the bureau, checks that his Colt is still in the drawer. Walks to the window and looks out at the night. You recognize the actions of a man who is unsettled, troubled, perhaps afraid for his own safety . . . Or: he is merely fidgeting, his mind elsewhere, sorting clues, testing first this puzzle piece, then another, seeing which fit and which do not, and what picture is emerging . . . Or: he is thinking of a woman, Emma Blake perhaps—it would be easy to walk down the hall to tap, lightly, on her door—or more likely Susan Burr, wondering how he could see her again, tonight, even though, he must admit to himself, she is quite clearly a suspect.

McAnnis reclines on the bed, fully clothed, smoking, ashtray on his chest. He is thinking, thinking, thinking, aided by nicotine, and you have some clues of your own to consider . . .

The detective lying about his client.

The conversation with Jonathan Gold.

Dr. Blake and the hidden metal box.

Duncan Mayer's silence about his wife's disappearance.

The appearance of the suicide note that supposedly didn't exist.

McAnnis lights another cigarette. The ashtray on his chest is filling with butts and ash. You recognize this type of scene from past mysteries: the Great Detective Pondering the Case. Sherlock Holmes withdrawn to his room, playing the violin, smoking furiously, shooting the occasional bullet into the wall, to emerge hours or days later, gaunt but with a gleam in his eye: "Watson—the game is afoot!" Or Hercule Poirot pacing about the balcony of his Mediterranean escape, complaining that his "little grey cells" have failed him, when a chance remark by his friend prompts the little egg-headed Belgian to spin around in alarm and triumph: "Mon Dieu, Hastings—do you realize what you just said? I've been a fool this whole time! Hurry, pray it's not too late!"

But there is no such epiphany here. The detective's fingers are drooping; the cigarette tip is one long column of ash; his eyes are closed. Once again, you are left to ponder these questions on your own. And you wonder, as you watch the sleeping man's chest rise and fall, whether fictional detectives dream. And if they do, do they dream of the living or the dead?

×

Claudia Mayer

Q:

A: For years. For years and years and years and years. Honestly, I don't remember ever *not* thinking about it. That was my secret, you see. I had to guard it from others. I knew they wouldn't understand. Not Duncan, not poor Otto. Not anyone. And they might try to take it away from me, my secret. That was my great fear. They would take it from me, if they could. They gave me pills, so many pills . . . pills and pills and pills and pills. It never did any good. It just let me pretend a little bit better. It made *them* feel better, not me. But I was still the same.

Q:

A: That's difficult to answer. Duncan talks about this Dylan concert he was at once where he said, "I have

my Bob Dylan mask on." Dylan said that, of course. Not
Duncan. Duncan didn't say that, except when he was
telling this story. It was Halloween, I guess. Well, every
day is Halloween for me. I have my Claudia Mayer mask
on. How does it look?

Q:

A: It feels like looking out through a window. You see
the trees, the lake, the grass, whatever's outside. But at the
same time, you're aware of the window frame, the rail, the
glass itself . . . You're looking *at* the thing you're supposed
to be looking *through*, if that makes any sense. And it's like
that all the time. Like the mime trapped in the invisible
box. You don't see it. But the mime, if he's any good—*he*
sees it. And you know, just know, standing there watching
him, that he shouldn't be able to break free.

Q:

A: No.

Q:

A: Yes.

Q:

A: I knew, I knew, I knew. Even if I didn't know, I
knew. Not everything, not about—

Q:

A: Yes, that boy. A man now, of course. Yet it still hurts
to think about. Should things still hurt now? I thought
all the hurt would go away, but it's still here. I don't
feel anything else. No regret, no sadness, no happiness,
nothing. But that hurt is still here. Perhaps the newest
passions are the last to fade?

Q:

A: Yes, sorry. No, I didn't know about that. But I knew
about their past, I knew about them as children, children
in love. A lovely phrase, isn't it? Children in love. But
children in love grow up. Not that I minded, really. Or
maybe I did. I don't know. It's so hard to know what one

thinks, isn't it? People ask you these things. "How do you feel about this? What is your response to that?" What is the right answer? Is there a right answer? It's a puzzle that you can try to solve, but you'll never know if you find the right solution, not really. "How do I feel?" How am I supposed to know? Wouldn't I be the last person to know?

Q:

A: No, everyone feels it, I think. We're all just sort of like chimes knocked about by the wind, aren't we? None of us making the music, at this point in our lives, that we'd hoped we'd be making. The notes are all there. They're just played in the wrong order.

Q:

A: Yes, things did change when he was born. Want to know something silly? For a while, when I was pregnant, I thought maybe the secret would come out, that I could hold it in my arms, cuddle it, nurse it, watch it grow on its own, outside me. And that I would be different. But that didn't happen. The baby was just a baby. And so I . . . Well, Duncan would say that I got worse. I don't think that's true. I got more *me*. And they just didn't like it. They would convince me, or try to convince me, that it wasn't me, that I was someone else, and they put another mask on my face. It would work, for a while.

Q:

A: They always blamed Otto. Because he was the one driving. And because he wore a seatbelt and Trip did not. I think Alex would have preferred that Otto had died, too. Not Amanda, though. She was just . . . It was awful. She was so sad. Sad, sad, sad. They couldn't bear to even look at us. And then after . . . Alex hated us even more.

Q:

A: I never liked it here. Duncan was born to this, of course, he's been coming here his whole life. Early in our marriage, while Duncan was working in the city, I would come during the week. He thought that I must have been doing so well—getting on and so forth. He believed, I think, that I'd become a West Heart Woman, spending my days sunbathing at the lake, walking in the woods, looking after the children. But I wasn't. I liked coming during the week, without him, especially after Otto left home, because then I could just stay in the cabin without seeing anyone, without talking to anyone, for days and days and days.

Q:

A: What is there to say, really? We slept in different rooms. That was my idea—I told him he thrashed around in his sleep, which wasn't true, I just wanted to be alone. And I knew he was going to bed early because he was going hunting in the morning.

Q:

A: Well, he *said* he was going to bed early, anyway. I don't know what he did after I left the house, obviously. Not that I care anymore. Like I said, I don't feel anything now. Except for the hurt from that one thing. I guess Duncan had a secret, too. Different from my secret, but still a secret. I got up. Put on that housecoat, the one with all the big pockets. I'd bought it specifically for those big pockets. And left. The moon was full so there was enough light to see. Though, honestly, I could have found my way in the pitch dark.

Q:

A: No, I didn't go to the clubhouse.

Q:

A: Quite sure.

Q:

A: Earlier in the day, at the lake, I asked some of the children to help me find stones. We made a game of it.

Smooth, round, perfect stones. They had to be just right. Then the kids and I piled them into a—what do they call that?

Q:

A: Yes, a cairn. I like that word. It feels like old magic. Cairn. We built a cairn, and then I made the children promise that they would leave it standing for me. They all swore, solemnly, like it was the most important promise they'd ever made. Children are such curious little creatures. But they kept their word. The stones were there, that night, at the lakeside. Waiting for me. In a way, it felt like they'd been there, waiting, my whole life. Old magic.

Q:

A: I told you, I feel nothing. Nothing, nothing, nothing. Except the hurt from that one thing. And I think that, soon, it will go away, too. And then there will really be nothing.

Q:

Q:

Q:

Q:

×

Murder, for instance, may be laid hold of by its moral handle . . .
or it may also be treated aesthetically . . .

SUNDAY

You begin these new pages with an advantage, or a burden: You know it's the final day of the story. How? Perhaps you flipped through the book—not to skip forward to see how it ends, you're not a sociopath, after all—but, rather, out of curiosity, noticing the ways in which this book fails to resemble other books, or not, realizing that "Sunday" was the last day marked in the text . . . Or perhaps you had read as much in a review, the one that convinced you to buy the book in the first place, the critic noting that the novel "takes place over the course of four days during the Bicentennial weekend" . . . Thursday, Friday, Saturday, Sunday . . . a review in which you eagerly sought out the reassurances of the genre: a plot that *leaves you guessing until the very end*, a *satisfying* twist that *you'll never see coming*, a climax to which only certain adjectives can be applied, depending on the aims of the writer and the whims of the critic—*exciting, ingenious, baffling, disappointing* . . .

It is with a certain elegiac mood, then, that you turn to Sunday morning, a feeling seemingly shared by the author, who begins the day in a different register, taking his time, as if he, too, were reluctant for the story to end . . . delaying his return to the plot by describing the West Heart grounds and the still-sparkling sunlight of dawn in a forest after a storm, the hush of wet leaves, a mute deer silently stepping across the road . . . idyllic descriptions that, you think, are meant to evoke an otherworldly indifference to the passing sins of women and men.

But at last, these meandering sentences finally curl back to the mortal concerns of a man walking down a gravel track. It's the detective, blearily surveying the evidence of the storm's fury: missing shingles, scattered tree limbs, overturned flowerpots, the torn and muddy bunting of the nation's half-forgotten birthday.

Adam McAnnis enters the clubhouse, alone again in the eerily quiet halls. His destination is the kitchen. While the coffee is brewing, he stands deliberating before the walk-in freezer. With a deep breath, he pulls open the heavy door and disappears inside, cold vapor billowing out behind him.

You hadn't expected this: Why would the detective return to the body? To see if it's still there? Or to see if something had gone missing? This late in the mystery, you are alert to the inevitable third-act twist—could this be it? The body has vanished. Or: the murderer has returned to retrieve incriminating evidence accidentally left on the corpse. Or: It's a trap. The murderer followed McAnnis to the clubhouse, waiting for an opportunity to stop these investigations once and for all . . . a hand entering the camera's frame to slam the freezer door shut, trapping the detective inside. The killer knows that no one will be close enough to hear his screams, weakening by the hour into silence, the crime discovered only later, when the police finally arrive and open the freezer to find not one corpse, but two . . .

Adam McAnnis walked out, shivering. He closed the door behind him, fumbling a bit with the metal latch to make sure it was securely fastened, then warmed himself with a cup of coffee. That was stupid. And unnecessary—bodies don't get up and walk away. Not to mention dangerous. He needed to remember that he was alone up here, with no one to trust. Certainly not his putative client. What he'd been able to pick up on him, back in the city, was not promising. Jonathan Gold was a man whom others were afraid to talk about, especially those on the fringes of crime and power: snitches, dope dealers, dirty lawyers. The less they said, the more concerned McAnnis grew. Was it really such a surprise, then, that death followed in his wake? McAnnis had known men like him before, in Vietnam, sergeants and captains with hollowed-out eyes for whom life back in the everyday world could never compare to the terrible delights of war and the freedom, finally, to test the limits of your will and your strength. Did Jonathan Gold somehow provoke this tragedy? Was he in fact counting on it?

McAnnis sipped his coffee. He felt, at times like this, like a thief with his ear pressed to a safe, straining to discern a click that might never come. But it was better than thinking about what he'd seen in the freezer. A body frosting over like a forgotten slab of meat. And in the back of the head, dimly illuminated by the bare lightbulb above, that terrible gaping hole of red-black ice.

With a final shiver, McAnnis left the clubhouse and set off down the muddy road that, he knew from Ralph Wakefield's map, led toward the dead man's home.

×

Jane Garmond was in a rocking chair on her porch when McAnnis walked up. She seemed to have been waiting for him. She had a cup of tea on a small wooden table next her. She didn't invite him to sit.

"I must be your first stop of the day," she said. "I'm flattered."

"Is your son home?" asked McAnnis.

"Ramsey?" she asked, a brief flash of concern crossing her face. "No. He said he was getting up early to go fishing. Apparently, the fish are biting after a storm. I think he just needed some time to himself. Anyway. What does it matter if he is here or not?"

"It matters."

"For what."

"For what I'm about to ask you."

"Ask away," said Jane Garmond. Her face unreadable.

"Did John know?"

She sipped her tea. "Is this relevant?"

"Everything is relevant. Did John know?"

"About what?"

"Please."

"Yes, he knew. Though we never talked about it."

"Did others know, here at the club?"

"What is there to talk about, up here but who we're all sleeping with?"

"You told me that Thursday night, the night of Claudia Mayer's death, you were home alone all night. But that wasn't true, was it?"

"No."

"Were you in Room 312?"

Jane Garmond's smile didn't reach her eyes. "How did you know that?"

"Because I was in Room 302," said McAnnis.

She laughed bitterly. "Congratulations," she said. "You should have stopped by to say hello."

"I imagine it gets crowded up there, some nights," said McAnnis. "Like a screwball comedy. Bumping into each other in the hall. Accidentally entering the wrong room. Do you talk about it, in the morning? Or do you pretend none of it ever happened?"

"The vices of night," she said, "vanish in the day."

"I thought as much," said McAnnis. "Doesn't it bother you that your lover is a suspect in the murder of your husband?"

"No. I don't believe it."

"Doesn't it bother you that you're a suspect?"

"No."

Jane Garmond began to rock back and forth, slowly, the chair creaking like a metronome. She was sitting in the shade, but a breeze rustled aside the tree branches so that, for a moment, she was bathed in morning sunlight. Her face seemed to glow, as if fired from within, save for the white of the long scar at her temple. She was very beautiful. Beautiful enough, perhaps, thought McAnnis, to kill for.

"When I asked you if John knew," said the detective, "I wasn't just asking if he knew about your lover."

"What, then?"

"I was asking if he knew about your son."

She'd steeled herself for this, clearly. Showing no reaction—which was more of a tell than denial, or anger, or shame.

"I don't know what you're talking about," she said.

"Claudia left a suicide note."

"The police were told she didn't."

"She did."

Jane Garmond stared at him defiantly. "And?"

"And in this note, which I have read, which in fact I possess, she makes some very specific claims about your son."

Jane Garmond stood and walked to the other end of the porch. She appeared to be searching for something toward the lake, but McAnnis suspected she was buying time. A scene flashed before him: the woman spinning around, pistol in hand, a fierce wildness in her eyes. Is she a good shot? Of course she is, she grew up at West Heart. And this is murder at close range. A desperate woman driven to protect her secret. She lifts the gun and fires a bullet into the detective's chest and then, hoping no one nearby is curious about the echo of that single shot, begins the grim business of hiding the body . . .

Jane Garmond turned and walked back toward him. She didn't sit down.

"Do you like this work that you do?" she asked.

"Sometimes yes. Sometimes no."

"And now?"

"Not particularly."

"I heard that you claimed John hired you," said Jane Garmond.

"Yes."

"And that people seemed to believe it."

"You do not?"

"No, I don't," she said flatly.

"Does it matter?"

"You call yourself a detective, and maybe you are, down in the city," she said. "But up here, you're nothing. Just some stranger who's been drinking our wine and sleeping with our wives and daughters."

"You're misinformed," McAnnis said, "about the latter."

"Emma is getting slow in her old age, then. Give it some time."

"It's true that you don't have to answer my questions," said McAnnis. "Nobody does. But I will tell you this, and it's a fact. The vast majority of murders that aren't solved in the first forty-eight hours are never solved. So you see, Mrs. Garmond, the clock is ticking."

"Do you really think I don't want to know who killed my husband?"

"I think, if you didn't kill him yourself, that you might be afraid to know who did. Because it could be someone you care about."

McAnnis had hoped to provoke a reaction, a grimace or another tell to betray the secret Jane Garmond wished to keep hidden, but she remained unreadable. She picked up her teacup and turned toward the screen door.

"You'll do whatever you think is best with this alleged suicide note. I can't control that. But I do ask that you at least consider the effect on those involved."

"I will," promised McAnnis.

"And there's something else I need to tell you," she said. "About the night John died."

"Please."

"I told you he got a phone call."

"Yes."

"You asked if the caller was a man or a woman. I said I didn't know. But that wasn't true." McAnnis waited. But he knew what was coming next. "It was a woman's voice," she said.

×

Case Study: The *Whowroteit*

W. H. Auden sniffed in a famous essay on the genre he adored that "the vulgar definition, 'a *Whodunit*,' is correct." Earlier detective stories, in which solving the puzzle was paramount, could more accurately be described as *Howdunits*. Later, when writers became more interested in character and psychology, the genre shifted into *Whydunit* mode. But these books often contained another mystery, hidden in plain sight (like Poe's purloined letter!) on their spines.

It cannot be a coincidence that the mystery, devoted to disguise and concealing the truth, has above all other genres been one in which the author's use of a pseudonym—an *alias*, to use the jargon of their texts—is customary. This began in the age of London hansom cabs and gaslight and continues today.

S. S. Van Dine was Willard Huntington Wright. Edgar Box was Gore Vidal. Nicholas Blake was Cecil Day-Lewis. Ellery Queen was two writers. Jane Harvard was four.

Some pseudonyms were adopted to disguise a prodigious output (Cecil John Charles Street published 144 novels as Miles Burton, another sixty-nine novels as John Rhode). Others due to professional obligations. But it must be said that many writers used pseudonyms because, essentially, they were slumming. "John Banville, you slut," that author admitted he said to himself when he first began writing his series of mysteries published under the name Benjamin Black. (Later, he killed off Black and began writing mysteries under the Banville name.)

Intellectuals have long been defensive about their attraction to the genre, like a secret vice (morphine, pornography, abstinence) that might embarrass them among their peers. The critic Edmund Wilson famously declared that he couldn't understand the appeal. Auden did, but asserted that the mystery novel could not be art. Graham Greene carefully classified his more suspense-oriented novels as mere "entertainments." G. K. Chesterton thought his true artistry was on display in the ponderous theological texts that nobody reads anymore, while his Father Brown detective stories continue to be cherished. T. S. Eliot wrote numerous reviews of detective novels but never attempted one of his own, though he quite consciously picked a title for his verse play *Murder in the Cathedral* that sounds like a mystery; for that play he also pilfered, nearly verbatim, a famous refrain from Sir Arthur Conan Doyle's Sherlock Holmes story "The Adventure of the Musgrave Ritual":

DOYLE	ELIOT
Whose was it?	Whose was it?
His who is gone	His who is gone.
Who shall have it?	Who shall have it?
He who will come.	He who will come.
What was the month?	What shall be the month?
The sixth from the first.	The last from the first.
[. . .]	[. . .]
Why should we give it?	Why should we give it?
For the sake of the trust.	For the power and the glory.

Of course, not all great writers were so coy. William Faulkner published several detective stories under his own name (it must be said, they're not very good mysteries; they're also not very good Faulkner). Also under his own name, Jorge Luis Borges wrote the astounding metaphysics that built his international reputation, including at least two famous detective stories ("Death and the Compass" and "The Garden of Forking Paths") as well as many others that could be described as mystery's cousins (including "Theme of the Traitor and the Hero," for which Borges should have more effusively credited Chesterton's "The Sign of the Broken Sword"). He only resorted to a pseudonym (Bustos Domecq) for the more frivolous detective satires, cowritten with his friend and literal partner in crime, Adolfo Bioy Casares, that were later collected and published in English as *Six Problems for Don Isidro Parodi*.

Interestingly, most women and writers of color have opted to write under their own names. Dorothy Sayers was Dorothy Sayers. Walter Mosley was Walter Mosley. Chester Himes was Chester Himes. Ngaio Marsh simply dropped her first name (Edith). P. D. James hid only behind her initials. And of course, Agatha Christie's pseudonym, Mary Westmacott, was used for what her—usually male—detractors later dismissed as *romances*, though not of the bodice-ripping type now conjured by the word; they were, in fact, pensive semi-autobiographical novels primarily devoted to a topic that many of those critics would no doubt have deemed as unworthy of literature: the interiority of the female mind.

×

The familiar rusty 4x4 was heading down the track straight for him. McAnnis held up a hand, half greeting, half signal to stop. Fred Shiflett leaned out the window.

"Shouldn't you be solving a crime somewhere?"

McAnnis didn't take the bait. "Working on it," he said.

"Glad to hear it."

"Actually, I've been looking for you," said McAnnis. "Can I ask you something?"

Fred Shiflett shrugged. "Depends."

"Do you know a secret way out of here?"

A crafty look stole across Fred Shiflett's face. He seemed immensely pleased with himself.

"You asking or saying?"

"I put it as a question, but really it's more of a statement," said McAnnis.

"How did you know?"

"A little creature in the woods told me."

Fred Shiflett spat into the earth. "That boy. I knew he was spying on me. Spying on everyone. Running around with those binoculars of his."

"So is it true?"

Fred Shiflett took his time answering. "Sure it is," he said slowly. "A path through the woods. It's not even a road, but you can get a truck down it if you're careful. I cut it myself, years ago, in case I wanted to get in or out of West Heart without anyone knowing."

"Why would you do that?" asked McAnnis.

"I have my reasons."

"And it's still open now, even with the storm?"

"It is."

McAnnis shook his head in disbelief. "You didn't say anything, even after the murder, when people were so desperate to get out and get help? You let us put John Garmond's body in a kitchen freezer, next to slabs of meat?"

"Nobody asked my opinion," said Fred Shiflett. "On this or any other thing. And by the time I learned about the freezer, he was frozen solid."

"But why didn't you say something?"

"What's it to me? I didn't kill anyone. Which meant one of these people did. And I wanted to see how it played out." Fred Shiflett cocked his head, studying McAnnis. "Have you ever spent time on a farm, detective? A real farm? Well, I grew up on one. And what people in the city don't know, or don't want to know, is that it's a bloody business. There are no 'natural deaths' on a farm. It's all murder, of one type or another. Ever hear about what happens inside a chicken coop when one of the birds is injured and the others see blood?"

"No."

"Cannibalism," said Fred Shiflett. "The chickens descend on the injured bird and tear it to pieces. Squawking like hell the entire time. If one of the attackers gets injured, the others kill that one, too. And so on. If you don't intervene, it can spread so fast that half your flock is dead or maimed within minutes."

"Are you the farmer in this scenario, Shiflett?"

"I'm nothing, is what I am. Nothing. You were right about that," said Fred Shiflett. "Want to hear something? Every Christmas, I get a bonus. An envelope with cash, handed to me in private, as if they're embarrassed, by the club president. Last year, it was about fifty bucks. Which means each family gave—what? A dollar? Two? None? For a year of fixing their roofs, delivering their wood, standing in shit up to my knees to fix their septic tanks? So, yes, I was happy to hear one of them was a killer. And even happier to see them tear each other apart trying to figure out who it is."

"John Garmond was the one who gave you this envelope?" asked McAnnis.

"Please. Other people have a lot better reasons to kill him than that."

"Shiflett, I understand how you feel—"

"No, you don't."

"Fine. I don't. But it's time. Someone else could get hurt. Someone who doesn't deserve it. You could stop it," said McAnnis. "Go to the sheriff's office. Tell them what happened. Bring them back here."

Birds were chattering at each other in the trees. McAnnis followed Fred Shiflett's gaze to see a blue jay land on a branch overhead, chirp at them angrily, then fly off in search of a nest to pillage.

"I'll think about it," said Fred Shiflett. "If I go, it won't be until after I feed my dogs."

"Thank you," said McAnnis. "Now I have another question."

"Yes?"

"Which way to Duncan Mayer's house?"

×

The Mayer house was on the other side of the lake. McAnnis wearily set off on a path whose name, he read from a wooden board nailed to a tree, was Talbot's Way, likely after a grandfather or great-grandfather of Jane Garmond née Talbot. With Ralph Wakefield's map in hand, he walked past various West Heart landmarks: the beach, still empty in the early morning, the rope swing dangling like a noose; a decrepit lean-to and crumbling brick firepit; the island where children battled pirates; a blackened and near-petrified, haunted-looking tree; a dam that no doubt explained the lake's existence, surging now with storm runoff; and the boathouse, stocked with kayaks and canoes, and by which, years apart, the bodies of two women had been found. At one point, before the trail led away from the water's edge, McAnnis spotted a lone figure in the middle of the lake, too far off to identify, swimming with long, easy strokes.

The trail underfoot was covered with a bed of pine needles, the earth beneath soft and damp, and McAnnis, whose feet were accustomed to concrete and blacktop, found himself, to his surprise, enjoying the walk. Finally, he saw the Mayer cabin up a hill, shrouded in trees; he guessed that it was in shade much of the time, only getting direct sunlight in the fullness of the day, and then only in the height of summer—a poor place, he thought, for a woman condemned to sadness.

When he reached the front door, McAnnis realized that this house, too, had a view of the lake, and he imagined Claudia Mayer gazing out from the porch, brooding on its depths, year after year.

No one answered the first knock, or the second. McAnnis delicately tested the doorknob—locked. He cupped his hands around his eyes to peer in a window. Fingers gingerly tugging upward on the frame.

"He's not here."

McAnnis turned to find Otto Mayer. "Who isn't here?"

"My dad. That's who you're looking for, isn't it?"

"Know where he is?"

"No. Not really," said Otto Mayer. "But if I had to guess, I would say the lake."

"Really?"

"I know it might seem odd to you. Returning to the scene . . . the scene of the crime, you might say. But he's a swimmer. Long-distance. A good one. Has been my whole life. He goes farther than anyone else, from the beach around the island."

"I think I saw him," said McAnnis. He hesitated. "Any regrets about telling me what you told me?"

"Only every second I've been awake since."

"Do you want the note back?"

"No."

Otto Mayer had the haggard look of a man who hadn't been sleeping. He rubbed his temples wearily. He had, McAnnis noticed with the satisfaction of snapping a jigsaw puzzle piece into place, the same slate-blue eyes as his father.

"I came for your father, but I actually have a question for you, too."

"I don't doubt it."

"Were you the one I was following Thursday night? From the clubhouse?"

Otto Mayer lit a cigarette, made a show of looking at it. "I'm down to my last pack. And I'm sure I'm not the only one. If they don't clear the road soon, people might really start killing each other." He winced. "Sorry. Yes, that was me. I knew someone was following me. But I didn't know who until you walked through a puddle of moonlight. I ducked down a trail, to lose you, and then doubled back to my house."

"You were in the hall, too?" asked McAnnis. "On the third floor?"

"Yes."

"Outside Room 312?"

"Yes."

"Why did you go there?"

"I don't know. I think I had some idea of interrupting them, catching them. My mother was hurting, and I wanted him to hurt, too. But I couldn't go through with it. Didn't want to go through with it." He cocked his head. "How did you know?"

"I was in a room down the hall."

Otto Mayer laughed humorlessly. "This goddamn place," he said. "As a kid, it seems idyllic. You spend summers up here, swimming all day, camping on the island, exploring the woods. In the winter you snowshoe and skate across the frozen lake. But then you realize, as you get older, that in fact everything is shit. Everyone is unhappy. Everyone is on something. Everyone is sleeping with everyone else.

And the worst part is, there's no escape. Everyone is stuck seeing the same people, people they hate or used to love, year after year. Maybe they should sell it after all."

"Why do you keep coming back?"

"Why does anyone do anything?" replied Otto Mayer. "Habit, I guess. And since the accident, something else. Guilt."

"Nobody I've talked to thinks it was your fault."

"That's because they weren't there," said Otto Mayer. "I hung upside down for an hour. Watching Trip bleed out. He never regained consciousness. If I were Alex Caldwell," he finished bitterly, "I would hate me, too."

×

McAnnis returned to the Blake house to find the downstairs empty: crumbs on the kitchen table, dishes piled in the sink, last night's wineglasses still scattered about the living room, ashtrays overflowing. The scenes of everyday life abruptly abandoned, as if the residents had received news of some impending apocalypse in the middle of breakfast. McAnnis felt like a ghost.

He discovered Emma Blake, still in her pajamas and those ever-present sunglasses, reading a magazine on the terrace.

"Where is everybody?"

"I don't have a clue," said Emma Blake. "They were all gone by the time I woke up. Have some coffee cake."

"Thanks."

"You look tired," she said.

"That's what people say when they don't want to say you look terrible," said McAnnis.

"All right, then." Emma Blake studied him over the top of her sunglasses. "You look terrible."

"I haven't been sleeping."

"Me neither. And just think," she said. "We could have been not sleeping together."

"Under your father's roof?"

"We could have gone to the clubhouse. Would you have preferred Room 302," she asked mischievously, "or Room 312?"

"Emma, please."

"Sorry. I can be a bit of a bully. Coffee?"

"Always."

They sat in a relaxed silence, McAnnis allowing himself to imagine meeting her again, in the city, when all this was over. He'll pick her up in his 1971 Pontiac Bonneville and drive her out to have dinner with the mobsters at Bamonte's in Brooklyn. The waiter will size up Emma, then look back at the detective—"A nice little number," that look will say, "how'd you pull it off?"—then ruthlessly suggest a bottle of red out of his price range. McAnnis will say yes instantly, of course, wincing inwardly as he calculates the cost in terms of clients and case hours. They'll have bread and olive oil while Emma asks about the mafiosi at the other tables, some of whom he knows by sight, some he doesn't, and for those he'll invent lurid stories about kilos of heroin sewn into cadavers flown into JFK and torture in warehouses in Greenpoint and bodies dumped in the marshes near Jones Beach. "You're making all this up," she'll say, laughing, and he'll swear it was all true, every last word. After dinner, they'll make out in the front seat of his car outside her apartment. When she invites him up, he'll say no. "There's such a thing as being *too much* of a gentleman," Emma will say, but he'll see that she's not disappointed, not really. For a few hours, he'll stay behind the steering wheel, watching the yellow rectangles in her building go out, one by one, the first and only time he's been on a stakeout for himself.

"What does Emma Blake do when she's not here?" McAnnis asked finally.

"When she's not a murder suspect holed up with a detective in an isolated hunting club brimming with weaponry, you mean?"

"Yes, that's what I meant."

"I have a job in the city. Share an apartment with two other girls."

"What kind of job?"

"I work at a magazine. I want to be a writer, or at least an editor."

"That's what you want to be. What are you now?"

"A secretary."

"What magazine?"

"*Esquire.*"

"I thought you'd say *Ms.*"

"No, but I met Gloria Steinem once."

"How was that?"

"She told me not to let the university brainwash me."

"When was this?"

"My senior year in college."

McAnnis laughed. "Good advice invariably comes too late. The first time I was arrested, for breaking and entering on a job, my boss came to bail me out. I was in a holding cell in the Tombs with junkies and hustlers and a crazy guy who took a shit into his own hands. My boss stood there, grinning at me through the bars, and said: 'I may have forgotten to tell you this, but being a private dick is a terrible career move.'"

"Was he right?"

"Mostly."

Emma Blake dropped her magazine onto the stone terrace. "Do you like being a detective?"

"People keep asking me that," he complained.

"And?"

"And what?"

"Do you like being a detective?"

"It's a ridiculous way to make a living," said McAnnis. "But the other ways are worse. And anyway, what would be a better option for a college dropout with nothing to his name but half a philosophy degree and a tour in Vietnam and a childhood spent hanging around cops?"

"You protest too much, I think," said Emma Blake. "I think you like it."

"Is that so?"

"I think you like to think that you're slumming by necessity, not by choice," said Emma, now serious. "I think you secretly enjoy the perverse. The abject depravity. The exposure to the worst elements of human nature. And I think you do it because it allows you to accept those elements in yourself."

McAnnis was silent a moment. Then, quietly, he said: "You talk as if you know me."

"I know men."

"There seemed a certainty in degradation," he murmured.

"T. E. Lawrence, right? Don't look so surprised. I had a good brainwashing in college, remember? But again: the Lawrence you read is not the Lawrence I read."

"What about you?" asked McAnnis. "How's *Esquire*?"

"Trying to change the subject?"

"Absolutely."

"The magazine is fine," said Emma Blake. "Except for the pretentiousness, vulgarity, misogyny, and ruthless capitalist exploitation of naïve young people working virtually for free."

"Sounds wonderful."

"As a liberated young woman on the Pill, the men hope or expect me to be sexually available at all times. Of course, if I am, then I'm a whore. If I'm not, then I'm a prude."

"Is the work interesting, at least?" he asked.

"This month we did profiles on John Ehrlichman and William F. Buckley. The latter written by William F. Buckley."

"That reminds me of the old definition of masturbation," said McAnnis.

"Which is?"

"Sex with someone you love."

Emma Blake laughed. "That's Buckley."

"Your parents must have loved that."

"The Ehrlichman was intended as a cautionary tale. But people around here"—hand gesturing to indicate *the club*—"probably see it as an instruction manual."

Their talk continues—idle, pleasant, commonplace, burdenless talk—and you think how different it is from last night, when the air crackled between them in the aftermath of the storm. There are a thousand and one ways to extinguish the spark of such a moment: a stranger interrupting to ask for a match, the wrong song on the radio, a train arriving one minute too soon. But you also suspect the influences of less tangible phenomena: a single millibar's drop in barometric pressure, a swallow's wing beating a hundred feet overhead, an echo of a footfall half a block away, one neuron among billions failing to fire . . . Eyes turn away, the pulse slows, and you realize that the tide you thought was coming in is in fact going out. Against such cosmic odds, what chance do we have? Isn't it proof that the moment when two magnets click together is even more miraculous than we'd imagined?

Suddenly you realize the two characters have circled back to talk of murder, and you must return to the text, lest you miss a new revelation.

"So do you have it solved?" asked Emma Blake.

"You say *it*," noted McAnnis. "But don't we have two bodies?"

"Yes, but Claudia— Everyone knows what happened."

"Perhaps," said McAnnis. "Perhaps not. At any rate, I think a suicide requires as much explanation as a murder."

"Fine, two bodies. Do you know what happened?"

"Very nearly, very nearly," he said. "The picture is almost clear. The clues are there for anyone to see."

"And what are they?"

"The clues?" McAnnis seemed amused. "You want me to list them for you?"

"Actually, yes."

"Okay," said McAnnis, considering. "I think I could do that. Yes. One moment."

Emma Blake had asked as a joke but now she waited, patiently. Surprised that he would do it. Or that he could do it.

"All right," said McAnnis. "Are you ready?"

"Yes."

He ticked them off on his fingers.

"*Madame Butterfly*. Henry Ford. Charles Lindbergh. The Oneida tribe. Room 312. A missing plaque. An unlucky gambler. The second shot. A midnight phone call. And a bruise on a woman's lower back."

"Those are clues?" Emma Blake gave him an incredulous look. Her blond hair looked almost white in the sunlight.

"Yes," said McAnnis. "Or maybe clues of clues."

"What are you going to do with all that?"

"For starters, take a nap," said McAnnis. "Or at least, lie down. I'm feeling . . . off. Probably something I ate."

"Maybe you were poisoned," suggested Emma Blake.

McAnnis shook his head. "Now, that would be a plot twist, wouldn't it?"

×

Ralph Wakefield was sitting on the shaded stone steps of the Burr house, doubled over a piece of paper, scribbling. He was rocking slightly back and forth and humming to himself, which he tended to do whenever he was concentrating and trying to block things out, like, for example, his aunt and uncle yelling at each other upstairs. There had been a crash; the sound of glass shattering; his aunt screamed "Liar!" and then the bedroom door was slammed shut. But Ralph wasn't worried. He knew this was just what grown-ups were like, because his mother and father acted the same way during those rare times when everyone was all together in the same city and country.

The piece of paper contained a newer, secret version of the West Heart map that he'd given the detective. On this map, Ralph had added everything that he'd discovered since arriving at the club, all that he'd learned peeping through windows with his binoculars or crouched in the crawl space beneath the stairs listening to adults gossip and argue and cry. When he didn't understand the words, he looked them up later in the dictionary. Ralph felt that this map, his secret map, was in fact the true map of West Heart.

So across his paper, the way other maps might note the directions of the compass, Ralph had added the labels:

SADNESS
HAPPINESS
LOVE
HATE

Next to three homes, he'd written one of his new words: ADULTERY.

Next to the clubhouse, he'd drawn a four-legged stick figure with a red squiggly line coming from it—he'd found a colored pencil for this—by which Ralph wrote: DEAD DOG.

He'd been unsure how to label the drowned woman in the lake, since he'd overheard people arguing about whether it was deliberate or accidental. And so, in the end, next to the boathouse he wrote: DEAD LADY.

At the clubhouse itself, he'd just finished adding his latest note: MURDER.

Ralph studied the map for a moment, as if committing it to memory. Then he carefully folded it up, shoved it into his jeans pocket, and pulled out his math workbook. He was annoyed, because he'd been struggling with the word problems for days. It was true what he'd told the new man, the nice man, the detective: They were easy for him. Usually. But these were different. He'd managed to solve the first two problems fairly quickly, writing down the solutions in his tiny precise block lettering, so small that his teacher had complained she couldn't read it even with her glasses, which Ralph knew she didn't like to wear. The answers he wrote down were:

1) THE ODDS ARE 1 IN 3
2) NO

The third problem was much harder. Ralph scrunched up his face. His pencil scratched across the page. Hesitantly, Ralph tried some concepts from the trigonometry textbook he'd stolen from his older brother. Then he realized the answer might be something he'd never encountered before: an irrational number. With much less certainty than he was used to, Ralph carefully wrote down:

3) NO LIMIT

The fourth and fifth problems had been comparatively easy; he'd finished them the night he met the detective. The fourth was just a question of adding up a series of numbers; the fifth, somewhat trickier, finally yielded its secrets when he was able to simplify its terms. Ralph's answers were:

4) 257 MINUTES
5) THE RATIO IS 10:1

That left only the last problem. Ralph was stumped. He felt like there wasn't enough information to solve it. He was hungry. He was getting bored. He had a book of mazes that he hadn't gotten to yet. Should he just guess? Ralph knew that there were two likely choices: YES and NO. He briefly considered MAYBE, which was sometimes an option in problems like this, but his gut told him that it was not the correct answer here. So—no MAYBE. That left YES and NO. Which was it?

His stomach growled. He could hear his aunt coming downstairs. Impulsively, in messier handwriting than normal, Ralph scribbled in:

6) NO

Feeling a sense of relief, he snapped his workbook shut. Then he hopped up and ran into the kitchen in his red Jox sneakers, a hungry child on a summer afternoon scrounging for something to eat.

×

Case Study: The *Whysolveit*

Whereas in "reality"—conceding, *pace* Nabokov, that the word has meaning only if restrained by quotation marks—unresolved mysteries are common, in classical detective fiction they are exceedingly rare. Raymond Chandler famously admitted (or claimed) that he didn't know who murdered the chauffeur in *The Big Sleep*. Thomas Pynchon's entire corpus may be said to consist of unresolved mysteries or, at least, unanswered questions (including his one explicit detective novel, the shambling *Inherent Vice*). Paul Auster's *New York Trilogy* offers no solutions and, it might almost be said, no crimes. Henry James, nearly a century earlier in *The Sacred Fount*, offers no crime, no solution, and *no detective*—yet still offered inspiration for decades of mystery stories featuring a protagonist probing the secrets and relationships of characters in a classic *Whodunit* setting (the elite country weekend getaway).

Roy Vickers used (real-life) instances of unsolved crimes as the basis for a series of (fictional) stories centered on Scotland Yard's (invented) Department of Dead Ends—a cold-case unit, before the term was invented by Florida newspapers in the early 1980s.

Conventional wisdom dictates that "Golden Age" mysteries required a solution, because the novels were dedicated to upholding or restoring the established social order. Later mysteries embraced ambiguous or unsatisfying endings for precisely the opposite reason: the established order was no longer seen as worth preserving.

Anthony Berkeley's *The Poisoned Chocolates Case* (1929) centers on a "Crimes Circle" club of armchair detectives who tackle a baffling mystery—*Who sent the poisoned chocolates to Sir Eustace?*—by each proposing his or her own solution, with a different murderer. The book exposes the essential arbitrariness of the genre by highlighting how one murderer's motives and methods are so easily swapped out for those of an entirely different killer: there is nothing sacred about the solution.

The greatest unresolved mystery is one that wasn't: the Agatha

Christie virtuoso performance *And Then There Were None*. Ten strangers are invited to a remote island and then murdered, one by one, seemingly in correspondence to an ancient (and, originally, astoundingly racist) nursery rhyme. The unique menace and dread of that novel, her finest, comes from the creeping suspicion that the victims are being killed by someone or something altogether unseen . . . an eerie fear fulfilled at the end, when all are finally dead, the last victim killed, impossibly, in a way that clearly requires another's hand.

It is a perfect and uncanny ending, and it should have been left there. But Christie evidently so feared it would baffle readers that she tacked on an epilogue—literally a message in a bottle!—explaining the whole thing in a way that manages to be both clever and disappointingly mundane.

Nonetheless, the miracle of *And Then There Were None* is that it's the only time in the entire Christie canon that the reader uneasily senses the influence that the fearful once ascribed to the Fates: the presence of unseen and potentially malignant forces manipulating or directing human destinies. It is of this feeling that Shakespeare's "star-crossed" characters fearfully murmur when they say, "It is the stars, the stars above us, govern our conditions" . . . when they mutter that "some ill planet reigns" . . . when they proclaim in awe that "the heavens themselves blaze forth the death of princes." We find it again in the anguished cry of *King Lear*'s Gloucester:

> As flies to wanton boys are we to the gods,
> They kill us for their sport.

A lament that readers might do well to remember when they start guessing who will be the next to die.

×

The detective enters his room, locking the door behind him. He opens the drawer into which he'd unpacked his clothes. He hesitates—has anything been disturbed?—then checks yet again that his revolver is still there. McAnnis rifles through the clothes and finds the little plastic container of pills, swallows two, without water, hesitates—what the hell, it's been a rough few days—fishes out two more, screws the cap back on, and slides it back under his socks. He flips through the pages of his club dossier: nothing is missing. His shoulders relax. McAnnis lies down on the bed, spreading the pages next to him like a student studying for an exam.

Over a cigarette, McAnnis broods on the case. The initial assignment that brought him here. And the tragedies that have since confused his purpose.

He closes his eyes. He thinks of Claudia, poor Claudia, alone on the clubhouse porch beneath her chimes, waiting in vain for the wind to change so she can hear the "Ode to Joy." Imagining her shivering in her housecoat, filling the pockets with stones, and sliding into the still, cold water.

McAnnis thinks, too, of the terrible hole in the back of John Garmond's head, and the quivering snout of a rat sniffing at the dripping black blood. And the night before, McAnnis watching as John's eyes followed his wife's gliding path across the terrace after dinner, the forlorn gaze of a man filled in equal measure with jealousy and guilt.

Did John know, then? Or is that simply what Jane wanted McAnnis to believe? He can't decide. He finishes his cigarette. Maybe it doesn't matter. He can act, or not. He can complete his case, or not. He can walk away.

"Just do the job," Horatio Brown used to tell him, swatting his qualms away like so many buzzing flies. "What they do after is not your concern."

That's what he'd been told. It seldom worked out that way.

McAnnis doesn't realize that his hands are trembling until he goes to light a second cigarette and it slips through his fingers. He wipes his brow. His clothes are drenched with sweat. He staggers to his feet, takes a step, then another, then falls back against the bed, sending the dossier papers fluttering to the floor. He slides down to his knees on the green chenille rug. The sunlight streaming from the window like the moonlight in Room 302, Susan Burr smiling at him in the shadows; he takes her hand the way he clutched his mother's hand as a boy, trying to be brave. Holding in his other hand a satchel with a change of clothes, looking up at her in a shabby hotel lobby, remembering how he'd lingered in the hall, watching through the cracked door as she stood with her back twisted toward the bathroom mirror, grimacing at the line of bruises up her spine. . . .

Bruises just like the needle tracks mottling the arms of the girl I snatched off the streets of Berkeley, she was screaming bloody murder as I handcuffed her in the back seat, thrashing and kicking against the windows the whole drive up into the hills as I raced through lights and stop signs because I knew that stopping would be the most dangerous part, but it was for her own good, that's what I told myself, even as she was howling like an animal with a leg caught in a trap. And then, later, her father's treachery, and then, later still, drinking alone in a squalid bar on the Oakland waterfront, knowing that I'd rescued her from one prison only to deliver her to another . . .

Shirley, I remembered. Her name was Shirley. Her father plunging the syringe into her arm and the eyes rolling back in her head and her body falling back on the couch like the soldiers falling back against the cushions in that dark basement in Saigon, grunts cycling in-country or out-country or to nowhere at all, the sweet white scented smoke curling from braziers and long wooden pipes, but, yes, also needles for those who needed a quicker fix. A month later, a bomb ripped apart the den and the bar upstairs, but all the mothers and fathers of those GIs were told was that they were KIA and never, ever coming home again. For me the screaming night terrors had already taken hold, and I knew why those soldiers were there and why I was there, too . . .

McAnnis groans and falls to the floor of the bedroom. His left arm is numb, and his mouth is dry. He tries to cry out—maybe Emma could hear him from the terrace—but he can't. He can't. His eyes turn to the papers on the floor. He crawls toward them. Not that one. Not that one. Damn it. Hurry. That one. There.

McAnnis grabs a page with his fist and rolls onto his back. He makes a sound that's close to laughter, the way you might respond to a cruel and humorless joke. And then, in the infinitesimal and ever-lasting moment between one breath and the next, McAnnis closes his eyes.

×

"What are we up to now?" asked Warren Burr. "One murder? Two? Three? Why stop there? Where's our ambition? If we apply our-selves, surely we can hit a baker's dozen . . ."

We were gathered in the great hall of the clubhouse. The word had spread fast. House to house. Neighbor to neighbor. The boy, Ralph, was seen sprinting down the gravel road with the news. The shock this time at a lower pitch. Tragedy, like comedy, loses its power through repetition.

Not knowing what else to do, we'd begun drifting wearily toward the clubhouse in ones and twos. Reginald Talbot. The Burrs. The Blake family. Jane and Ramsey Garmond. Duncan and Otto Mayer. Jonathan Gold. By this point, Dr. Blake and his son had already moved the new body into the freezer.

We were feeling bad that we didn't feel worse, but, after all, the detective had been a stranger. We didn't know him. He wasn't *one of us*. We were also acutely aware, though we tried not to think about it, that, to at least one person, the end of the detective's questioning would come as a relief.

No, we didn't care about Adam McAnnis. But still we shuddered when we heard the news. The true horror of this latest tragedy, we realized, was that it invited the prospect of a *series*, like in a chil-dren's nursery rhyme. *And then there were none.*

"At least we're spending some quality time together," said War-ren Burr. He slumped onto a leather sofa.

"That's enough, Warren," said Dr. Blake.

"Who found him?" asked Susan Burr.

"The kids and I did," said Dr. Blake. He recounted the scene: Knocking at the door, calling his name. No response. Trying the door, finding it locked. They'd thought perhaps he had fallen back asleep. James walked outside to try the window, but it was fastened shut.

"He's lying on the floor," James reported. "We need to get in there."

"The door or the window?" asked Emma.

They thought for a moment. "The door," their father said finally.

"Smash it open?" his son said.

"I guess."

They tried first with their shoulders, explained the doctor, but the door was an old one, solidly built, and the hall wasn't long enough for a running start; if there was a trick to bashing a door open, they didn't know it. In the end, at Emma's suggestion, they unscrewed the doorknob plate and were able to jimmy the lock that way.

They found the detective lying in the center of the room. No signs of violence on the body. His eyes were closed. One arm rested on his chest, fist clenched; the other extended by his side, like a signpost arrow pointing down a path.

"Stay back," the doctor had said. He crouched down next to the body and placed his fingertips gently on the neck. "No pulse."

"Jesus Christ," said James. "What happened?"

"I don't know. But the body is still warm. Can't have been dead more than hour."

"Did he . . ."

"Maybe." Dr. Blake looked up at his son. "Was he the type?"

"Is there a type?"

"Was he depressed, did he have manic highs and lows, did he talk about killing himself in our goddamn guest bedroom?" snapped the doctor. "That type."

"Not really. I don't know. Honestly, I feel like I barely knew him anymore."

"If he committed suicide, then how did he do it?" asked Emma.

"I don't know."

Without a word, as her father and brother watched, she walked to the bureau, opened the top drawer, and pulled out the Colt Detective Special she'd seen McAnnis hide there. She popped open the cylinder. "It hasn't been fired," she said. "If he was going to kill himself, wouldn't this have been the way to do it?" Without waiting for a response, she replaced the revolver and slid her hands back into the drawer.

"I don't think you should rifle around in his things," said James.

Emma extracted the pill container with a magician's flourish.

"No label," her father observed. He took the container from Emma, tipped a few pills into his palm. "I doubt these came from any pharmacy."

"What's in it?" asked James.

"No clue," said Dr. Blake. "Anyone with a tablet press can make pills containing just about anything."

"It would have been easy to switch these pills for something deadly," said Emma.

"What are you suggesting?" asked James.

"There's already been at least one murder," Emma had said. "Why not two?"

"Or is it three?" Warren Burr said, after the Blakes had finished with their story.

"Claudia killed herself. We all know it," said Meredith Blake. She nodded toward the dead woman's husband and son. "I'm sorry, but it's true."

"If I may," said the doctor. Heads nodded. "There is some evidence, in the literature, that people who are vulnerable to the idea get inspired, though that's not really the right word, they get inspired to act when they see others—"

"McAnnis didn't kill himself," interrupted Susan Burr.

We'd been watching her carefully from the moment she stepped into the great hall. We knew about her and John, of course. And we'd seen her and the detective slip into the woods at the bonfire. *Susan caught a new one*, we'd said. *She and Warren have quite the arrangement.* But now Susan looked exhausted and hollow-eyed in a way that no makeup could hide, and we studied her face the way a fortune-teller studies lines on a palm. Why was she so certain that McAnnis wasn't a suicide?

"What else could it have been?" asked Reginald Talbot.

"Anything. I don't know his medical history," said Dr. Blake. "He said he had a heart murmur—maybe it was related to that. Or perhaps he had a stroke, though his age doesn't fit the profile. Maybe it was something freakish—a blood clot in his leg. Maybe he overdosed accidentally on whatever was in those pills. Or maybe—"

"Or maybe someone killed him," said Susan Burr.

"The door was locked from the inside," said James Blake. "How did the killer get in?"

"And how did they get in without anyone in the house noticing, in the middle of the day?" asked Reginald Talbot. He glanced around the room. "Unless someone in the house was the murderer, of course."

"Reg?" said Emma Blake.

"Yes?"

"Go fuck yourself," said Emma Blake.

"Emma!" exclaimed her mother.

"Let's not pretend it's some deep personal tragedy," said Reginald Talbot. "After all, none of us knew him. Except James," he added. "Sorry."

"I hadn't seen him in years," admitted James Blake. "I'm not sure why he called."

"He called because he'd gotten a job and needed to maneuver you into an invite," said Jane Garmond. "That's probably *why* he got the job. He could come here without raising suspicions. You played right into his hands."

"The hell I did."

"He had a file on us," interjected Emma Blake. "On the club."

This was unexpected; we all stirred uneasily. "A file?" Warren Burr asked finally.

"We found it in his room," said Emma Blake. "A folder filled with papers. Property records, it looked like. Legal documents. Newspaper clippings. Some handwritten notes." She paused. "Also individual reports on some of you."

"Who?" asked Warren Burr.

"Could I see it?" asked Reginald Talbot.

"Why?" asked Emma Blake. "Are you worried about what's in there? Guilty conscience?"

"Don't we have more urgent matters to discuss?" Dr. Blake asked impatiently.

"Meaning?"

"Meaning—who's going to play detective now?"

×

Play

A large room, recognizable as the great hall of the West Heart clubhouse. The massive stone fireplace lies upstage, against the back wall. On the floor near the fireplace is a stain, the size you'd expect would be left by a gunshot wound to the head, a few hours after being halfheartedly scrubbed. Scattered leather sofas and chairs throughout, along with whatever small tables and rugs are necessary to convey a sense of staid, indifferent luxury. A telephone is on a table. The lighting is slightly dim (running off generator power); it should be noticeable when they brighten, later, as electricity is restored.

In the Prologue and Scene 1, the styling for wardrobe, hair, etc. for Reader should be contemporary to that of the Audience, and clearly separate from that of the Characters.

Reader is a woman.

PROLOGUE

*Stage empty. Before the action begins, the house music should cease
long enough for the Audience to feel uncomfortable. Staging for
Reader may vary according to the house and experience of the
company. If Reader is seated in the front row, she should stand,
walk quickly to the apron, and turn to address the Audience. If
Reader is seated in a box seat, then she should simply begin speaking down to the Audience. In either case, Reader should try to
pass as a member of the Audience prior to speaking: reading the
playbill, conversing with those around her, etc.*

READER: [*To Audience*] This murder drama, like
    all murder dramas, begs a suspension of belief, the
    acceptance, or, rather, insistence, that what you're seeing
    is not real, and that these poor players do not live or
    die upon this stage. The poet wakes from the dream
    not knowing if he is the poet who dreamed of being a
    butterfly or the butterfly now dreaming of being the
    poet. You are all actors; you are each like Alice afraid to
    wake the Red King, who, you've been told, is dreaming
    of you—because where, then, do you suppose you'd be?
    Are you so certain, as you look upon this stage, that you
    know where it ends? And is it with hope or fear that you
    puzzle the notion that someone, somewhere, is sitting in
    a darkened theater—watching *you*?

*Lights dip to black after the Prologue; enter the Characters.
When they are settled, lights come back up.*

SCENE 1

READER: Shall we start at the beginning?
WARREN: As opposed to the end?

READER: Some mysteries start that way. They reveal the killer right at the beginning. The suspense, such as there is, lies in watching the detective search for a solution, and the killer try to evade one. This is not that kind of mystery. So we start at the beginning. Let's review the crimes here. Or at least, potential crimes. Murder. Attempted murder. Suicide. Suborning suicide. Lying. Infidelity. Blackmail. Extortion. Three people are dead. I say *crimes*, but you might say, rather, that some of these are more properly considered *sins*. Do we still believe in sin? For our purposes here, let's say yes. Furthermore, there is the business about the sale of the club, and about the admission of a new member who would be . . . unusual for this organization.

JONATHAN: [*Bowing his head mockingly*] Guilty as charged.

READER: We also need to address the question of the detective. Who hired him and why was he here?

MEREDITH: He said he was hired by John.

READER: I have reason to believe that is not true. I'll get to that in a moment. Let's consider each incident from these past few days. A dog is killed. A man is shot, but survives. He's later found dead in the clubhouse—in this very room, in fact. A woman is found dead in a lake. Another man is found dead in a private home. How do these connect? Do they connect? The detective was wary of false solutions—the coincidence turned into a clue—and we would be wise to follow his example. Let's turn now to the morning of the murder.

WARREN: Which one?

READER: Sorry. The murder of John Garmond. Friday morning. We did not then know about Claudia's death. Nor did we know about the deaths ahead. Most of us, anyway. Obviously, the killer or killers did. But at that time, West Heart was in a state of innocence, if you will.

OTTO: [*Bitterly*] That's a laugh.

READER: It was on this morning that several of the men went on this illegal hunt. A Garmond tradition, I understand. Reginald Talbot. John Garmond. Ramsey Garmond. And Duncan Mayer. As I think we all know, John was shot. The detective was very interested in this incident. He was present for its aftermath. He was able to read the faces of the men involved. And he asked many questions about it. Duncan?

DUNCAN: [*Ironically*] What? Me again?

READER: It does you no credit that you're at the center of so many of this weekend's uncertainties. If I were you, or someone close to you, that would worry me. You told the detective that you shot John accidentally, correct?

DUNCAN: The alternative being that I shot him on purpose?

READER: The alternative being that you did not shoot him at all. [*Turning to Reginald*] Reginald, you said that you didn't know who chose the hunting pairing, but, when pressed, said Duncan had picked them. Why did you say that?

REGINALD: I suppose because I thought that's what happened.

READER: You thought so? But you weren't sure.

REGINALD: No, I was.

READER: Did you say this because you thought it would make the detective more suspicious of Duncan?

REGINALD: Of course not. And I don't like what you're insinuating.

READER: You also told the detective something very interesting, the significance of which I only realized later. You said that you were distracted, when John was yelling after getting shot, because you had just fired at a deer yourself.

REGINALD: That's right.

READER: And where is this deer?

REGINALD: Excuse me?

READER: You fired a shot at this deer; where is it? Is the head mounted on a wall, somewhere here in the clubhouse, and I failed to notice?

REGINALD: Of course not. No, I don't know where the hell it is. Somewhere in the woods.

READER: In the woods—alive—because you missed?

REGINALD: Yes.

READER: Was Ramsey Garmond with you when you fired at this deer?

REGINALD: No, we had separated by this point.

READER: So nobody but you saw this deer. Is it not possible, then, that this deer . . . was imaginary?

REGINALD: Are you saying I hallucinated the deer? [*Laughs nervously*] We'd barely started drinking!

READER: I'm saying the deer did not exist. I'm saying you invented the deer because you needed a reason to fire your rifle. The woods are quiet; a shot echoes through the trees. The other men hunting that morning would have heard this other shot. [*To Duncan*] What did you think you were shooting at?

DUNCAN: I thought it was a buck.

READER: Were you surprised to discover instead that it was a man?

DUNCAN: Very.

READER: Human psychology can be very powerful. Enough so that it can overwhelm the senses. Let us set the scene. It is early morning. You did not, I suspect, sleep very well. You were worried about your wife. Your marriage was at a breaking point. For reasons we'll get into presently, your long friendship with John was strained. When you saw him, lying bloodied in the brush, did a wave of doubt threaten to overwhelm you? Did you begin to question what you saw, looking down the sights of your rifle, or at least, to question the memory of what you saw? To think, Maybe I shot this man after all? And to wonder if you did so, on some level, deliberately?

DUNCAN: [*Slowly*] It was something like that, yes. I didn't know. I didn't think . . . but then I saw him there, bloody . . . and thought . . .

READER: Thought maybe you shot him?

DUNCAN: Yes.

READER: But I think that's not what happened. [*To Reginald*] When you shot John that morning, did you shoot to kill?

REGINALD: I didn't—

READER: Did you plan to do it all along, or did you seize your chance when you saw it? Was he a target of opportunity?

REGINALD: I didn't shoot him.

READER: You were desperate to sell the club, were you not?

REGINALD: I wanted to sell, yes, but—

READER: Did you mean to kill John when you shot at him?

REGINALD: I didn't mean to—

READER: It was an accident, then?

REGINALD: Yes. No. I didn't shoot him—

READER: When you shot John that morning, did you shoot to kill?

REGINALD: No, I didn't want that—

READER: Did you wake up that morning planning to shoot him?

REGINALD: No, it wasn't like that—

JANE: For Christ's sake, Reginald, shut up!

[*A few moments' silence. We should be able to register that Duncan Mayer is angry, Warren Burr is smirking, Jane Garmond is disgusted. Jonathan Gold is watching impassively.*]

DUNCAN: You're a goddamn bastard, Reginald.

REGINALD: It's not my fault you had a guilty conscience. If I hadn't done it, you probably would have. [*To Reader*] But I didn't kill him.

READER: The detective questioned you quite extensively about this very scenario. How unlikely it is that the person who failed to kill John in the morning would have circled back to finish the job in the evening. I believe he knew you fired that earlier shot when he was questioning you. He was offering you a chance to come clean. But you didn't take it. Of course, some mysteries rely on the "double bluff"—the most likely suspect is the one who committed the crime. Is that you, Mr. Talbot?

REGINALD: I'm telling you. I didn't kill him.

READER: Young Ralph Wakefield was doing word problems the other night. I have one for you. Imagine a man with a gambling addiction. He is deep in debt. His wife is seven months pregnant. What is the minimum amount of that debt, in dollars, needed to entice him to murder?

REGINALD: It's not like that.

READER: Did you start skimming funds from the club just recently, or did it start as soon as you became treasurer?

REGINALD: I'm not—

READER: Did you become treasurer precisely *because* you wanted to steal the money?

DR. BLAKE: You're a snake, Reg.

REGINALD: It's not true.

DR. BLAKE: You had two sets of books!

REGINALD: That was for the club! Not for me! The club couldn't get the loan with the real numbers. I had to do it.

DR. BLAKE: That loan was three years ago. Why keep the fake accounts going?

REGINALD: I was . . . I was worried we might need them again. It was easier just to keep it up than invent from scratch.

READER: [*To Jonathan*] Mr. Gold, what do you think of these accounts?

DUNCAN: What does he know about any of this?

READER: Mr. Gold currently possesses both sets of books. Unless he's decided to destroy them. He was given the accounts by the detective.

MEREDITH: Why would McAnnis do that?

READER: Because Jonathan Gold hired him to investigate the club.

SUSAN: He did?

WARREN: [*To Jonathan*] You did?

SUSAN: Why?

DR. BLAKE: And why did the detective lie to us?

READER: [*Sighs*] We are taught not to speak ill of the dead, but I'm afraid this reflects poorly on Mr. McAnnis. He saw John's death as an opportunity, I believe. The isolation caused by the storm left him as the logical person to begin queries. It essentially gave him free rein to the property.

DR. BLAKE: And to all of us.

READER: [*Nods*] And to all of you.

DUNCAN: But why did Jonathan hire the detective?

READER: Mr. Gold?

JONATHAN: [*Evenly*] I was merely doing my due diligence. *Caveat emptor.* Inspecting the horse's teeth before you ride away on it.

DR. BLAKE: You're buying the club?

JONATHAN: Let us say, rather, that I represent clients who are interested in buying the club.

READER: How much does Reginald Talbot owe your organization?

JONATHAN: [*Studiously ignoring Reginald*] For us, it's a rounding error. For him, of course, it's quite substantial. He was worried about it, and we let him worry. We had many productive conversations with him about repayment scenarios. [*Smiling*] Expectant fathers being an especially pliable sort of creature.

READER: And it was during one of those . . . conversations . . . that he revealed this land was originally Oneida, and shared his idea for a casino property?

JONATHAN: We were initially skeptical, of course. And as surprised as anyone that it all checked out. The idea, as it turns out, is quite sound. [*Smiling*] They say that God favors fools. At least on occasion.

READER: But there was only one problem. There was a person with veto power who was refusing to sell.

JONATHAN: Obstacles are meant to be overcome.

READER: Or murdered.

JONATHAN: Please. Do you really think me such a coarse instrument?

READER: I think you're capable of anything.

JONATHAN: My talent, if you want to call it that, lies in mustering the will to do what is necessary.

READER: Regardless of whether it's right or wrong?

JONATHAN: [*Waving his hand dismissively*] Like our dearly departed detective, I'm a bit of an amateur philosopher. It's a vocational hazard, perhaps. Absent a deity, right and wrong—or good and evil, if you prefer—are of course just artificial constructs. It's an agreement between you and me, no different than signing a lease on a piece of property. Or a contract for goods or services rendered. The only thing that compels adherence to the contract is the threat of violence, if broken.

READER: But that works only if you respect the threat of violence.

JONATHAN: Indeed. If you can evade the threat, by lawyer or lobbyist, or thwart the violence with violence of your own—then you are, truly, free.

READER: Did you ask Reginald Talbot to murder John Garmond?

JONATHAN: Of course not.

READER: Did you suggest to him that his debt would be forgiven if he ensured that the sale of the club went through?

JONATHAN: We merely stated the obvious—that it would help Mr. Talbot's financial condition if the club was sold.

READER: But you knew he was desperate. You were, in fact, the reason why he was desperate.

JONATHAN: Reg Talbot is a weak man. If I were to embark upon a task like murder, it would not be in so leaky a vessel.

READER: Nonetheless, it's my view that you insinuated that murder would save him. And so he tried.

JONATHAN: You're entitled to your view, of course. This is America. What is this great nation but a land of belief and myth? [*Looking at Reginald*] But I don't believe you'll get much out of that quivering rabbit.

READER: To ask the obvious: Did John Garmond know that you were misrepresenting yourself when you applied to be a member? Did he know that your clients were interested in buying the club?

JONATHAN: What did John Garmond know? What did

he suspect? What did he admit only to himself, alone,
late at night, in the darkest recesses of his heart? You
might ask his wife or lover, I suppose. But I have no
idea.

READER: [*Exasperated*] These aren't metaphysical
questions.

JONATHAN: Aren't they?

READER: These are questions of fact and public record.
Words, gestures, expressions. Who said what to whom,
and when. What was done, and how. The quip at a
cocktail party. The glance across the room. The letter
written but not sent. These all get us to motive. So I'll
ask you again. Did John Garmond express enthusiasm
about your application to join the club?

JONATHAN: I suppose so.

READER: Is that because he thought the addition of
a new wealthy member might forestall the sale of the
club?

JONATHAN: Perhaps.

READER: And perhaps also you led him to believe that.
He knew you were Jewish, of course.

JONATHAN: I would assume so.

READER: We'll return to that. Now, on this question of
the disposition of the club—may I assume that everyone
in this room was in favor of the sale?

[*Nobody dissents.*]

SUSAN: Including you, Jane?

JANE: Yes. I thought . . . a fresh start was necessary.

WARREN: She wasn't going to stay, in other words.

READER: Good. That's motive, for those who care about
such things. For all of you. Let's consider. The detective
pursued several different questions which, I believe, are
related to this issue. For example, who served as club
president from 1935 to 1940?

MEREDITH: How could that possibly matter?

READER: It matters because someone thought it mattered. The plaque covering those years is missing from the upstairs library. Someone removed it. Why?

REGINALD: It's been decades. Maybe some kid stole it. Maybe it just got lost. Who the hell knows?

READER: I believe it was removed recently, as part of an attempt to alter the history of this club. [*To Dr. Blake*] Why did you lie about your father's term as club president?

DR. BLAKE: I don't believe I did.

READER: The detective asked you about it directly. I didn't know why he was so interested in this plaque, and these questions, but it's clear to me now. Unfortunately, too late to do anyone any good. Why did you lie to him?

DR. BLAKE: I must have misunderstood the question.

READER: Your father, Dr. Theodore Blake, was president of the club from 1935 to 1940, was he not?

DR. BLAKE: He was president; I'm not sure about the dates.

READER: Those are the dates. And during that time, he used his position to foster a certain . . . political agenda, did he not? [*Dr. Blake is silent*] For example, he invited a physician inventor who had devised a machine he claimed could differentiate between the blood of different races. [*To Jonathan Gold*] Mr. Gold, did you know that your blood vibrates at a much lower frequency than the blood of Dr. Blake here?

JONATHAN: [*Dryly*] I did not.

READER: [*To Dr. Blake*] A total crock, of course. But such theories were *en vogue*, back then, among a certain set. Were you aware that your father also managed to secure visits from Charles Lindbergh and Henry Ford?

DR. BLAKE: West Heart members are well connected.

Celebrities and powerful people have been frequent guests. [*To Meredith*] Who was it that came last year? The actor?

MEREDITH: Bill Holden?

DR. BLAKE: No, the other one.

MEREDITH: Charlton Heston?

DR. BLAKE: That's right. Charlton Heston. [*To Jonathan Gold*] Moses!

JONATHAN: Never saw it.

READER: Celebrities have certainly passed through this club over the decades, but those two men, visiting at that particular time, are especially interesting. The West Heart records indicate that they were speaking on the "situation in Europe." Those records also state that their speeches were "well attended" by a "supportive audience." Tell me, doctor, have you ever heard of the Service Cross of the German Eagle? Or of the Grand Cross of the German Eagle?

DR. BLAKE: No.

READER: Both were medals created by Adolf Hitler. Henry Ford had the latter pinned to his chest by the German consul. Charles Lindbergh was awarded the former personally by Hermann Göring while touring the Reich. In Berlin, actually. Lindbergh later testified to Congress that we should negotiate with Hitler. Ford published anti-Semitic tracts, including *The Protocols of the Elders of Zion*. I believe they were invited by your father to share their views on these subjects with the good people of West Heart. To this "supportive audience." [*Silence; Reader now addressing the entire room*] I realize these are . . . inconvenient facts. The sort of facts that Americans are usually quite good at forgetting. Unless we don't want to forget. [*To Dr. Blake*] Do you have a hunting cabin, Dr. Blake?

DR. BLAKE: It's a family cabin. We've had it for years.

READER: It's remote? Out of sight? Would it be wrong to call it hidden?

DR. BLAKE: It's not hidden.

READER: The detective found something under the rug there. A metal box. Would you like to describe what's inside the box? [*Silence*] No? Then allow me. [*Reader again addressing the entire room*] It's a metal box full of Nazi memorabilia. It includes a pin worn by the Schutzstaffel, better known as the SS. There are also several newspaper clippings, one of which includes a photograph of Dr. Theodore Blake with Hermann Göring. The type of souvenir a proud son would preserve, carefully, to honor his father's memory. [*To Dr. Blake*] Were you proud of your father's beliefs?

DR. BLAKE: This line of questioning is ridiculous.

READER: Do you share those beliefs?

DR. BLAKE: I'm not going to disown my father.

READER: Were you unhappy at the prospect of Mr. Gold joining West Heart?

DR. BLAKE: [*Proudly*] Yes. [*To Jonathan Gold*] Nothing personal.

JONATHAN: [*Coldly*] Of course.

DR. BLAKE: I just believe that like-minded people should stick together. People should be with their own kind.

READER: You mean with people whose blood vibrates at the same frequency as their own?

DR. BLAKE: Mock if you want to. But you know I'm right. [*Addressing the room*] You all know I'm right.

READER: This box also includes a Luger pistol. Did you use this Luger to shoot John Garmond?

DR. BLAKE: Of course not.

READER: Did you know that John Garmond met Lindbergh during that visit?

DR. BLAKE: [*Surprised*] I did not. I wasn't here. At that time, I was in medical school.

READER: He was very young, obviously. The West Heart records have a photo of them together. As a boy obsessed with aviation, who later became an amateur pilot, meeting the hero of the *Spirit of St. Louis* must have seemed like a dream come true. But, of course, Lucky Lindy eventually fell to earth. John, like a lot of Americans, must have been disappointed. But the point is, he likely knew about this aspect of the club's past. [*To the room*] Like many of you, I suspect. A shared guilt. Or perhaps a shared amnesia. At any rate, it must have worried him. The club was facing an existential problem. John had spent his childhood here. Married his teenage sweetheart here. Raised his son here. But now it was under threat. There are logging trucks out on the main road—selling lumber is something the club hadn't done since the Great Depression. Reginald Talbot had to obtain a loan just to keep the club going, using fraudulent accounts. Back in New York, before the detective came here, he did some homework; I wouldn't be surprised if he found a lien on this property. [*Glancing at Reginald, who says nothing*] Perhaps a copy of the lien is in that manila folder back in his room. So John knew the club was in trouble. If he thought Jonathan Gold could save it, he'd be eager to remove or hide any obstacles that might get in the way. Including signs of a Nazi past that might give a Jewish applicant pause. [*To Jane*] I'm guessing that back in your house, in a closet somewhere, there is a plaque for the years 1935 to 1940, bearing the name of Dr. Theodore Blake.

JANE: [*Dismayed*] But none of it mattered. [*To Jonathan*] He was worried about nothing. You weren't going to be a member. You wanted to buy. And he was in the way.

READER: Mr. Gold, would your clients be concerned about this past?

JONATHAN: Our concern is future-focused. Results-oriented, you might say.

READER: I thought as much. [*To the room*] So now we know certain things. The treasurer was deep in debt and under pressure to arrange for the sale of the club. The prospective buyer was here, lying about his intentions. His hired investigator was also here, also under false pretenses. And poor John Garmond dodged death in the morning only to be murdered that very night. Anyone disagree? [*Silence*] Now we turn to the dog.

JAMES: [*Incredulously*] The dog?

READER: Yes, the dog. It matters little whether Alex Caldwell meant to kill the dog or not, and, frankly, it's possible that Alex himself may not even know. We don't care if that dog barks or not, if you will. What matters is that the dog was the first thread on a string that led to Claudia Mayer's death. It revealed tragedies that seeped through everything else we've been talking about, like a secret rot in the wood. [*To Jane*] But the key clue to Claudia's death came from the aria that you sang on the night of the bonfire. Why did you choose that particular song?

JANE: I told the detective about this already.

READER: Humor me. Tell it again.

JANE: I felt like it. And I knew the words.

READER: But you were a professional opera singer. You probably know the words to many songs. Yet you chose this one. McAnnis was interested in this question, and I didn't know why. But I believe I know now.

JANE: Do you?

READER: Might I suggest that it was a gesture of sympathy, perhaps even an apology, aimed at two

different people? One who was there, and one who
was not.

JANE: I don't know what you mean.

READER: *Madame Butterfly* is about a woman whose
husband loves another woman. It's also about a parent
losing a child. Claudia Mayer was the former. And your
husband, John, was the latter.

JANE: [*Anguished*] Please.

READER: I'm sorry, but the truth will out,
Mrs. Garmond. [*To Duncan*] Claudia was a troubled
woman, was she not?

DUNCAN: Yes. I think everyone here knew that.

READER: The detective asked you about her state of
mind before her death. But you failed to tell him that
Claudia had disappeared, suddenly, for weeks, and
returned just days before her death. Why did you keep
that from him?

DUNCAN: I don't know.

READER: But of course you do. We are not children
who say "I don't know" when we want to skirt a painful
subject. You also told the detective that you were home
all night on Thursday, the night of Claudia's death. But,
of course, that wasn't true. Where were you? [*Duncan
doesn't answer*] Perhaps your silence is borne of some
misguided or outdated gentleman's sense of decorum,
the impulse to protect a lady's honor. But this particular
lady has already spoken. [*To Jane*] Isn't that right?

JANE: The detective already knew, Duncan.

READER: I daresay half the club knew, when it came
down to it. Duncan Mayer, do you love Jane Garmond?

DUNCAN: Yes.

READER: How long have you loved her?

DUNCAN: [*Defiantly*] My whole life.

READER: You asked her to marry you when you were
both young?

DUNCAN: Yes.

READER: But she married John Garmond instead?

DUNCAN: Yes.

READER: And then you married Claudia?

DUNCAN: Yes.

READER: And you were both unfaithful that whole time?

DUNCAN: Not the whole time . . .

READER: At the beginning?

DUNCAN: Yes.

READER: And at the end?

DUNCAN: Yes.

READER: Were you in Room 312 on Thursday night? [*Duncan hesitates*] With Jane?

JANE: [*Answering for him*] Yes.

READER: Just to put the matter as bluntly as possible: The night of your wife's death, you were in another woman's arms. And you lied to the detective about it. Why?

DUNCAN: [*Wretchedly*] Shame, obviously. Wouldn't you lie?

READER: That night in Room 312, did you know there was someone outside the door, listening?

DUNCAN: [*Surprised*] No. No, we didn't know that. [*Pauses*] Was it Claudia?

READER: That's who I assumed it was, at first. That's who I was led to believe it was. But we'll circle back to that in a moment. The main thing is that you had an alibi for the night of your wife's death, an alibi that you would not have had if you were faithful to her. Or put another way: your guilt proves your innocence. Did you provide the sheriff with this alibi?

DUNCAN: No.

READER: You also told the sheriff that she didn't leave a suicide note.

DUNCAN: Because she didn't.

READER: I believe, or at least I think I believe, that you believed that. But it wasn't true. Claudia did leave a suicide note.

DUNCAN: [*Shocked*] She did? How—what did she say?

READER: The note contained secrets. Why she disappeared, and why she came back. Or so I surmise. I haven't read it myself.

DUNCAN: Where is it?

READER: Most likely, in the kitchen freezer. Somewhere on the body of the detective. But it's not necessary to search the corpse. Not when there's someone here who's read it.

DUNCAN: [*Glances at Jane*] Who?

READER: The person who found it. Otto? [*Otto Mayer struggles to his feet*] You don't have to stand. This is not a courtroom.

OTTO: I prefer it.

READER: Otto, where were you Thursday night?

OTTO: Outside Room 312.

DUNCAN: Why?

READER: Why?

OTTO: [*Ignoring his father*] I knew he was in there. With her. I knew how much it hurt my mother. Or I thought I knew. I didn't really, though. Not until the next day. But that night . . . when he left the house, I knew where he was going. I thought maybe I'd interrupt them, or catch them. Shame them.

READER: But you didn't.

OTTO: No. I lost my nerve. Or thought better of it. I left instead. The detective followed me. I went partway down the trail to the lake, then doubled back. If I had just continued down the trail . . . I might have seen her. [*Emotional*] I might have stopped her.

READER: And the next day, you found the note?

OTTO: Yes. I didn't know what to do with it. I didn't know who to share it with. Finally, I gave it to the detective.

READER: What did the note say?

OTTO: [*To Duncan*] She apologized to us for living a lie. Trying to fool us into thinking that she could be a normal wife and mother. [*Blinking away tears*] But she accused you of living a lie, too.

READER: Otto, do you know why your mother disappeared last month?

OTTO: Yes. I didn't then, but I do now.

READER: And why is that?

OTTO: Because my father told her . . . he told her that he was leaving her.

READER: What else?

OTTO: [*Deep breath*] He told her that I was not his only son.

READER: Did her note make it clear who that was?

OTTO: Yes.

[*An uncomfortable pause here, during which some Characters should indicate dawning understanding. Other Characters should remain in the dark until it's also clear to the Audience.*]

RAMSEY: [*Shocked*] Jesus.

JANE: Ramsey—

DUNCAN: Now is not the time—

RAMSEY: [*Glancing from one to the other*] I don't believe this.

JANE: Ramsey, we can explain—

RAMSEY: You can all go to hell. [*Looking around*] Who else knew about this? [*To Jane and Duncan*] How did this happen?

JANE: No one wanted it this way.

DUNCAN: It was an accident.

RAMSEY: That's comforting.

JANE: It's not like that.

RAMSEY: I think it's exactly like that.

EMMA: My God.

WARREN: [*Smirking*] This is fantastic.

DUNCAN: Go fuck yourself, Warren.

RAMSEY: [*To Duncan*] Did you know?

DUNCAN: Not until recently.

RAMSEY: [*To Jane, dismayed*] Did Dad know?

JANE: No.

RAMSEY: Were you just going to keep this a secret forever?

JANE: I thought so. And I did. [*Takes a deep breath*] For years and years. Women keep their secrets. At least, women of my generation, and the generations before me. My mother knew girls who grew up not realizing that their much older sister was actually their mother, made pregnant much too young. [*Hesitates*] I didn't want to hurt anyone.

RAMSEY: Well, you have.

JANE: When I realized that I couldn't be with your father—

RAMSEY: [*Bitterly*] Which one?

JANE: When I realized that I was leaving John, only then did I tell Duncan.

RAMSEY: When were you going to tell me?

JANE: I—I wasn't sure.

RAMSEY: Were you *ever* going to tell me?

JANE: [*Glances at Duncan*] We weren't sure. It's . . . complicated.

RAMSEY: If Dad hadn't been killed, would you have told me?

DUNCAN: Probably not.

RAMSEY: Jesus. [*To Otto*] You at least should have told me.

OTTO: I only just found out. And it's been a fucking ruinous weekend for me, too.

RAMSEY: [*Taken aback*] Sorry. This is all so . . .

JANE: It's a lot.

RAMSEY: It's a melodrama, is what it is. A cheap theatrical twist, at my expense. [*Looking around the room*] I don't have to stay here for this. Enjoy the rest of the goddamn show.

JANE: Ramsey—

[*Exit Ramsey*]

READER: Let him go.

JANE: Why?

READER: Because we have a lot of work left to do. But at least, now we understand poor Claudia a bit better. What was done to her may not have been a crime. But it may have been a sin.

DUNCAN: [*Gruffly*] Get on with it.

READER: We must turn to the question of what we now know was the first murder here at West Heart. Who killed John Garmond?

[*Curtain*]

×

Entertainments

"These violent delights have violent ends" is the phrase from Shakespeare, neatly encapsulating (though this is not how Shakespeare meant it) the dilemma that has vexed artists, moral philosophers, and civic-minded prudes for centuries. Although the average reader harbors no qualms about the macabre enjoyments of murderous fiction, there is something faintly unsettling about the entire enterprise. If one surveys the full canon of humanity's creative output, it's easy to write off generations of mankind as a bloodthirsty and lip-smacking horde of sadists cheering as Hector is mutilated, Lavinia raped, and Fortunato entombed—all while Hannibal Lecter tucks in his napkin to savor his latest meal.

In this regard, the rare reader who pauses, uneasy about the characters in a mystery who archly joke over the corpse of the (very) recently deceased, is much like that reluctant Roman in the arena who couldn't bring himself to turn his thumb either up or down. (One also suspects that Dante's *extremely* detailed accounts of the tortures of Hell, while ostensibly warning about the perils of leading a sinful life, in fact serviced baser impulses for both him and his readers: they enjoyed the suffering.)

But of course, storytellers have exploited murder for millennia, and it has not yet brought civilization to ruin. And though intuitively it seems permissible and perhaps even desirable for people to consume death as a form of entertainment, the precise explanation for why that should be the case has proved elusive.

Thomas De Quincey's satirical essay "On Murder Considered as One of the Fine Arts" helped frame this debate; it was principally inspired by the real-life (quite grisly) murders apparently committed by John Williams in 1811. De Quincey describes them as the "sublimest" crimes ever committed, and praises Williams as a "solitary artist" who by the "blaze of his genius" has "exalted the ideal of murder to all of us." De Quincey, in full tongue-in-cheek mode, cites Aristotle in his defense, who in the *Poetics* spoke of a "perfect thief" and a "good thief," suggesting that we can admire an immoral criminal's skill—that is to say, we can have an aesthetic appreciation of his crimes.

The latter part of De Quincey's essay, written years later, is a meticulous re-creation of the Williams murders, which inaugurated "true crime" as a literary genre. Accounts of crime, often quite gruesome, had delighted the public for centuries; cheap pamphlets detailing the latest crimes and arrests filled the muddy streets of London in Shakespeare's time. Later, entire tomes were filled with stories of "outrages upon the law," and much enjoyed by the reading populace.

Robert Alison's *The Anecdotage of Glasgow* (1892) relates the tale of James M'Kean, who was, in a delightful phrase, "a master shoemaker of easy circumstances," but who nonetheless in 1796 murdered a man with a razor, nearly severing the head from the body, apparently over a matter of some 118 pounds. M'Kean had also been suspected of his mother's death, years earlier, and, when asked about it on the eve of his execution by a clergyman, was supposed to have said, "Doctor, can you keep a secret?" The priest said yes, to which M'Kean replied: "So can I."

This is a fine anecdote with a marvelous punch line. Are we, then, to feel bad for enjoying it? How many of us *actually* thought of the poor victim, blood spurting from his neck in the final seconds of his life, of the friends and family who will never see him again? And should we blame this omission on a lack of imagination or a lack of empathy?

There are also, it must be noted, more practical considerations to consider. Agatha Christie, one of society's most prolific (fictional) murderers, was horrified by the prospect of a (real-life) "copycat" crime that took place near the end of her life. Graham Young poisoned several victims using thallium, a technique Christie had employed a decade earlier in her novel *The Pale Horse*. Whatever the likelihood that the novel inspired the killer (Young claimed not to have read it, but thallium was quite esoteric before Christie), it certainly led to his capture—a doctor consulting on the case identified the victims' symptoms based on his memory of her book.

Despite the fears of these violent delights, one could fairly definitively settle the matter by noting that only a tiny fraction of us ever shoot, stab, bludgeon, strangle, drown, defenestrate, or poison anyone else. What, then, is the utility of murder as art?

The earliest, and still most convincing, rationale for the metaphysic nutrition of murder comes, again, from Aristotle. In his *Poetics*, he introduces the concept of *catharsis*. Writing in the context of classical Greek theater, Aristotle conjectures that experiencing certain feelings vicariously—he cites pity and fear, though centuries of criticism have expanded this to include any emotion—can allow the audience members to purge themselves of those feelings in a kind of psychological "cleanse." It's why we enjoy a "good cry" from a sad film or book; it's also why we may laugh in delight during a horror movie. The mechanism for *how* this works remains opaque, though Freudians and other occultists have done their best to explain it. But there's little doubt that catharsis *does* work; it's perhaps the obverse of Bertrand Russell's claim for the ontological proof of God's existence: "It is easier to feel convinced that it must be fallacious than it is to find out precisely where the fallacy lies."

The limits of this debate were discovered at the Cherry Lane Theatre in New York City on May 25, 1952, at the premiere of Paul Goodman's Roman gladiator play *Faustina*. After its horrifying climax, the actress playing the empress addresses the spectators, out of character (Goodman allowed the actress to devise the precise words herself), rebuking them for failing to thwart its bloody dénouement: "We have enacted a brutal scene, the ritual murder of a young and handsome man. I have bathed in his blood, and if you were a worthy audience, you'd have leaped on the stage and stopped the action." The audience was unmoved by her appeal; in fact, they grew angry and resentful. The actress, Julie Bovasso, was mortified by this moment in the play: that first night, she confessed to the audience, "I have some lines to say that are so ghastly, I don't think

I can continue . . ." and left the show after just a few performances. The director, Judith Malina, then played the part of Faustina. In the play's program, justifying the production and referenc... audience, Malina wrote: "We are creators in an art where ev... night hundreds of people are ignored . . ."

The production closed after two weeks.

×

Play

Great hall of West Heart clubhouse, as before. The Characters should be located exactly where they were at the end of Scene 1. Reader is now dressed and styled contemporaneously to the Characters, not the Audience.

SCENE 2

READER: [*To the room*] This is a grim business, isn't it? Playing the murders. But I think we're getting somewhere. We've revealed a love affair. Explained a suicide. Uncovered a decades-old secret. Unmasked a Nazi. Exposed a thief and his blackmailer. And we've discovered how a would-be murderer was saved only by his poor marksmanship. But of course, our principal task remains. Who is the murderer? [*Pause; then to Susan*] Susan Burr.

SUSAN: My turn, is it?

READER: When did your husband ask you to make that call to John Garmond? [*Susan looks down, then looks over at Warren*] Don't look at him, look at me. A call was placed to the Garmond house at midnight, just before the murder. John went to the clubhouse afterward.

When did your husband ask you to make that call? [*Silence*] Answer, please.

WARREN: Susan—

READER: Please.

WARREN: Careful, Susan.

SUSAN: [*Hurriedly*] When we got home. [*Warren visibly angry*] After the bonfire.

READER: Did he say why?

SUSAN: He said . . . [*Glances at Warren again*]

READER: Don't look at him. Look at me. Why did he say he wanted you to make that call?

SUSAN: He said he knew everything. Which I knew, that wasn't the surprise. The surprise was that he was talking about it. We'd never done that before, not directly. He said that he needed to talk to John about the sale of the club. He needed to convince him to do the right thing.

WARREN: Susan, I'm warning you—

READER: Ignore him. He can't hurt you anymore. What was "the right thing"? To approve the sale?

SUSAN: Yes. Warren said we needed it. He said we were in trouble if it didn't happen. There were debts I didn't know about. He said he was in trouble.

WARREN: [*Rising from his chair*] Susan, so help me—

DUNCAN: Sit the fuck back down! [*Warren astonished*] If you lay so much as a goddamn finger on her, I swear to God I'm going to break it off.

WARREN: [*Coldly*] You don't know what you're talking about here, Duncan. You should be careful.

DUNCAN: I'm sure I should be. But I don't really care anymore who you know or claim to know down in the city. I want to hear what she has to say. [*Pause*] I want to hear what happened to my friend.

[*Warren hesitates, then sits down, sneering*]

READER: [*To Jonathan*] Do you have anything to say about all this, Mr. Gold?

JONATHAN: [*Exaggerated perplexity*] Me? Why would I?

READER: [*To Susan*] What sort of trouble? What did you take that to mean?

SUSAN: I took that to mean that something very bad would happen. The people he deals with . . . they don't mess around.

READER: People like Jonathan Gold?

SUSAN: He's just the messenger. The face of Death when it rides through the village.

READER: [*To Warren*] You told the detective that you move money around. For whom do you do this, Mr. Burr?

WARREN: If you think you know all the answers, why do you ask so many questions?

READER: Do you do it for Mr. Gold's concern?

WARREN: I have many clients.

READER: You told the detective that you didn't know Mr. Gold before this. But that wasn't true, was it? Your wife revealed to the detective that in fact you were business associates.

[*Murmuring among the Characters*]

DR. BLAKE: [*Icily*] I don't appreciate being lied to, Warren.

WARREN: Such pillars of morality, here at West Heart. Please.

DR. BLAKE: [*To Jonathan*] Who exactly do you work for?

READER: Would you like to name names, Mr. Gold? In the interest of advancing the cause of justice?

JONATHAN: Of course I have a deep, long-standing

interest in the processes of justice. However, my hands are tied in this matter. Surely we all have an interest in protecting the time-honored tradition of attorney-client privilege?

DR. BLAKE: Convenient.

JONATHAN: Quite.

JANE: Is it the Mafia?

JONATHAN: [*Disdainfully*] If your criminal concern has a name, then you're doing it wrong. [*To Reader*] But by all means, continue. Don't let my reticence stop you. These . . . speculations are fascinating.

READER: [*To Susan*] You said you were afraid something bad would happen. To Warren? Or to yourself?

SUSAN: Warren made it sound like, whatever was going to happen, it was going to happen to both of us. And I believed it.

READER: Was that the only reason you made the call?

SUSAN: I'm sorry?

READER: Was there also a threat? [*Silence*] Let's move on. What did you say to John on the phone?

SUSAN: I said I needed to see him.

READER: You needed to have a rendezvous, you mean.

SUSAN: That's how I made it sound, yes.

READER: Was he reluctant?

SUSAN: He was never reluctant. [*Gestures toward Jane*] Do we have to do this in front of her?

JANE: It's fine. [*Wearily*] Go ahead.

READER: [*To Susan*] Did you know what he was going to do?

SUSAN: I didn't know. I swear to God. [*To Jane*] Jane, I didn't know.

READER: Were you awake when he got home? Afterward?

SUSAN: Yes.

READER: What did he say?

SUSAN: Nothing.

READER: Does your husband frighten you, Mrs. Burr?

SUSAN: [*Emotional*] Yes.

READER: Has he given you cause to be frightened, in the past?

SUSAN: Yes.

READER: [*Gently*] Do you currently have a bruise on your lower back, the size of a tennis ball, blue-black in the moonlit shadows?

SUSAN: [*Nods*]

READER: [*To Warren*] Mr. Burr.

WARREN: Yes.

READER: The questions, at last, come round to you.

WARREN: Obviously, I won't answer.

READER: There is merit, I believe, sometimes, in simply asking the questions. The gambit of the scientist or philosopher. So, Mr. Burr. Shall we begin?

WARREN: If you like.

READER: Mr. Burr, are you in debt to criminal elements? [*Silence*] Did you ask your wife to call John Garmond? Did you threaten her? Do you beat your wife, Mr. Burr? [*Silence*] Did you force your wife to call John Garmond so you could surprise him at the clubhouse? Did you kill him? [*Silence*] Did you kill John Garmond to ensure the sale of this club? Did you kill John Garmond in revenge for sleeping with your wife? [*Gestures toward Jonathan*] Did he put you up to it? Did he demand you do it? Threaten you? Did you do it quickly, afraid you'd lose your nerve? Or did you draw it out? Take your time? [*Reader moving to stand next to Jane*] Did you enjoy it? Did you explain to him why you were doing it? What did he say? Did he ask for mercy? Did you enjoy that? [*Silence*] Did you kill John Garmond with the sharp snare-drum crack of a pistol shot in the back of the head?

[*The room is quiet for several long moments. Are Jane and Susan crying, softly?*]

WARREN: [*Slowly, to Reader but also to the room*] Is this the part where I confess? Where I sink to my knees, begging forgiveness? I think not. You have, of course, no evidence. None. A supposed phone call. Speculation. The testimony of a frightened and hysterical woman who's also known to be a promiscuous drug user. Where's the gun? Where's the evidence of my alleged financial distress? Where's the evidence of my association with Jonathan Gold? You have nothing. And nothing will happen to me. The sale of this club will still take place. These people need it too much. John Garmond's death will have served its purpose. And soon all of this will seem like a dream. A half-forgotten story from a book we read by chance and have since cast aside. You have nothing. Nothing. [*Glancing around the room*] So many old friends here. So many emotions. Fear. Anger. Disgust. Perhaps a hint of admiration? Soon you may be thanking me. Postcards at Christmas.

DUNCAN: You're delusional.

WARREN: Am I? [*To Susan*] And of course, dear Susan, I forgive you. [*She flinches*] We'll discuss this later. [*Studies her closely, then addresses the room, looking at each member of the cast in turn, and smiles*] Do any of you know the art of beating a woman? How to inflict pain, deep pain, without leaving behind evidence? It seems like a brutal business, but it's actually quite delicate. Obviously, you don't want a ruptured organ or internal bleeding; that would lead to a hospital visit. Perhaps even the involvement of the police. So you avoid creating bruises where they would show: The face, of course, and the arms. The legs in summertime.

Always be mindful of the season. And monitor your alcohol intake. A whiskey or two, to get you loose, is wise. Anything more than that and it's too easy to make a mistake. And of course you have to choose the right tools. Some men swear by a bag of oranges. Others, a sock filled with a few bars of soap. I find that the old ways work best. Fists give you more control. More control, and more satisfaction.

JANE: [*Furious*] You're a monster.

WARREN: [*Feigning surprise*] Did John never give you a whack, to set you straight? When he was deep in his cups?

[*Duncan leaps to his feet in anger. Warren pulls a revolver from his jacket pocket and points it at him. Duncan freezes.*]

JANE: Don't!

WARREN: Take another step, Duncan. Please. Self-defense laws in New York are very strong. And so many witnesses, too. Would make it so much easier to get off. Take a step.

DUNCAN: She's right. You are a monster.

WARREN: I'm a man, same as you. Maybe they're the same thing.

READER: How many rounds are in that cylinder, Mr. Burr? Is there one missing? [*Warren grimaces*] Care to hand it over for inspection?

WARREN: I think not. In fact, now that the gun is out, I think I have only two options. I can either shoot someone or I can leave. Which do you all prefer? [*Silence*] Nothing? Okay, then.

[*He cocks the hammer on the revolver and points it at Duncan, who closes his eyes*]

SUSAN: Warren. Please.

WARREN: So now you're talking to me?

SUSAN: Please.

WARREN: [*Still looking at Duncan*] Say you'll come home
with me.

SUSAN: I will.

WARREN: Say it.

SUSAN: I'll come home with you.

WARREN: [*Keeps the gun pointed for a few more seconds,
then lowers it, grins, whistles appreciatively*] Jesus Christ.
Now, that's an experience. Is your pulse racing,
Duncan? Mine is. The adrenaline. Almost worth doing
it again. [*Feints pointing the revolver again; Duncan stiffens
instinctively; Warren lowers the gun*] Joking, joking.
Violence is an addiction, like everything else. I could
get used to this. [*To Susan*] Ready, my love?

SUSAN: Yes.

[*Warren takes her by the hand, kisses her knuckles, then lightly
slaps her wrist.*]

WARREN: Naughty girl.

[*Exit Warren and Susan*]

[*The remaining Characters are quiet for a certain period of
time—however long people in a room would naturally hold their
breath until they're sure an armed man has left and the danger
is over. Duncan slumps back in his chair.*]

JANE: [*To Duncan*] You okay?

DUNCAN: At least I didn't piss myself.

[*The lights flicker, then surge brighter with an audible whoom!
The faint hum of the generator abruptly clicks off.*]

MEREDITH: Power is back. Maybe the roads are cleared?

JANE: What do we do now? About him?

READER: This seems like a good time to say that the police are on their way.

JANE: How?

READER: Fred Shiflett had a back way out of the club that only he knew about.

DUNCAN: Sneaky bastard.

JANE: But thank God.

READER: Police should be here any minute.

JANE: They need to get Susan away from him.

DUNCAN: They will.

JANE: And then he should rot in Hell.

READER: Yes. Though he's right in that the evidence against him is tenuous. He very well could go free. [*To Jonathan*] I'm sure your concern has recourse to the best in legal representation.

JONATHAN: We do, of course. [*Shrugs*] But our interests now diverge. Mr. Burr, at this point, is on his own.

REGINALD: So that's it, then?

READER: Not quite.

REGINALD: What?

DR. BLAKE: The detective?

READER: Yes.

JANE: The poor man is dead, and it feels like an epilogue.

REGINALD: Why would Warren want to kill him?

READER: I don't think he did.

JANE: Who, then?

READER: We have three deaths. Three bodies. All very different. A drowning. A shooting. That we understand. What we have with the detective is . . . unusual. I don't understand it.

JANE: Maybe he found something that his client didn't like.

READER: Mr. Gold? Any thoughts on that?

JONATHAN: I appreciate the aesthetics of murder, like anyone else. But the practical side is another matter. Wet work is not my expertise.

READER: [*To the Blakes*] The room was locked from the inside?

EMMA: Yes.

READER: Windows, too?

JAMES: Yes, I checked.

READER: [*To Dr. Blake*] You were the first one into the detective's bedroom, correct?

DR. BLAKE: All three of us went in.

READER: But as the doctor, you examined the body first? And asked the others to stand back?

DR. BLAKE: Yes.

READER: As those of you familiar with the classical traditions of the Locked Room know, special attention must be paid to the first person to enter the room and examine the body. Especially if they have some expertise in anatomy, such as a butcher or a veterinarian. Or a doctor. [*To James and Emma*] When you entered the room, did your father block your view of the body with his own?

JAMES: What you're suggesting is ridiculous.

READER: Is it possible that your father, while apparently checking to see if the detective was still alive, was in fact killing him?

JAMES: Absolutely not.

READER: Emma?

EMMA: I don't . . . I don't believe he could do that.

READER: At dinner on Thursday night, when the detective was lying about his service in Vietnam, he'd claimed to have a heart murmur. Perhaps that part was true? [*To Dr. Blake*] As a doctor, it would have been

simple for you to replace the pills in his drawer with
something else. Something that you knew would make
his heart condition worse. Maybe even kill him. Or
maybe you had a different plan. Maybe you swapped in
some sort of sedative that you knew would knock him
out, that would give you a reason to be first into the
room, to examine the victim, to quietly inject a lethal
poison? If we examine the body [*gestures in the direction
of the kitchen*], would we, perhaps, find a little pinprick
bruise in the left armpit?

DR. BLAKE: [*Defiant*] Why don't you roll him out and
check?

READER: If it wasn't you, doctor, then who was it?
[*Reader begins to stalk the room, pausing in front of each
Character in turn; first to Meredith*] Was it the zealous
wife, perhaps, eager to protect her husband's reputation?
[*To Jane and Duncan*] Or the illicit lovers, desperate
to hide a decades-old secret? [*To Reginald*] Or the
crooked accountant, afraid that more misdeeds would
be brought to light? [*To Jonathan*] Or was it the client,
worried that his detective's unexpected and expanding
inquiry threatened a profitable business transaction?
[*Reader circles back to where she began, now addressing the
entire room*] It's a difficult problem. What we're missing,
unfortunately, is a final clue to the murderer's identity
left by the victim himself. In the canon, this is known
as the Dying Message: the torn corner of a book, or
initials scratched into wood, or a hoarse misunderstood
whisper—"paradise" instead of "pair of dice," for
example. But it appears the detective didn't leave such
a message. [*Pause*] Or did he? [*Turns to Emma*] Did you
find anything on his body?

EMMA: No, I don't think so.

READER: Who transported the body to the freezer?

EMMA: James and my father.

READER: [*To James*] Did you find anything on the late
   Mr. McAnnis?

JAMES: No.

READER: Are you certain?

JAMES: Yes.

READER: So you didn't find a piece of paper crumpled in
   his fist?

JAMES: [*Silence*]

EMMA: [*Apprehensive*] James?

READER: [*Insistently*] I'll ask again. Did you find a piece
   of paper? Was it from the detective's dossier on the
   club?

JANE: We really need to see this dossier.

READER: [*To the room*] I haven't seen it, either, though
   of course I know of its existence. A detective's dramatis
   personae, if you will. I assume that many of you are in
   the dossier. Background checks. Financial issues. Liens,
   loans, debt. Moral failings. Sexual deviations. I'm sure
   it's all in there.

DUNCAN: What a bastard.

READER: All part of his work for Mr. Gold. But now we
   turn back to the question at hand. [*To James*] Whose
   name was on this piece of paper, James? [*Silence*] What
   did you think, James, when you found the report on
   your father crumpled in the dead man's fist?

EMMA: How could—

JAMES: [*Abruptly*] It doesn't mean anything.

DR. BLAKE: James—

JAMES: Seriously. It doesn't mean anything. It could
   mean nothing. He could have grabbed it for any reason.
   Or no reason at all.

READER: When did you find the paper?

JAMES: In the freezer.

READER: And where was your father?

JAMES: Outside. I told him I needed a minute.

READER: And then you found the document.

JAMES: Yes.

READER: And then what?

JAMES: Then I stuffed it into my pocket.

READER: And where is it now?

JAMES: I burned it in the kitchen sink.

EMMA: Jesus.

READER: [*To Dr. Blake*] If you committed this murder, then your son became an accessory after the fact. Do you have anything to add now, doctor?

DR. BLAKE: [*Evenly*] I did not kill Adam McAnnis.

REGINALD: That's a laugh.

JAMES: Go to hell.

READER: [*Long silence, then to Dr. Blake*] I believe you.

EMMA: Really?

READER: Yes. There is opportunity but no motive. Why would you murder the detective? Because he had discovered your father's odious beliefs, beliefs that you share? Perhaps. But it feels insufficient. A recipe in which the key ingredient has been forgotten. So we are left with the riddle of this death. What can't be denied is that we have been led to believe that you *could* have done it. We were given a Dying Message that feints in your direction. We were made to understand the parameters of a corpse found in a Locked Room. We were primed to be suspicious of the first person to check the body, especially if they professed certain vocations. It's natural to be wary of doctors: they are reminders of our own mortality. A single word of diagnosis, a scrawled test result on an illegible form, can prove a death sentence. They are as close as we get, most of us, to a judge pronouncing a verdict. So doctors make great villains. And, indeed, I think you are a villain. But not for the murder of this detective.

JAMES: You're saying that my father was set up?
READER: Yes.
DR. BLAKE: By whom?
EMMA: And who killed the detective?

[*Curtain.*]

×

"Why did I ever invent this detestable, bombastic, tiresome little creature?"

CONFESSION

The message in a bottle. The letter mailed to the newspaper or to Scotland Yard. The manuscript left in a country manor drawer for the Watson character to read. We must acknowledge, you and I, here at the end, that we are enriching a venerable tradition. The moment, at last, when all the cards are turned over.

The perils are clear. Do we really want the illusionist to explain the trick? The humorist to deconstruct the joke? Does this not kill the magic, if there is any to be lost?

Nevertheless.

Who doesn't permit themselves a little cheat, when seeing the puzzle solution printed upside down at the bottom of the page?

×

The motives of the classic murder mystery are those driving Shakespearean, if not Aristotelian, tragedy—love, hate, fear, greed, jealousy—along with a panoply of lesser vices—lust, ambition, rage, vanity, shame, cowardice. The young man *loves* his fiancée, so he stabs the villain trying to blackmail her out of *greed*. The mother *fears* the exposure of her son, whom she *loves*, and so poisons the investigator probing her son's crimes of *ambition*. The failed entrepreneur is *jealous* of his more successful rival, who, driven by *greed*, cheated him in their first shared enterprise, and so exacts his *revenge*. The son *lusts* after his mother and so kills her from a sense of *shame*. The *vain* public hero in a *rage* murders the one soldier who knows of his true *cowardice*. The clerk *hates* the store owner. The son *hates* his father. The wife *hates* her husband. The suicide *hates* herself . . .

> Q: So—what was your motive? Why did you kill Adam McAnnis?
> A: [. . .]
> Q: How did you do it?
> A: With the same mysterious force by which an ancient deity turned a woman into a pillar of salt. That is to say, a combination of magic and myth and belief.

×

I didn't hate Adam McAnnis—why should I? Rather, I pitied him for the miseries I inflicted upon him. Nor did I hate Claudia Mayer or John Garmond. If you credit this confession at all, then you may trust this: these were crimes of logic, not passion. Once I understood my plot, their deaths were a necessity. I could not do otherwise *but* kill them.

I didn't know that McAnnis had to die until well after he arrived at West Heart. My plan to kill Claudia Mayer also came later, even though she was the first to die. John Garmond I determined to kill from the start.

Of course, in these crimes, I followed many illustrious and exemplary models of homicide.

Arthur Conan Doyle killed Sherlock Holmes at the Reichenbach

Falls and let the world grieve for ten long years before his miraculous and improbable resurrection (young men walked the streets of London wearing black armbands, in mourning). Agatha Christie savaged Hercule Poirot—inflicting him with a terminal illness and finally, cruelly, turning him into a murderer—in a fit of revenge that she kept buried in a drawer for three decades (*The New York Times* printed a Poirot obituary when the book was finally published).

But no cruelty surpasses that of Shakespeare, who breathes softly on the embers of his creations just so that he may kill or torture them a few pages later. The death of Cordelia. The blinding of Gloucester. The poisoning of Hamlet. What moves a man to murder a character named after his own dead son?

So:

Did I weep when I forced Claudia Mayer to fill her housecoat with rocks? Did my hand tremble when I aimed Warren Burr's gun at the back of John Garmond's head? Did I hesitate before I wet my fingers to snuff out whatever Promethean flame fired Adam McAnnis?

How do I plead to such accusations?

I plead guilty.

So why did I do it? Shall we blame the pursuit of fame and fortune? Or is it something else? Intellectual curiosity? Aesthetic bliss? The indulgence of sociopathic or sadistic-erotic fantasies? Am I now, like Iago in the famous Coleridge explanation, merely "motive-hunting," searching for an explanation, *ex post facto*, for all these endless hours spent alone, meditating on murder?

Consider the world's first mystery story, in which Oedipus sets in motion a dire inquiry—the investigation into who killed the former King of Thebes—that results in the discovery that the culprit is himself, and his anguished realization that he's the author of the plot that leads to his own apocalypse.

Or consider a more recent case: the example of Eugène François Vidocq, the nineteenth-century criminal who became a chief of police in Paris, and who then later started the world's first private-detective agency—which, it was rumored, would often *commit* crimes so they would be paid to solve them later. A rat constructing the labyrinth from which I plan to escape.

Or consider W. H. Auden's plot tip to Raymond Chandler (which he ignored): a club of assassins who, suspecting that one of their number is killing for sport instead of money, hire a private detective to find this killer among killers.

Who better to interrogate the writer of murder, than the reader of same?

×

This murder mystery, like all murder mysteries, ends with what readers understand to be its dénouement, the revelation, or refusal of revelation, in which the problems are resolved, or not—for in truth, there are neither rules nor betrayals for this kind of story. All we have, you and I, are these guilty memories of bloody crimes in which we are both complicit; for every writer is a murderer, and every reader a sleuth.

Acknowledgments

First, I must express my gratitude for their hospitality to the good people of the real-life "West Heart" that inspired this book: they are nothing like the rotten creatures in these pages and (as far as I know!) are not harboring any murderers in their midst. The geography, history, and characters of my fictional West Heart are, of course, purely imaginary; and to readers who suspect I've altered the historical calendar, weather, and lunar cycle to suit my own purposes—I plead guilty.

Most of the research for this novel came from primary sources (i.e., reading), but, among many other texts consulted, I must acknowledge my particular debt to Julian Symons's *Bloody Murder* and to *The Oxford Companion to Crime & Mystery Writing* (Rosemary Herbert, editor). Fans of T. S. Eliot's *The Waste Land* (1922) will recognize Thursday's epigraph; Friday's epigraph is from John Dickson Carr's *The Hollow Man* (1935); Saturday's is G. K. Chesterton's "How to Write a Detective Story" (1925); Sunday's is Thomas De Quincey's "On Murder Considered as One of the Fine Arts" (1827); and the Confession epigraph quotes Agatha Christie's "Hercule Poirot—Fiction's Greatest Detective" (1938).

Special thanks must also go to my literal partners in crime, David

Black, Susan Raihofer, Paul Bogaards, and Jennifer Barth. And to my friends Sebastian Cwilich and Anne Hellman, who in different ways did much to make this book possible.

Finally, and most important, I thank my wife and children for their patience, love, and support.

A   NOTE   ON   THE   TYPE

This book was set in Janson, a typeface named for the
Dutchman Anton Janson, but is actually the work of Nicholas Kis (1650–1702). The type is an excellent example of
the influential and sturdy Dutch types that prevailed in
England up to the time William Caslon (1692–1766) developed his own incomparable designs from them.